overkill

also by eugenia lovett west

without warning

the ancestors cry out

overkill

eugenia lovett west

Minotaur Books

A Thomas Dunne Book

New York

This is a work of fiction. All of the characters, organizations, and events portrayed in this novel are either products of the author's imagination or are used fictitiously.

A THOMAS DUNNE BOOK FOR MINOTAUR BOOKS.
An imprint of St. Martin's Publishing Group.

OVERKILL. Copyright © 2009 by Eugenia Lovett West. All rights reserved. Printed in the United States of America. For information, address St. Martin's Press, 175 Fifth Avenue, New York, N.Y. 10010.

www.thomasdunnebooks.com
www.minotaurbooks.com

Library of Congress Cataloging-in-Publication Data

West, Eugenia Lovett, 1923–
    Overkill : an Emma Streat mystery / Eugenia Lovett West.—1st ed.
        p. cm.
    ISBN 978-0-312-37114-2
  I. Title.
    PS3573.E818O84 2009
    813'.54—dc22

                                                            2009012747

First Edition: December 2009

10   9   8   7   6   5   4   3   2   1

To wonderful family and friends who
help and support in so many ways.
Love you!

acknowledgments

It takes the proverbial village to move a book from a blip in the author's imagination to completion. My special thanks to peerless editor Ruth Cavin, associate editor Toni Plummer, agent Ann Rittenberg, and publicist Susan Schwartzman.

Muchas gracias to my longtime mentor, Joseph W. Hotchkiss, and advisers Robbin Reynolds and Rebecca Sinkler.

Merci infiniment for the expertise and support of family. Among them are my brother, Rev. Sidney Lovett, my daughter, Victoria West, and my niece, Anne Lovett.

overkill

Human beings are disguised by their bodies and only God can look through the lattice of the flesh and see what we are.

—Saint Augustine

He sat at a state-of-the-art computer and studied the monitors on the wall. All his goods in transit were moving on schedule. Number 107 was halfway between Dubai and Turkey. Number 323 left Islamabad at 4:00 A.M. their time. Number 112—the goods were arriving in Venice today. He frowned, trying to see beyond the impersonal numbers connected to number 112. Over the years he had learned to trust his primal instincts. There was something about number 112 that spelled risk.

After a moment, he looked down and tapped a few words on the keyboard. Number 112's illegal goods now in transit must proceed. Then, as soon as the money was in hand, he would terminate account number 112.

As always, his identity was hidden behind a solid firewall. Nothing in this transaction had his signature. On the other hand, a hazardous operation was only as strong as its weakest link.

part one

one

October 8

Boston, Massachusetts

Strange, really, that fifth-grade Greek mythology should ever come back in my life, but today, instead of walking around my rented apartment, I imagined that I was climbing Mount Olympus. Looking at twelve ancient seated gods. Listening to them as they decided where to throw their thunderbolts. Argued about who should be punished.

"Not me," I said to them. "Not me again. I've already appeased you. In spades." This morning I was aching for my dead husband. Aching for my beautiful old house on the Connecticut River, now a pile of bombed-out rubble. Right now I should be putting in daffodil bulbs for next spring; moles always made short work of tulips.

After a moment, I went to the window and looked out at the narrow brick houses, the old, uneven sidewalks that gave Beacon Hill its unique character. By nature, I was not a moaner. After all, the jealous gods had left me my health. My money.

My boys. Jake, the overachiever, was a sophomore at Brown. Laid-back Steve was just starting his freshman year at Harvard. The nest was empty—and I missed being a hands-on mother, with boys and their friends needing food and rides and well-disguised affection.

Last June my godmother had lectured me about letting go. "You're forty-seven, Emma. You've got half your life ahead of you. You had a great singing career until you lost your voice. Then you married Lewis and brought up those superb hunks. They're men now, out of the nest. Cut the cord. You've got looks, brains, energy, money to burn. Do something important with the rest of your life." That same night Lewis had come home holding in anger. The start of the stripping away.

Turning from the window, I stood still and looked around my expensive rented living room, a comfortless place of slippery white leather sofas and tubular steel chairs. The boys hated this apartment. Right now I should be looking for a house, beginning to make a new home for them. Instead, I seemed to be in limbo, as if my feet were nailed to a foot walk on a bridge.

"Move it," I said aloud, and pushed back my hair. The best antidote against the vengeful gods was to put on sweats and go for a fast jog on the Esplanade, the wide promenade along the Charles River.

I was heading for the bedroom when my cell rang, demanding attention.

"Is this Mrs. Streat?" An unfamiliar voice. I hesitated. Not many people had my number.

"Who's calling?"

"Mrs. Streat, it's Cathy Riordan." A young voice with a lilting Irish accent. "Ye'll not know me, but I'm your niece Vanessa Metcalf's assistant." My brother Ned's daughter was a rising young opera star. The wheels in my brain did a fast spin.

"Cathy Riordan. Yes. I know exactly who you are." Last winter Ned had talked about his gifted, volatile daughter: "Vanessa's stretched too thin, her schedule is a killer, but at least she's got a new assistant. Name of Cathy Riordan, fresh out of Ireland, with that soft tongue and a good head on her shoulders. They seem to be getting along very well."

"I'm that sorry to bother you, Mrs. Streat, but the truth is, I need help."

My hand tightened on the cell. Calls like this spelled trouble. "What's wrong? Was there an accident?"

"Ah no, not an accident, but someone in the family should know before it's too late. I've tried to reach the parents, but they're away, out of the country." There was no mistaking the distress in her voice.

"Too late for what? Tell me."

"I will, so. Ye'd have heard of Seth Barzalon, the millionaire playboy. He races cars. Ye'd have seen his picture in the papers."

"The name doesn't ring a bell, but that doesn't mean anything. I'm not much into racing."

"This man—he and Vanessa—the two of them met in Paris last week after her *Traviata* at the Opéra Bastille. A party for the cast. I'm told 'twas like putting a match to a can of petrol. Since then ye'd not be able to pry them apart with a knife."

Not a car crash. Not a fatal illness. "Where are you now?" I asked. "In Paris?"

"In Venice. She has a Rescue Venice benefit recital two nights from now. He brought us here today in his fancy plane."

I shook my head. "Cathy, to be honest, it doesn't sound all that bad to me. Men have been following Vanessa around ever since she was fifteen. You wouldn't believe what her mother went through, keeping those sexed-up teenagers in line."

"Begging your pardon, but you have it wrong, Mrs. Streat. She wants to give up her singing. Cancel all her engagements. Fly off with him to Sardinia."

I jumped. My hand went to my throat. "Did you say—give up her *singing?*"

"I did, so. They won't be separated, not for a single day."

"But . . . that's . . . that's—she *can't* do that."

"She can. She will, unless someone makes her see reason. I'm told ye used to be a singer. An opera singer like Vanessa. I was thinking ye might know what to do."

"It can't be his money. Vanessa doesn't give a snap about money. It sends her father up the wall."

"Ah, the money isn't in it. Ye'd have to see for yourself; he looks like a prince in a fairy tale. He's sweeping her off her feet, promising her the world."

"Good God." Fairy-tale prince and impetuous, romantic Vanessa. A lethal combination. But . . . was the new Irish assistant given to exaggeration? Painting too lurid a picture? "Wait," I said. "Does Vanessa know you're calling me?"

"Never. She'd have my head, but 'twould be a sin for me to sit back and do nothing. I've been with her since last February. She's been that good to me, but I'm only her assistant. Someone in her family ought to come. Talk sense into her before it's too late."

Outside a police car went screaming up the street. I closed my eyes. For most of her life Vanessa and I had been close. I had helped her to make the initial plunge into the world of opera. But then I had zeroed in with unwanted advice about self-discipline and the need to build a solid foundation. Vanessa had backed away.

"Look," I said. "I'm beginning to get the picture. You want me to to come over and talk to Vanessa, but it's not that simple.

We both know she can dig in her heels. The last thing she'll take is advice about a man. Especially from me. We haven't seen much of each other lately. Where is her next engagement?"

"London. Covent Garden. They're expecting her to start rehearsals for *Manon*. Now she's off to Sardinia after the recital and the divil take the hindmost."

"Oh God," I said. "Big houses won't stand for that kind of thing. Does her manager know?"

"She does not."

"Hold on; I have to think," I said, and went back to the window. The last thing I wanted was to fly off to Venice for an emotional encounter. Sheer madness to imagine that I could march in and lecture Vanessa, the spoilsport aunt who had come to burst her bubble of happiness. On the other hand, Metcalf family loyalty went very deep. My brother, Ned, and sister-in-law, Cassia, if asked, would walk the last mile to help my boys. I pushed back my hair and spoke into the cell.

"Cathy. Look. It may not do any good, but I'll come. You say the recital is two nights from now?"

"Thursday night. At a private palazzo."

"Where are you staying?"

"We have a suite at the Hotel Dordona. Will I get you a room there?"

"Yes. Oh, and give me your number. I'll call you back as soon as I have a flight."

"Saints be praised. I've been that worried."

"Don't thank me. Vanessa will be furious with both of us."

No time now for jogging. I sat down at the black steel desk and opened my small computer. A pop-up was asking me to renew a firewall. I sent it into space and rested my fingers on the keys. What if Cathy *had* exaggerated the situation? I should have asked more questions.

After a moment, I lifted my hands. The truth, plain and simple, was that I loved Vanessa. At age two she used to climb into my lap and press her face into my neck. When she was five, we had invented a private dialogue: "Love you to infinity. . . . No, love you to infinity *plus* infinity."

"Suck it up," I said, clicked onto Travelocity, and began to scan airline schedules. After all, when push came to shove, this rescue mission, whatever the outcome, wouldn't last long. It might take four days out of my life. No more.

two

The Rescue Venice benefit was scheduled to begin at eight o'clock. At two minutes after eight, I slid into a gilt chair like a runner stumbling to the finish line. My plane had circled Marco Polo Airport for an hour. The hotel *motoscafo* had raced me across the lagoon to one of the finest palazzos in Venice. A close call, but not my fault.

The dais was still empty. I sat back, catching my breath. Tall candles and Murano glass chandeliers shone gently on blurred frescoes; long mirrors were dark from centuries of smoke; a plaster angel in the corner had lost her arm. Around me, people were talking in rapid-fire Italian. The women were bedecked and bejeweled. I was still in my black travel pants and jacket.

There had been time, as the plane droned over the Atlantic, to plan a strategy for my talk with Vanessa. Count on the fact that, along with her Chilean mother's volatile temperament,

Vanessa had inherited her father's strict New England sense of fairness. I had rehearsed my speech:

"Look, I totally understand that you're head over heels in love and you want to be with this man. I'm happy for you, really happy, but why not do London first? It's just a few performances, but if you cancel now the Covent Garden people will be frantic; your manager will be furious. Don't forget, there are a lot of singers out there ready to jump into your shoes." In other words, appeal to her fairness—and her drive to be at the top of the operatic ladder.

Ten after eight. The audience was growing restless, looking at their programs. I twisted my fingers together, willing Vanessa to appear. Had something gone wrong? For me, recitals had been far more challenging than operas. No supportive conductor, no prompter, no other singers to cover a slip.

At last the accompanist was walking onto the small dais banked with red and white flowers. He bowed and sat down at the piano, a small man with shiny black hair plastered to his skull. A long pause, then Vanessa walked forward. Tonight she was wearing a long, sleeveless white dress that showed off her enviable figure. The mass of red hair was pulled back and fell in a cascade down her back. She acknowledged the muted applause with a slight smile, folded her hands, and nodded to the accompanist.

"Dove sono" from Mozart's *The Marriage of Figaro* was a daring choice for an opening aria; the sostenuto called for perfect control. I let out my breath as Vanessa's effortless phrasing trailed off to a soft finish. In some mysterious way, the odd gene in our family had emerged again. This voice, far more compelling than mine, was a unique God-given gift.

A Brahms, another Mozart, a Schubert. Vanessa sang with a faraway expression in her eyes. No hand waving or head tossing, no attempts to win the approval of the audience. She held them because she didn't need them. She sang to the heart of the music, to the genius of the composer. Last came the poems written by Wagner's lover Mathilde set to music by the composer, an outpouring of restless love that filled the great *salone* with vibrating sensuality. Silence, then loud, spontaneous applause. The recital was over—and the highly critical audience had been captivated.

People were getting up, moving toward doors that led to another *salone*. Before I left Boston, Cathy had given me an update:

"She'll come back to the dressing room after the performance. The countess who owns the palazzo is giving a reception in her honor."

"That won't give us enough time to talk. Have you told her I'm coming?"

"Not yet."

"Maybe you should. She'll never believe I'm just passing through."

The chandeliers in this *salone* were strung with blue glass beads. Gilt chairs covered with worn brocade lined the walls; gilded cherubs flew overhead. Waiters were passing champagne to a gathering of top-layer Venetian society.

I took a glass and went to a window that looked out over the Grand Canal, an outsider who didn't speak the language; my throat was scratchy from the bad air on the plane. I raised the fluted glass and sipped, still under the spell of Vanessa's superb singing. Somehow I must reach her, my beautiful talented niece who once had wanted to be another Callas.

A distinguished-looking man passed by, glanced at me, and then again—a sign that, even in a pants suit, I could hold my own in a room filled with overdressed Italian beauties. There were no pounds in the wrong places. My hair was a darker red than

Vanessa's, the same heavy mass, but cut above the shoulders. Her eyes were greenish hazel. Mine were a bright blue. "Ma's blow-torch eyes," my boys used to say. And in my press clippings: *Eyes that mesmerize up to the third balcony . . . Metcalf has presence. Vitality. Brio.*

Small groups were forming. As people shifted, I saw that the small accompanist had appeared. He was facing a tall man with a tanned face.

"Keep away from her, Barzalon," he said loudly in a nasal British voice. "You'll ruin her life, you bloody bastard."

People around me stopped talking. I stared—and my resolve began to waver. Cathy hadn't exaggerated. The man had the look of a princely Nordic hero. Thick, fair hair. Even features. A magnificent specimen—and tomorrow he was taking her off to Sardinia. No wonder the little accompanist was upset.

"Leave her alone or I'll kill you. I swear it." The little man was dancing around, fists raised. Barzalon looked down, a Great Dane tolerating a yapping terrier. Then he shrugged his shoulders and walked away. After a few seconds, people began to talk again. The accompanist disappeared.

The waiter was presenting another tray of filled glasses. I shook my head, aware of movement in the center of the room. Vanessa had arrived and was standing beside a formidable-looking woman in a black velvet dress and a pearl choker. The countess, no doubt, whose palazzo was on loan for the evening.

Vanessa was still wearing the white dress, and she was carrying a red satin stole. She blew a kiss as Barzalon came up to her. Around me, everyone was watching this spectacular couple. *"Che bella figura,"* a woman said. Others nodded.

The line of people waiting to meet Vanessa grew longer. She was smiling, shaking hands. Barzalon stood behind her, looking bored. Suddenly he leaned forward and whispered in her ear.

She laughed. Seconds later they were crossing the *salone,* running hand in hand toward the loggia. Their heads disappeared as they raced down the grand staircase, like children escaping from a grown-up party.

I stood still, unable to believe that Cassia and Ned's daughter, my niece, was capable of displaying such incredibly bad manners.

"How *could* she?" I said under my breath. There was a set smile on the countess's face. Murmurs and raised eyebrows around me. It was easy to guess what they were saying: "What else can you expect from Americans?" In two minutes, Vanessa had managed to insult her hostess and Venetian society. Carefully, I put the delicate glass down on the nearest table. It was high time to go and find Cathy Riordan.

Behind the dais, a small paneled room had been converted into a temporary dressing room with a table and mirror. A young woman with sturdy legs was holding a worn Paddington bear, his furry legs enclosed in signature red shorts. I had given Vanessa that bear when she was four, one of my most enduring presents. I cleared my throat.

"Cathy?"

The woman turned. Her face was closer to plain than pretty. She had freckles and gray eyes with thick black lashes. An Irish face, round, with wide-set eyes.

"Saints be praised, ye're here. I checked just before we left the hotel and there wasn't a sign of you."

"The plane was late. I didn't have time to change, but I made it. My bags went on to the Dordona. Is Vanessa expecting me?"

"I told her there'd been a message and you hoped to be here for the recital."

"What did she say?"

Cathy looked away. "Ah, she's always inside herself before she sings."

"So she wasn't pleased. Too bad. All I can say is, right now I'm disgusted with her. Furious."

Cathy dropped the bear. "What in the world?"

"It wasn't the recital. *That* was lovely, a huge success. It was the reception. I decided to keep out of her way until we could talk, but—"

"She saw you?"

"No. First the accompanist came in. He went up to Seth Barzalon. Called him a bloody bastard who would ruin her life. Said he was going to kill him."

Cathy shook her head. "Wild talk. Mark Dykstra wouldn't kill a fly."

"Barzalon brushed him off—like a fly. Then Vanessa came in. She stood there, shaking hands. Suddenly she and Barzalon took off across the room and down the stairs. They literally ran away. Like children. Everyone saw them go. The guests won't remember the singing, just her rudeness. I tell you, I wouldn't have believed it if I hadn't seen it with my own eyes. I think it was his idea, but she went along like . . . like a puppet on a string. Honestly, I could have *smacked* her."

"Holy Mother." Cathy touched the silver cross at her neck. "I told you, Mrs. Streat, she's not herself. Not herself at all."

"You did, but this is worse than I thought. Much worse. Where do you think they went?"

"He's staying at the Grillo. They'll likely have gone there."

"Oh Lord." I leaned against the red brocade wall. "For how long? Will she be there all night? Will I have a chance to see her?"

"She'll have to come back to the suite to change and pack."

"But there's no telling when *that* will be."

"You have the right of it there. Will I be giving her a call at the Grillo, then? Tell her you're here?"

"Not until I simmer down. I'll go back to the hotel with you. Maybe you could let me know when she comes in, whatever time that is."

"I can, so. Your room is just down the hall, a hop and a skip away. Will you sit while I finish here?" She turned, picked up a roll of cotton and a bottle of water, and put them into a big canvas carryall.

I sat down on a gilt chair. "I see she has special water," I said. "I remember. Special water and spray for the temperamental throat."

"Heaven forbid we run out. I always keep an extra supply."

Jet lag was beginning to dull my brain. I leaned back and watched Cathy as she moved around. Large feet crammed into high-heeled shoes. Pierced ears and a small silver crucifix at her neck. A young Irish girl in the process of bridging two cultures. I had always loved the Irish, starting with my old nurse Biddy McGee. Loved their warmth and easy humor. "Aren't you the clever one," Biddy's sisters would say when I visited their little house in South Boston. This Cathy had the same warm smile, the lilting voice.

"That's everything, then," she said at last. "I'd best leave the flowers. She doesn't like them too close."

"Allergies. How are you getting back to the hotel?"

"The hotel said they would send a boat. All these little canals and alleys, I'd be lost before I took a step, and me not speaking a word of the tongue."

I got to my feet. "How would you feel about walking? It's not far and I know the way. Right now I could use some fresh air and stretch my legs."

"Will it be safe, then, after dark?"

"Of course. Venice is one of the safest cities in the world. The police have strict orders to keep the tourists safe and happy."

A manservant in a white coat was moving chairs in the big *salone*. I went up to him.

"Good evening. Do you speak English?"

He made a small bow. "Si, signora. Very good America speak."

"Will you show us the way to the street?"

"Si, si, signora. No boat?"

"No boat."

"Si, signora." He took us to the end of a long hall. Stone stairs led down to a courtyard lined with statues; pebbled paths were bordered by clipped boxwood hedges. As he opened the gate to a side street, I hesitated. My sense of direction was a standing family joke: "If Ma says go right, go left."

The streets were dark; the shutters on the houses were closed. As Cathy and I hurried along, a cat crossed in front of us, a gray shape in air that was growing cool and misty.

Cathy shivered. " 'Tis bad luck when a cat crosses your path at night. Are we right?"

"We're right. The arrows on the walls are pointing to San Marco. That's the big piazza. Our hotel is just beyond."

"Sure and I'd never want to hear someone walking behind me. Those shutters. Why would ye want to lock yourself in?"

"It's safe, I promise you," I said, rubbing my arms. Cathy's uneasiness was contagious. No need to tell her that the city had a long history of murderous intrigues and assassinations, maybe some on this very street.

As we turned a corner, I glanced at Cathy, my partner in an intervention that seemed headed for disaster. Vanessa would rush in, impatient to be off. I would make my little speech about contracts and Covent Garden. Family ties might keep her from telling me to mind my own business. Maybe not. When had cool reason ever trumped hot passion?

"This Seth Barzalon," I said. "He's good-looking, all right. What do *you* think of him?"

Cathy made a noise in her throat. "He'd not give me the time of day. He wants me out of her life. Out of his way."

"So he's arrogant *and* rude. You know, nothing about this affair makes sense. Vanessa worked so hard to get where she is. How *could* she throw it all over?"

Cathy hesitated. "I've watched. It's hard to get your head around it, but the fella makes her feel as if she is the only woman who ever lived. He has her thinking all he wants is to make her happy, but sure and that's what he says to them all. I know."

I turned my head. "You know? How?"

"Terry Gallagher, his pilot, he's from my county; that's Waterford in the west part of Ireland. He took me out for a drink in Paris. A lovely little bar it was, near Notre Dame. He says Seth Barzalon has a string of beautiful women. He likes to be seen with celebrities. Nothing lasts long with him."

"Oh God."

"And doesn't he have the money to wave a wand and make the magic happen. Ye've never seen anything like that plane, a crew of four. Terry's the head pilot. The top man."

"I see." It was too dark to catch Cathy's expression, but drinks with a pilot in Paris would be heady stuff for a country girl not long away from home. "What else did you find out?" I asked. "Where does Barzalon live when he's not flying to races?"

"He has an apartment in New York. Other places. There's a sister who lives in Venice, a sort of recluse. He doesn't like her, but he has orders to check on her once in a while."

"Orders?"

"Terry says there's a family foundation in Boston. Something to do with medicine. Terry takes him there for meetings, but mostly it's fancy car races around the world."

"How do he and Terry get along?"

"Ah, well, he says a pilot goes wherever he's told. That's the way of it, he says."

"True." I frowned, trying to absorb this information. "I'm beginning to get the picture, but it still doesn't make sense. There *has* to be another reason why she's lost all the manners her mother drummed into her. That running away at the reception—it was almost as if she needed to escape from everything. The success. The applause. The people."

Cathy shifted the carryall. "Ye picked up on it soon. The truth is, the poor thing is going faster and faster, like a whirly machine at a fair. All those people hanging around with their hands out. Recordings. Rehearsals. A fan club. A pushy publicist. All wanting their slice of the cake. She's being torn into little pieces."

We were passing an all-night *farmacia*. I stared at the lit window. "That makes sense," I said slowly. "I can understand the feeling. It's like being on a wheel, not able to get off. The question is, how to keep her from ruining her life."

We were coming into a large piazza; a tan mongrel with a muzzle over his nose sniffed at a piece of torn paper. By daylight the place would be filled with boys and soccer balls. Tonight it was shadowy and deserted. I had never walked these shuttered narrow streets after dark.

As we went over a little bridge, Cathy shook her head. "Nasty sort of place. Garbage and worse floating all around. Houses falling into the water."

I laughed. "Venice does seem a bit sinister tonight. But it can be beautiful."

"You know Venice, then?"

"Not well. I was here for a few days last summer," I said, and stopped. There was no need for Cathy to know about my one-time indulgence of the senses.

"Staiii . . ." A long, eerie cry in the darkness. I jumped.

Cathy gasped. "Ah, God, what was that?"

"Just a gondolier, a signal at a blind corner, like sounding a horn. Tell me about yourself," I said quickly. "I've never been to Ireland."

"There's not much to tell. My mam and da live in a little place called Castledown. One street down the middle, a shop and two pubs. There's plenty of jobs in Ireland these days, but I decided to come over and take my chances. I was working for one of those temp agencies and Vanessa needed a secretary. Last February that was."

"She's lucky to have you. What will you do if—when—she goes to Sardinia?"

"I'll go back to her apartment in New York for a while, any-how. Pay bills. Stay as long as she needs me."

"You're very fond of her."

"I am, so. She can try your patience, but she has a big heart. She'd give you the shirt off her back. And it's grand to see all these foreign cities. The fine hotels and all." A pause. "Are we right?"

"We're right. Almost there."

A bell was striking the quarter hour as we walked into San Marco piazza. The enormous square lined with tall colonnades. A few people sat at the little tables, but waiters were beginning to pile up chairs. By the far colonnade, a small band was playing a lethargic rendition of "My Way."

"We made it," I said. "You were sure we were going to be lost or mugged."

" 'Twas those closed shutters gave me the shivers. Eyes watching from behind. But this—I wish my mam could see it."

"You can send her postcards."

We walked on past an anchored white cruise ship, a looming bulk in the night, lights blazing. As we reached the entrance to the Dordona, two carabinieri strutted by, a handsome pair of policemen in tight-fitting black uniforms and shoulder epaulettes.

The Hotel Dordona was once a fine old Venetian palazzo. In the lobby, stained-glass windows were set in ornate walls of dark wood, carved as if Renaissance workmen had been ordered, on pain of death, to leave no inch untouched. Great stairs led up to the mezzanine. Overstuffed armchairs stood in stiff groups.

Cathy led the way to the front desk. The glossy-haired young clerk was wearing a black coat and a gray striped vest. He greeted Cathy with a smile.

"Good evening, signorina."

"Good evening. The key, please. And a key for Mrs. Streat. Her bags came by boat earlier."

"They are in your room, signora. Room four-thirty-two. Welcome to the Hotel Dordona," he said, and handed me an electronic card.

As Cathy and I went up in the gilt and wood elevator, I swallowed and touched my throat. My voice, always fragile after the operation that ended my singing career, was fading. "Would you happen to have any spare lozenges?" I asked. "It's nothing serious, just the air on the plane."

"And aren't we a traveling pharmacy for the throat?"

The elevator opened onto a long hall. A little maid went by, carrying a pile of towels.

"Buona sera," she said with a smile.

Cathy nodded as she unlocked the door. "Not a word of English, but the service is grand. You can't drop a towel on the floor but it's whisked away."

"And Vanessa uses a dozen at a time. It used to drive her mother crazy."

The small foyer was paneled in dark wood. A tall vase on the table was filled with purple gladiolus.

Cathy pointed to a *salone* beyond. "Will ye sit while I find the lozenges? Will ye be wanting aspirin?"

"Just the lozenges," I said, longing to get to my room. First a hot shower or a long, soaking bath. I could order café au lait from room service and drink the hot milk.

The unlit *salone* was dark and shadowed. I sat down, glanced at the heavy furniture, then closed my eyes.

After a moment, I opened them and yawned. Where was Cathy?

Curtains had been drawn over the long windows. Nothing unusual about that, but suddenly I was aware that a dark shape was hanging from one of the high rods. An odd, extended shape, like a duffel bag with legs.

I sat forward, looked again, then turned and felt for a switch on the wall behind me. Instantly, the chandelier blazed into light. The delicately colored glass shone down on an overturned chair. A black toupee lying on the parquet floor. A bald head dangling from a gold curtain cord. The head of Mark Dykstra, Vanessa's accompanist.

three

The brain struggles to reject what the eye sees. I stared up at the chandelier. At the obscene bald scalp.

"Will six lozenges do you, Mrs. Streat?" Cathy's voice behind me. I pointed to the window. The lozenges fell to the floor.

"Holy Mother have mercy." She crossed herself. "Jesus have mercy." Every freckle stood out on her white face. "Jesus have mercy."

The words came out in a whisper. We stood motionless, as if our feet were fastened to the parquet floor. The blood was going from my head.

"*Permesso,* signora?" The little maid was coming through the foyer, holding the towels. I jumped, jolted from shock, and tried to block her view. Too late.

"*Alla Madonna.*" A piercing shriek. She ran, scattering the towels.

Cathy swayed forward. "To kill himself . . ."

I caught her arm. "Sit down."

"The boat—if we'd taken the boat we might have saved him." A rising wail of hysteria.

I shook Cathy's shoulder. "Never mind the boat. We have to get help. Where's the nearest telephone?"

She raised her head and touched the silver cross. "Poor creature, poor soul—it's in the foyer."

The door from the foyer to the outside hall was open. The maid and a young waiter were standing there. She was still sobbing, calling on the Madonna.

"*Scusi,* signora," the waiter said, shifting from leg to leg. "Is trouble here?" Clearly, the news about a man hanging from a curtain cord was spreading like wildfire sweeping down a canyon.

"The manager is coming," I said, and shut the door in their faces.

There was an old-fashioned black telephone on a table. I picked it up and pushed the button for the front desk.

"It's Mrs. Streat. I'm in Miss Metcalf's suite, I don't know the number," I said, forcing myself to speak slowly. "There's been an accident. A very bad accident. Please ask the manager to come here at once. Do you understand? At *once.*"

"I will inform him, signora."

"Thank you." I closed my eyes and leaned against the wall. Less than two hours ago I had watched the little accompanist's fingers fly over the keyboard. Watched as he confronted Seth Barzalon and threatened to kill him. Why, *why* had he decided to hang himself? Why do it *here*? I swallowed, fighting faintness, wanting my dead husband. Oh God, Lewis, I need you. How can you be dead when I need you?

After a moment I took a deep breath and straightened. In the haze of shock, one thing was becoming clear: I was in charge. There was no one else.

Back in the *salone*, Cathy was standing in the same place, holding the little cross in one hand, muttering a prayer.

"The manager is coming," I said, looking away from the window. "Where's the bedroom?"

Cathy looked at me blankly.

"Cathy. The bedroom. We can't stay here."

She turned and led the way down the hall and into a high-ceilinged room that was reminiscent of a greenhouse. Green walls and carpet. Green and gold furniture. Green brocade bedspreads on two enormous beds.

"You'd better sit down," I said. "You're in shock. I didn't know him. You did."

She put her face in her hands. Tears were running through her fingers. "It's the shame of it. If only I'd talked to the poor soul. Holy Mother, I should have talked to him after Vanessa gave him the rough side of her tongue. Straightened him out."

"Straightened him out?" I pulled up a carved chair and sat down. "Did something happen with Vanessa?"

Cathy raised her head. "Oh God, didn't she come back to the dressing room to take off her makeup. There wasn't much, not for a recital in a private house. She drank a bottle of water and sprayed her throat. 'Now for the meet and greet,' she said. 'I'll see you back at the hotel, I'm not sure when.' Then she opened the door. He was standing there."

"The accompanist."

"Waiting for her to come out. Lately he'd taken to following her around like a little dog. Even before Barzalon, she didn't like it. But tonight—didn't she lay into him good and proper. Told him she was going off to Sardinia with Barzalon. Told him that he wouldn't be playing for her again."

I winced. "No wonder he was upset."

"He went to pieces. He was crying like a baby, begging her

to stay. She said it wouldn't change their contract. He would be paid the whole."

"All the same, it does seem hard, to hear it like that. I mean, he *was* her accompanist. And he was good."

"She had others. He was the best until he began to make a nuisance of himself."

"You mean, he fell in love with her."

"Poor man, he couldn't see his own foolishness, the idea that she could ever fancy him. The wig, and his sinuses were bothering him something chronic. We used to laugh about it behind his back, but now—"

"You wish you hadn't." I leaned forward. "You say he was crying, but a few minutes later, at the reception, he was *angry*. Very angry. Everyone heard him threatening to kill Seth Barzalon. It was ridiculous, but maybe—I wonder—just maybe he was angry with Vanessa. Angry enough to come and do it here. Just to cause trouble for her."

Cathy's eyes rolled. "The wonder is he could do it at all. He was that fearful about himself. Hurting his hands."

"He must have climbed up onto the chair, then kicked it away—no, sorry."

"He committed a mortal sin. 'Tis a mortal sin to take your own life. His poor family." Cathy was crying again, crossing herself, rocking her head from side to side.

I sat back and closed my eyes. Disasters had a way of spreading, like spilled paint.

"His family," I said, after a moment. "Whoever they are, they'll have to be told. Do you know how to reach them?"

"He's English. The payments go to an agency in London. The Cromwell Road Agency. I have the address in my files at home."

"Not much use. Besides, right now, we need to think about Vanessa. How to tell *her*."

Cathy straightened. She wiped her face with her hand. "She'll be destroyed entirely, knowing what she said to him. She'll never forgive herself."

"But we still have to—"

The bell in the foyer was chiming. We both jumped.

"I'll go," I said. "It must be the manager."

The man at the door was small and neat, with a neat, gray mustache. He stepped in and made a little bow.

"Signor Landgrau, assistant manager. The manager is in Milan. I'm told a man has hanged himself here."

"He's in the *salone*," I said. Signor Landgrau looked like a Swiss, maybe an Austrian. Definitely not Italian. In a moment he was back.

"Regrettable. You recognize him?"

"Yes. He's—he was—Miss Metcalf's accompanist. His name is Mark Dykstra."

"You are?"

"Emma Streat. Miss Metcalf's aunt. I have a room here. Her assistant and I came back from her recital a few minutes ago and found him."

"He had a key?"

I hesitated. Dear God, how *had* Mark Dykstra unlocked the door?

"I . . . don't know."

The manager pressed his lips together. "The hotel doctor will be called. That is protocol. The police must be informed." He picked up the foyer telephone and spoke in rapid Italian. I listened, sensing annoyance under the brisk manner. People were not supposed to kill themselves at the Dordona. Protecting the hotel would be his first priority. Protecting Vanessa was mine.

"I'm sorry, but there's another problem," I said as he hung up.

"Yes?"

"Miss Metcalf is over at the Grillo. Her assistant is going to call and tell her what happened. This will be a shock. She'll want to come back, but it mustn't be through the main entrance."

"Why not the main entrance, madam?"

"As you know, Miss Metcalf is a well-known opera singer. The fact that her accompanist committed suicide in her suite will be a big story. Someone, maybe someone on your staff, is sure to alert the media."

"The media will not be allowed to annoy other guests, madam."

"Fine, if you can keep them from crowding in. Camping out in the lobby. The sleaze press is the worst. I know the damage they can do."

"Indeed." He gave me a quick look. "I will make arrangements for Miss Metcalf," he said stiffly. "I will send the hotel boat for her. With an escort. They will use a back entrance. Ah, here is the doctor. You will excuse us, please."

"I'll be in the bedroom," I said, and went back down the hall.

In those few short minutes Cathy had catapulted from stunned shock into frenzied activity. Suitcases lay open on the floor.

"I might as well start packing," she said in a high voice. "If I keep moving I'll not see him hanging there. Was that the manager?"

"His assistant. The doctor just came and the police are on the way. The manager is going to send a boat for Vanessa. Now she has to be told. I think it had better be you."

"Will she believe me?"

"Tell her to come alone. The press mustn't see Barzalon with her."

"She may not listen."

"If she argues, I'll talk. Where's the number?"

"In here," and she pulled a notebook from the carryall. "The number for his suite at the Grillo. If it doesn't answer, I'll try her cell."

"And if they aren't answering, we'll send someone up," but a moment later Cathy was talking to Vanessa. I went to the window and listened.

". . . by the grace of God your auntie was here when we found him. She's talked to the manager and he's sending a boat; they'll bring you in a back way. No, no, you *must* come alone. Why? Because the the news is all over the hotel. Someone may have called the press. You don't want them pushing into yer faces, taking pictures of the two of you."

A boat was pulling up to the quay, lights flashing. A dark-colored boat with red stripes and a little cabin. Two carabinieri stepped out, followed by two men in plainclothes. As they walked toward the hotel, lights flashed. The press *had* arrived. I closed my eyes, seeing last summer's flaming headlines: *Suspicious Death in Stately Home . . . Tragic End as Two Women Fight.* Since then my fear of the press had become a phobia.

"Brace yourself," I said to Cathy. "The press is outside, and the police are on the way up."

"Police, is it. Foreigners. On my own I'd be choked in me throat, and they not understanding a word."

A few moments later, five men stood in the foyer, filling the small space.

"Miss Riordan and I will be in the bedroom," I said to the manager, and went back to Cathy. I listened as heavy feet went into the *salone*. There was a long pause. I dug my nails into my palms. Were they lifting the body down, picking up the toupee? Would they put it back on his head?

The door opened and the manager appeared. He touched the little mustache and spoke to me.

"Signora, this is Commissario Filardi from the Questura— police headquarters." I held out my hand as a middle-aged man wearing a dark suit came forward. Please, God, let him speak English.

"How do you do," I said in a formal voice. "I'm Mrs. Streat, and this is Miss Riordan, Miss Metcalf's assistant."

The *commissario* took my hand in a firm grip. "Good evening, Mrs. Streat. My sincere regrets."

"Thank you." I let out my breath. I should have known that a high official in Venice would speak excellent English.

The *commissario* nodded to Cathy. "Please sit down, ladies." He looked at me. "You know this man?" His manner was grave and polite. The manager hadn't expressed any sympathy.

"No, I don't," I said. "I just got here; I mean, I arrived in Venice tonight. I think Miss Riordan will be more help."

"I understand." He turned to Cathy. "Tell me, please, what you know about this person."

As they talked, my mind veered to Vanessa. How would this death affect her plans to go off with Barzalon? In any case, I must be prepared for anger and resentment.

Cathy was telling the *commissario* that Mark Dykstra had been the accompanist at the recital. I closed my eyes. So many questions remained. Why had the little man come here to kill himself? How had he managed to get in?

From the foyer, the tramp of heavy feet meant that the police were finally leaving. The *commissario* was still talking to Cathy.

"When did you plan to leave Venice, Miss Riordan?"

"In the morning, sir. Miss Metcalf is going to Sardinia. Mrs. Streat will be flying back to Boston."

There was a long pause. The *commissario* cleared his throat.

"I'm afraid that will not be possible."

"What?" I opened my eyes. "Excuse me. Are you saying we can't leave Venice?"

"That is so."

"But . . . *why?*"

"Signora, you must understand. This is a serious matter. An autopsy must be performed. There may be more questions. Until you hear from me, I must ask you to remain in the city." The *commissario* folded his hands.

"More questions?" I stared. Was this Italian law or the *commissario* throwing his weight around?

"Yes, signora." The brown eyes were steady, revealing nothing.

"Even so . . ." I hesitated, trying to keep my voice steady. "I don't know your laws, but in the case of a suicide, why should there be more questions?"

"I regret the inconvenience, ladies. I will be in touch as soon as possible." He stood up. Exchanged a quick word with the manager and disappeared through the door.

"Mrs. Streat." The manager came forward. "If you wish to use the *salone,* it is now . . . restored." He touched the little mustache and frowned. "I regret to say that there are now reporters in the lobby wanting information."

"And they'll do *anything* to get a story. Anything. They may even try to get into this suite—"

He held up his hand. "Calm yourself, madam. I assure you, they will not commit a trespass in this hotel. I will warn my staff. Anyone who accepts a bribe from them will be dismissed immediately."

"All the same—"

"I suggest that you order meals from room service. A special waiter will be assigned. One of my security people will be posted outside your door. Around the clock."

"Thank you," I said, trying to smile. "I realize we're causing you a lot of trouble, but believe me, I appreciate your help." In fact, the way things were shaping, we would need a great deal of support from this man—and nothing would please him more than to see us all disappear into the lagoon.

"A most unfortunate occurrence. Please call on me if I can be of further service." He made a little bow. For a second I thought he was going to click his heels and kiss my hand.

As the door closed behind him, I shook my head to clear it. An hour ago Cathy and I had walked through narrow streets to the hotel, wondering how to handle the volatile Vanessa. Now we were being held prisoners at the whim of the Italian police.

Cathy was still sitting down, still plucking at her little silver cross. "Do I have it right? We can't leave tomorrow?"

"Not until we hear from the *commissario*. Which could mean days. Cathy, I'm sorry to bother you, I know how upset you are, but did Mark Dykstra have a key? I mean, how did he get in?"

"A key." She put a hand to her head. "He wouldn't have had a key, but he was here twice yesterday afternoon. The second time with some music."

"So the man at the front desk might have recognized him. Given him a key. Or sent a hotel person up with him to let him in. The manager will find out. Or the police. Never mind. It can wait."

"Barzalon." Cathy was on her feet. "Will we be telling him Vanessa can't leave? He'll tear us apart, limb by limb."

"He won't. He can't. And at least Sardinia is off, for the moment. We'll get through this. I promise you—" I stopped in midsentence as the bedroom door swung open.

"Emma." A choked whisper. Vanessa ran forward. She threw herself into my arms and buried her face in my neck. "I was so awful to him after the recital. I told him I wouldn't need him anymore. I never in this world thought he would do *this*."

"No, no, of course you didn't." I put my arms around her. Tears were running down my neck.

"I feel so terrible. As if I'd killed him. So *guilty*."

"I know. I know." I held her tightly, stroking her hair. One small mercy in all the horror—there would be no confrontation with Vanessa. She was *glad* to see me.

For a moment we stood there, holding each other. Finally she lifted her head. This was not the gifted singer who had delighted the critical Venetian audience and then insulted them. Vanessa's face was distorted and blotched with tears. The white dress was crumpled. She was shaking, on the verge of collapse. I looked at Cathy, a wordless plea for help. She crossed the room and took Vanessa's arm.

"There now. It's no good working yerself into a state; ye need to be tucked up in bed. Besides, yer auntie's had a long day, what with flying here and walking into a hornet's nest. She's dead on her feet."

"Cathy's right," I said. "Dead" was not the word I would have chosen, but once again Irish warmth had come to the rescue, the warmth that had eased my childhood nightmares.

"Emma. Love you." Vanessa unwound her arms from my neck.

I gave her a final hug. "Get some sleep. We'll talk in the morning. Love you. To infinity."

My room was at the end of the long hall. The blue brocade curtains in my room had been drawn, the bed turned down. I threw my leather handbag on the floor and collapsed into the nearest chair. An endless night—and it was far from over.

"We'll get through this. I promise you," I had said to Cathy. Fine words from the captain of a sinking ship with a cargo of escalating disasters: Vanessa's accompanist dead by his own hand in her suite. Orders from the police not to leave the city. Paparazzi gathering in the lobby like sharks in a feeding frenzy. By the time they finished with Vanessa, nothing would be left of her career, let alone her reputation. I needed help—and there was only one person who could give it.

Lord Andrew Rodale and I had met last July during my search to find my husband's killer. He had come toward me in the House of Lords, tall and arrogant in a pinstripe suit. A peer whose seat in the House of Lords was a cover for his double life as consultant for one of the secret services. A man who expected women to jump when he said jump.

In spite of initial mutual dislike, we had become colleagues. Working together, we had put together the last piece in a lethal puzzle, a puzzle that ended when I was nearly burned alive. He had taken me to Venice—a salvage operation to alleviate shock. There had been four days of healing in an old palazzo. Nights of exploring mind and body.

We had parted at Marco Polo Airport with good memories and no commitments. He went back to his double life. I had gone home praying that my boys would never know that their mother had slept with a man so soon after their father's death. It was a onetime aberration. There had been no reason to think Lord Rodale and I would ever meet again.

I closed my eyes and saw a tanned, muscular neck on strong shoulders. Two deep vertical lines in a strong-featured face. Perceptive gray eyes. A tiger between the sheets. Dangerous—stupid—to stir up tamped-down fires, but helping Vanessa came first. Andrew Rodale was a big player in the shadowy police world. The only card in my hand.

It was after midnight in London. I picked up my bag and pulled out the cell. Two rings. Three. Please, God, please let him be there, not on the other side of the world, ferreting out terrorists and spies.

"Rodale." The familiar deep voice.

"It's Emma." I cleared my throat. "Emma Streat."

He laughed. "You don't have to introduce yourself. Where are you?"

"In Venice. I'm in trouble and I need your help."

A long pause. "Is this some sort of joke?"

"No. Not a joke. A man just committed suicide in my niece's suite at the Dordona. The police won't let us leave. It's a nightmare and I don't speak Italian."

"Sorry. Take it from the top."

"The top. I have a niece, Vanessa Metcalf. You may have heard of her; she's a singer with a *beautiful* voice. I flew over today for her Rescue Venice recital, but that wasn't the real reason."

"Which was?"

"It's hard to explain, but the thing is, she's lost her head over this rich race car driver. He's pushing her to break her contracts, go off with him to Sardinia. The scandal would *ruin* her career."

"And?"

"We—her assistant and I—came back to the hotel after the recital. We found her accompanist hanging from a curtain rod in the *salone*. That was three hours ago. I called the manager, who called the police. A *commissario*. He says there has to be an autopsy. He says we can't leave until he gives us permission."

"That seems clear enough."

I pressed my hands to my head. "But it *isn't*. My niece is in shock. We're holed up in this hotel like prisoners; we don't know for how long. What's more, the press is camping out in the lobby. Waiting for the next installment."

"Not surprising. About this call. Exactly what did you have in mind?" A wary note in his voice.

I hesitated, feeling my way. "I know it's asking a lot," I said, "but you know the ropes. I was hoping you could get in touch with this *commissario*—his name is Filardi—and find out what's going on. If he gets a call from someone like you, he might press on faster. Aren't there things like reciprocal agreements, mutual aid?"

"There are, but it's complicated."

"This whole situation is complicated. I don't know the laws over here, but the more I think about it, the more I have a feeling that this *commissario* is hiding something. I mean, this wasn't a homicide. We aren't suspects. We answered all his questions. So why not let us go?"

"Can't answer that. I'd say you'd better be in touch with your consul in Venice."

"Oh." I pushed back my hair. I wasn't getting through. "I could, but there's another problem. The accompanist is—was— English. Vanessa's assistant has no idea how to reach his family. She just sends money to an agency, but *someone* has to be notified. *Someone* has to take care of the body. Is that the consul's job? I've never had to do anything like this before. Not in a foreign country."

A pause. Rodale cleared his throat. "Very well. English, you say. That changes the picture. Give me his name and the name of the agency."

"His name is Mark Dykstra. The agency—oh God, let me think. Oliver Cromwell—it's the Cromwell Road Agency."

"I'll look into it, but frankly, it's a bit off my turf. I don't know how far I can push the Questura."

"But you'll try?"

"Do what I can. I must say, you haven't wasted much time getting yourself in another mess."

"I know. The last thing in the world I needed, but Vanessa's assistant called me in Boston two days ago. Told me that Vanessa was about to throw away her career for this poster boy. Andrew, she's a gifted singer. She's *family*. I love her. I don't want her to be hurt."

"And now you're in over your head."

"Feet touching the bottom. I'm sorry, really sorry, to bother you, but I didn't know who else to call."

"Relax. I'll contact the *commissario*. Find out what's going on. I've learned, the hard way, to respect these gut feelings of yours."

"When do you think you'll know anything?"

"I'll get onto it in the morning. Put out feelers, but mind you, no promises."

"I understand. You've still got my cell phone number?"

"I do. By the way, how are your boys?"

"Very well. Back in college."

"Have you found a place to live?"

"Not yet, but I'm working on it. What about you?"

"Work is fairly intense at the moment. One rat hole gets plugged and three more appear. We seem to have a surplus of bad actors stealing, smuggling, and planning havoc." He cleared his throat again. "It's good to hear from you, even if it's a call for help."

"I—well, thank you," I said, blocking out the image of a carved bed in a borrowed palazzo. A man at the height of his physical and mental powers. Challenging. Addictive. Just hearing his voice was activating nerve endings that should be dormant.

"It's late. Go to bed. Anything else I can do for you?" A change in that deep voice. I could tell he was smiling.

"Nothing. I mean, isn't this enough?"

"We'll see, but don't forget one thing."

"What's that?"

"You owe me, Emma." The phone clicked off.

four

October 11

Like an endless movie, unnerving sequences revolved around and around in my head: A dark, narrow street. A bald head hanging down like a broken puppet. The street again. Cathy holding her little silver cross. The street again.

When I woke, the bedside clock was blinking eight o'clock. I rolled onto my back and lay still, breathing deeply. Last night I had thrashed around, feeling helpless and confused. Today I must be calm. Exude authority. "Count to ten before you panic," I had lectured my little boys. "Look before you leap."

Eight fifteen. I got out of bed and pulled back the brocade curtains. The day was beautiful, Venice at her best. In the lagoon, under a brilliantly blue sky, a swarm of seagulls swooped in tight formation. The shiny black prows of gondolas bobbed up and down. The great white cruise ship had sailed off.

I turned away, needing a jolt of caffeine, but first the call to Cathy.

"It's Emma," I said. "I just woke up. What happened after I left?"

"She was on and on, blaming herself for the hard words. I gave her a double dose of sleeping pills. That was around three o'clock. There hasn't been a peep out of her since."

"I'll have a shower, get some coffee, and come down. Have you heard anything from Seth Barzalon?"

"I have, so. The man has called five times since seven o'clock. The plane is waiting, he says, ready to go. I tell him that herself is asleep, but he won't be put off much longer. He'll be here, breaking down the door, guard or no guard."

"Oh God. Did you tell him we can't leave?"

"I didn't have the nerve. He wouldn't have listened to me."

"If the phone rings again, don't answer it. I'll be down in a few minutes."

At eight thirty, the waiter from room service appeared with pots of café au lait. *Cornetti* and rolls. Butter and jam.

"*Buon giorno,* signora," he said with a curious, sideways look, then put the tray on a nearby table and left.

An Italian newspaper lay beside the tray. I glanced at it without interest, then picked it up. There was a large picture on the front page. A close-up of Vanessa and Seth running out of the palazzo, holding hands, looking into each other's eyes. Another picture of a boat ambulance leaving the Hotel Dordona. Underneath the pictures, translatable words like *suicidio* and *gelosia* and *amore*. All the ingredients of a sensational love triangle. I threw the paper onto the floor.

"Scum. Bastards." My resolution to be calm and controlled flew through the open window and out into the lagoon. "I could *kill* them. I could kill them with my bare hands."

Standing in the shower, I reminded myself that my son Jake wanted to be a journalist. There were brave reporters in war zones. It was these greedy celebrity chasers who gave the profession a bad name. Somehow, someway, I must keep them away from Vanessa.

My clothes were still in the big suitcase. I pulled on a pair of black slacks and a deceptively simple striped designer top I'd found at a sale on Newbury Street. Whatever the next crisis, I must look—and act—like a woman of substance. A woman who wouldn't be pushed around by the press *or* the police.

Dark glasses. Cell phone. It was too soon to expect a call from Rodale, but from now on this little piece of high tech would be attached to me like a third arm.

No photographer lurked in the hall. A thick-necked man in a dark suit stood at the entrance to the suite. As I came up, he moved to block the door.

"No one goes in, signora."

"I understand, but I'm Miss Metcalf's aunt."

"No one goes in, signora."

I raised my chin. "Please find her assistant."

He hesitated, then disappeared, shutting the door in my face. A moment later, he and Cathy came out.

"It's all right," she said to the man. He gave a surly nod and let me pass.

The vase of purple gladiolus was still standing on the foyer table. I picked it up and handed him the vase.

"For you," I said, and closed the door.

Cathy put a hand to her mouth. "The look of him holding the vase—"

"He was rude and I can't stand gladiolus."

Today she was wearing a neat blue dress, her hair was combed, but there were dark circles under her eyes.

"I can see you didn't have much of a night. Is she still asleep?"

"Waking up. Will you be telling her about the police?"

"I'll have to."

The curtains in the green room were closed. Vanessa was lying in the vast green bed. Her bright hair was spread out on the pillow.

"Vanessa?"

She turned her head and clutched my hand. "He was standing by the door, waiting for me like . . . like . . . a little dog. I didn't mean—" An uneven voice. Slurred words. Was she too groggy to take in the bad news?

I reached down and smoothed her hair. "Vanessa, there's a problem. The police came last night. They say we have to stay in Venice."

"Police." Her eyes were closing.

"Italian police. We have to stay here in the hotel. We can't leave today."

"Can't leave." She turned on her side, drifting away. I looked at Cathy.

"One thing is for sure. She's not fit to go *anywhere.*"

"She's not, but how will you tell Mr. Barzalon?"

"God knows. I'll talk to him when he calls again."

Sun was coming through the long windows in the *salone.* We went in and pulled two high-backed chairs toward the door to the foyer. The heavy hand of death had been lifted, but it could never be erased.

"About Vanessa," I said slowly. "This has hit her hard—harder than I would have expected. On the other hand, she's always been unpredictable. I remember when she turned fifteen. One day cargo pants, the next sequins. Her mother had to do a juggling act."

"Poor soul."

"It wasn't easy. Vanessa always danced to her own music. She hated team sports, but she loved to fish; she'd stand for hours on a bank, casting. Boarding school lasted a week. Dull, and the girls were boring. Singing gave her a little discipline, but maybe not enough. I made the mistake of talking too much about the galley years; that's what singers call them. Getting a foundation. Not what she wanted to hear."

"*Permesso,* signora?" A maid was at the door with a huge bouquet of long-stemmed white roses wrapped in cellophane.

Cathy took them and looked at the card. "Barzalon," she said. As if on cue, the telephone began to ring. We looked at each other and went into the foyer.

Cathy picked it up. "It's him," she said under her breath. "He's altogether riled. He'll speak to Vanessa and he won't take no for an answer."

"We'll see about that." I took the receiver. "Mr. Barzalon? This is Emma Streat, Vanessa's aunt from Boston. I arrived last night for the recital. Vanessa's had a bad shock. She's still asleep and she can't be disturbed."

"Wake her. She can sleep on the plane."

I took a deep breath. Over the years I had learned that there was only one way to deal with bullies. Stand firm. Beat them down.

"The plane will just have to wait."

"Aunt, are you?"

"I am. Let me tell you something, Mr. Barzalon. The police were here last night. There's going to be an autopsy. The *commissario* says Vanessa can't leave Venice until he gives his permission. It may be days."

"Autopsy? The little poof hanged himself. What's the name of this *commissario*? I'll go to the Questura and straighten him out. Then I'm coming to the hotel."

"His name is Filardi, Commissario Filardi, but there's another problem. You may have seen the picture in the paper this morning."

"Crap. I want to talk to Vanessa and that Irish peasant is giving me a runaround."

My hand tightened on the old-fashioned black receiver. "Did you hear what I said, young man? Vanessa is not allowed to leave Venice. Police orders."

"Bunch of dagos. Get her packed."

Dagos. Get her packed. The stiff-necked aunt approach wasn't working.

"Look," I said in a softer voice. "I don't mean to sound sharp, but it's been a nightmare." A pause. "I think you need to be put in the picture. Hear exactly what's been going on."

"Fine. Tell me."

"I mean, we should talk, but not here or at the Grillo. The press is camped out in the lobby. There must be a place off the beaten track where we can meet for a few minutes."

"Waste of time."

"Not if we come up with a plan."

"Hold on." I could hear him talking to someone nearby. In a moment he was back. "My head pilot is here. Terry Gallagher. He'll pick you up in fifteen minutes."

Ten minutes later, Terry Gallagher arrived wearing a uniform with inches of gold braid on the sleeves. There was a fancy emblem on his hat and a grin on his face.

"Commander Gallagher, U.S Navy. Around here they don't know the difference."

"Emma Streat," I said, trying not to laugh.

"At your service, Emma Streat." He made a sweeping bow,

then turned to Cathy and blew her a kiss. "Morning, mavourneen. I hear the boyos in Waterford put on black when you left."

"Fine talk," she said, tossing her head. Suddenly there was color in those white cheeks. The drink in Paris had made a major impact.

"We'd better be on our way," I said, and checked to make sure the cell phone was in my handbag. I hadn't told Cathy about the call to Rodale. No point in raising hopes.

Across the Grand Canal, the Basilica di Santa Maria della Salute stood etched against the blue sky, a monument to the end of a fearful plague. Even in operas, *Otello* and *La Gioconda*, Venetian themes were apt to be death and destruction. Wagner had composed his tragic *Tristan und Isolde* in a borrowed palazzo. Today I was painfully conscious of the two sides of Venice: the romantic and the sinister. Beauty and depravity.

"This way, milady," Terry said, taking my arm and leading me toward a side street, a cheerful young man with a compact build and curly brown hair. The type who would bounce through life like a beach ball.

A battered red and blue canal barge filled with empty Lora bottles chugged by. A man passed, pushing a tilt cart filled with groceries. Working people going about their ordinary routines.

As we reached a little stone bridge, a black gondola came gliding toward us, a pole sweeping the water. The gondolier was wearing a navy-and-white-striped jersey and a straw hat with a red ribbon. He raised a dripping pole and saluted Terry.

"Ho there, man," he shouted.

Terry touched his cap. "Ho there, Fausto."

"We meet usual place?"

"On my way."

"Si." The gondolier saluted again and swept by. The pilot and this gondolier seemed to know each other very well.

"A friend of yours?" I asked, hiding surprise.

"The boss likes Fausto. The man sings the finest 'O sole mio' in town. Even the Japanese crack up." I smiled, remembering a party of Japanese sitting stiffly on upholstered seats with lace covers, looking straight ahead with serious faces, listening to "Jingle Bells."

"Are you in Venice often?" I asked, keeping my voice casual. This was my golden chance to find out more about Seth Barzalon.

"Once in a while. The boss has a sister who lives over on the Lido. A recluse, not right in the upper story. He has orders from their trustees to check up on her."

"Well, better Venice than Bangladesh. How long have you had this job?"

"It'll be two years, now."

"What kind of plane do you fly?"

"G Five. Gulfstream Five. A real sweetheart. Crosses the ocean non-stop."

It was the right button to push. He was off and running, an Irishman with a gift of the tongue. I listened, remembering the days when Lewis and I traveled in the Galbraith company jet. Our head pilot, Chet, once told me that there was a brotherhood of men who flew private planes and met at stopovers while their bosses played or did business. No doubt some of the pilots swapped stories about their employers.

The next alley was so narrow that we had to move against the wall as a priest wearing a long brown habit passed by. Lines of washing hung out of the upper-story windows.

"I gather you were planning to leave today," I said, wanting to get back to Barzalon. In warfare, information was a major weapon. In a moment I would be meeting my enemy face-to-face. Trying to find out what made him tick.

"Noon sharp."

"So when did you hear about Mark Dykstra?"

"Who's he?"

"He is—was—Vanessa's accompanist. He committed suicide in her suite last night. A tragedy."

"The one who screwed us up. I was off duty because of the recital. Went down to a beach where the water smells clean. Any road, I was back early to do the routine checks and arrange for food for lunch. Then I get a call from the boss to go to his hotel. He was cursing a blue streak, calling the Dordona every half hour."

"I know. I was at the other end. Is he always like that?"

Terry glanced at me and shrugged. "Ah, well, he doesn't like to be crossed, but he pays top dollar. When he gets me down, I think of the money and put up with his mouth."

"I see," I said, making a mental note. No love lost there. Money the key to this relationship.

The long alley was ending in a large, cobbled *campo*. A bronze statue of a soldier stood in the center; two women with babies in strollers sat talking on the pedestal steps.

"That's him over there," Terry said, and pointed to a small trattoria with a bar and a number of tables outside. "The one with the dark glasses. Tell him I'll be in the bar if he wants me."

"All right." I took a deep breath. God give me strength, I thought, and went forward.

Seth Barzalon was sitting at a table, a glass in front of him. Today he was wearing a rough navy linen shirt and white linen trousers.

"Mr. Barzalon? I'm Emma Streat," I said.

He turned his head and looked at me. Looked again. Not a tight-ass aunt from Boston. This woman was tall, with hair almost the color of Vanessa's. Bright blue eyes. Dressed for a power lunch at Cipriani's.

"Sit down," he said, and made a vague gesture toward an empty chair. "Have a Bellini."

I hesitated. Was this a challenge? The peach-and-champagne cocktail, a specialty at Harry's Bar, was apt to go to the head. "Fine," I said.

As Barzalon gave the order to the waiter, I did my best to assess Seth's appeal. There was the Nordic hero look. A sense of physical power barely held in check. The primordial man who could rescue a woman from overwhelming pressures and carry her off to his cave.

The waiter was back with my drink. Barzalon frowned. "Okay. So why are we here?"

Deliberately, I took a sip of the chilled Bellini. "The *commissario* says that we—Vanessa and Cathy Riordan and I—have to stay in Venice until the autopsy is done. He wouldn't say when."

Barzalon put down his glass. "Shit. I knew I should have gone to the Questura. What's the name of that *commissario* again?"

"Filardi."

"Yeah. Filardi." He picked up an ashtray with the Spumanti logo, then slammed it down. "Okay. Here's the deal. I straighten Filardi out. You go back, get Vanessa packed and on her feet. Terry goes to the airport."

"What about the press?"

"What about them?"

"They're not going to be cheated out of a good scandal."

"Jesus. Forget the press. By tomorrow they'll have another story."

A child on the steps began to wail. A mother stopped talking and picked it up. Another child threw a toy on the pavement and screamed for attention.

"There's more," I said, and stared at the battered ashtray. Confrontation on an adult level wasn't working. I must cut through the swaggering bravado. Treat him like one of the screaming toddlers in the *campo,* a child fighting to keep his toys.

"What?"

"Just this." I took a sip of the Bellini and tried to ignore the tension in my neck. "Why are we sitting here fighting? We should be on the same page. After all, we both want what's best for Vanessa."

"Then back off. Let her alone."

"How can I? She's my niece." I leaned forward. "Look. I've loved Vanessa from the day she was born. You've known her for a few days. That's a short time. How much do you care about her?"

Silence. He shifted in his chair, then shrugged. "None of your business, but I'll tell you this. She's spinning out. I'm good for her. I can make her happy."

"Then put yourself in her place. She and Mark Dykstra had hard words after the recital. She lost her temper and fired him. Now she feels guilty. Horribly guilty. It'll be worse when she reads that the press is calling this a love triangle. Hinting that the two of you may have caused his death."

"All the more reason to leave."

"But not on your plane. These people could be watching the airport. They might even follow you to Sardinia."

"Like I said, tomorrow there'll be another story."

"Maybe, but a lot of people heard Mark Dykstra threaten you at the reception last night. You and Vanessa bolt down the stairs. Believe me, people were talking about *that.* A few minutes later Dykstra goes and kills himself. Now the two of you go running off to a resort hideaway. It all adds up to a very nasty story. Very damaging."

"Wait." He held up his hand. "You've got it wrong. We're flying first to Boston. Then to Sardinia."

I stared. "You're flying to *Boston*?"

"Emergency board meeting of my foundation. Got word. One day and one night."

"I see." The cell in my handbag began to ring. I pulled it out.

"Emma." Rodale's voice. "Can you talk?"

"Not right now."

"It's fixed. You can leave Venice, but there's a problem. How soon can you ring me back?"

"Within the hour. Half an hour."

"Use this number."

I fumbled in my bag and found paper and pencil. "Got it. I'll call you back."

Barzalon was drumming on the table with his fingers. "Good news," I said. "That was a friend of mine in England. He has connections with the police here. I called him last night and asked him to help. He just told me we can leave."

Barzalon took off his dark glasses and looked at me. "He did that? Who's he?"

"Just a man I know in London."

"He must have pull. What's his name?"

"It doesn't matter," I said flatly.

"Maybe it does. A guy with connections with the police can be useful."

"It's done," I said, and put the cell back in the bag. Could Cathy and I slip away with Vanessa? No, too risky, but another thought was beginning to form in my overworked brain.

Barzalon was still drumming on the table. "Okay. Terry picks Vanessa up at the Dordona. Sneaks her out and takes her to the plane. That satisfy you?"

"Not if the press is already there." I paused. "On the other hand, your going to Boston changes everything. Here's a thought."

"Which is?"

"Very simple. No one's going to follow *me*. I'm just Vanessa's aunt. What if Vanessa and Cathy fly back to Boston with me? Vanessa spends the night in my apartment. You meet her there the next day."

He shook his head. "No way. I'm not running from any low-lifes."

"You're not running. You're beating them at their own game. There's something else. Vanessa is very close to her family. Having her name dragged all over the news would upset them terribly."

"That's their problem."

"Your problem if it upsets Vanessa."

"Nice try, but no dice. She goes with me."

The children were chasing each other over the cobblestones. I took a deep breath and studied the horse in the statue, front legs pawing the air. Oh God, how to break through this fire-wall of self-interest. This frightening need for instant gratifica-tion. Didn't the man have family? Friends who cared about him? I pushed my glass away and leaned forward.

"Never mind Vanessa. What about you? There must be peo-ple who don't want to see the name Barzalon smeared all over the tabloids."

"Not many."

"But I heard you're head of a foundation. What kind of foundation?"

"Research. Vaccines. My grandfather Comstock set it up for me before he died."

"Comstock. He was Comstock Pharmaceuticals?"

"The giant founder of the giant. He wanted me to quit racing and go into the business. Didn't work. I turn up for meetings and write checks. Problem is, my shitty trustees are looking for an excuse to put me on a tight rein."

"I see." This was interesting. My awareness antenna went up a notch. "Why would they want to do that?"

"A little trouble last spring in Europe. Any more bad publicity, they say, and *finito* the plane. *Finito* racing." He picked up his empty glass and put it down with a thump that rattled the tin table.

"That *would* be a problem," I said, needing to feel my way. "I guess racing can get in the blood. The speed. Taking chances. The adrenaline running."

He gave me a quick look. "You some kind of shrink?"

"No, but I can see it would really hurt to lose all that, especially if there's a way out."

"Your way, you mean."

"I mean, what's more important to you? My way or your lifestyle?" I leaned down and picked up my handbag. "I'm off. All I can say is, good luck with your trustees if they read the papers."

A group of young tourists with backpacks crossed the *campo*. The mothers and the children were leaving with a flurry of waves and kisses. Suddenly Barzalon pushed back his chair. "You win. Vanessa goes with you to Boston. For one night. One night only. Is that clear?"

"Yes."

"Good. By the way, when you get back to the Dordona, tell that Irish cow to put me through to Vanessa." He looked around.

"Where's Gallagher? I should fire him, always off making deals when he's needed."

"He said to tell you he'd be in the bar."

Outside the trattoria, men in V-necked red sweaters were playing cards at a table. Terry and the gondolier were standing by the door. I looked at them, then looked again. A few moments ago these two had been acting like buddies. Now their heads were together. They were talking fast, faces exuding anger. Terry raised his fist and shook it.

"I know the way; I don't need Terry to take me back," I said quickly, wanting to escape before Barzalon changed his mind.

Back in the Piazza San Marco, the tourist line in front of the basilica had doubled. I paused, then went toward Florian's, the eighteenth-century establishment where generations of Venetians had dined at the marble tables, sat on the red velvet banquettes. Rodale and I had come several times for coffee.

There was an empty table outside on the piazza; aside from observing cell phone etiquette, the discovery of high-tech listeners in my old house had taught me to talk in the open whenever possible.

"Signora?" A white-jacketed waiter was hovering.

"Um . . . a small espresso." The Bellini had given me a distinct buzz.

"*Grazie,* signora." He left. I punched in the number Rodale had given me. After a few seconds he answered.

"I'm alone now," I said. "At Florian's. Outside."

"Right. First the good news. My outfit is running a joint operation with the Questura. Nothing to do with your situation, but it gave me an edge with Commissario Filardi. He's not happy, but he agreed to let you go. A personal favor, you might say."

"Arm-twisting, you mean." Rodale had never told me if his

seat in the House of Lords was a cover for MI5 or MI6 or Special Branch. In any case, I would never ask.

"Now for the bad news. Your gut instinct about the *commissario* holding back was right. Tell me again what you know about the accompanist Mark Dykstra."

"Not much. I saw him in the distance at the reception, threatening Barzalon. An hour later he was hanging in the *salone*. According to my niece's assistant, he was sickly and very careful of his hands. She was amazed he had the strength to do it. What I can't understand is, why do it there—and how did he get in?"

"We'll get back to that. Filardi is no fool. He suspected what the autopsy confirmed. Mark Dykstra's death was caused by a blow that ruptured the spinal column between the first and second vertebrae."

"My God." I put down the cup. Coffee spilled into the saucer. I closed my eyes. Murder. The deliberate taking of life. The ultimate, unforgivable sin.

"Emma?"

"I . . . I can't believe it. That pathetic little man. I can't imagine why anyone would want to kill *him*."

"It happened, and not long before you arrived."

"Witnesses." The skin on my back contracted as cold ran up my spine. I could see a faceless man coming from behind the heavy furniture in the *salone*. If Cathy and I had walked in a moment earlier he could have panicked. My boys would have had to fly over and take my body home.

". . . you asked how he got in. The accompanist told the clerk at the front desk that Miss Metcalf wanted him to fetch some music for her. Right away. The clerk had seen them together earlier and he gave Dykstra a key. The man's been given the sack."

"Not surprising."

"As for suspects, Barzalon and your niece were at the Grillo. You and the assistant have been ruled out, even though the timing was close. Do you remember meeting a maid in the hall?"

"She was carrying towels. She came back and had hysterics all over the place."

"But that meeting puts you in the clear." A pause. "About the body. It's gone to the Civil Hospital. We've located a sister in a London suburb. She'll be notified officially. The consul in Venice has been alerted. He'll cope as best he can, but some informer may spot the switch from suicide to homicide. Sell the story to the press."

"More fuel for the fire."

"Another reason why the Questura isn't happy. Foreigners. Celebrities. No suspects. Forensics hasn't come up with any evidence."

"Nothing?"

"Not as yet. I advise you to get out of Venice before the *commissario* changes his mind or there are more developments."

"I will. Believe me, I will. I'll start hounding the manager for reservations. He'll be all too glad to get rid of us."

"What about the race car driver?"

"I met him just now. In a *campo* away from the hotels."

"And?"

"Imagine a Norse god who acts like a caveman. I've never met anyone like him. The extreme good looks. The extreme rudeness—it's almost like an act. Anyhow, I *think* I've persuaded him to let Vanessa fly back with me to Boston. Avoid the press. After that it's out of my hands."

"One more thing. I wouldn't pass this news along to the assistant or your niece. Let them think it was a suicide. No point in frightening them until we have more facts."

"Is that a warning?"

"A man was killed. We can't read the killer's mind. He knew his job, but Filardi outwitted him. Now he's in trouble. What should have been a straightforward case of suicide is now a homicide. Under investigation." He cleared his throat. "That's it, then. Safe trip back."

"Wait." A small boy ran across the piazza, chasing a ball, and the pigeons rose in a flock. "Wait. I haven't thanked you." Rodale had produced. I owed him—and he knew it.

"Right. You owe me." Once again, that unnerving trick of reading my mind. "Perhaps we should plan another meeting. Strictly for consultations, of course."

I swallowed. Game playing with this man required a light touch.

"No promises. One condition."

"Which is?"

"I will never, *ever* set foot in Venice again."

He laughed. "Paris, then. Or the Bahamas. Ring me when you get back," and he was gone.

"Signora?" The waiter was hovering.

"No. Grazie."

I wrapped my hand around the small espresso cup and stared at two pigeons fighting over a few grains of corn. High above me, the bell tower sounded the hour; for four centuries the two Moorish figures had emerged with hammers to hit the bell.

I sat in the warm sun, trying to take in this ominous new landscape. First the frustrating enigma of Seth Barzalon. My battle for Vanessa had ended in a short reprieve. Nothing more. Then Rodale and his veiled warning about a killer on the loose: "We can't read the killer's mind." Did Rodale know a lot more than he was telling me?

The pigeons returned. Three young girls with eyebrow rings sat down at the next table, chattering and tossing their hair. I put some euros on the table and stood up, knocking over the chair. Two words were drumming through my head: Get out. Get out. Get out.

five

The crowded plane was starting the final run over Boston Harbor. I tightened my seat belt and gazed down at the Bunker Hill Monument and the spire of the Old North Church. Symbols of my sturdy colonial heritage—and a welcome contrast to lagoons and piazzas and canals.

The flight attendant was coming down the aisle for a last-minute check. I looked around. A few rows behind me, Cathy was trying to wake Vanessa.

"Signorina suffers from stress and shock," the hotel doctor had said yesterday. "Here are pills to keep her sedated."

We had followed his directions. The crying and shaking had stopped. There had been no protest about the change of plans. All she wanted to do was sleep.

But this morning, as we were leaving the Hotel Dordona, she had emerged from her trancelike state. "There's press in the lobby? I'd better speak to them, not sneak away as if I had something to hide." It was the right thing to do. At the hastily arranged interview, her words about the loss of a valued colleague had been sensitive and moving. Pictures in the papers would show a suitably drawn white face. And "I'm going home to Boston with my aunt; she's standing right here" was hardly sensational news.

The water below us changed to runway. The wheels touched down with a manageable thump. The engines roared and stopped. Sheer relief was making my hands clumsy as I unfastened my seat belt. At last, no more fear that a carabiniere would step forward, shaking his head: "You are not free to leave, signora." No need to climb in and out of boats. Everyone spoke English.

The hired limousine was waiting, but it took a few minutes to find and load all of Vanessa's bags—the encumbrances of a singer on tour. Rush-hour traffic was heavy as the driver maneuvered his way through downtown Boston, along Charles Street, and up Beacon Hill. As he stopped in front of my old-fashioned building, I turned to Cathy.

"We'll get Vanessa upstairs; then the car can take you on to your cousin's apartment. Are you sure she'll have you?"

"Ah, she's glad of the extra money."

A chilly wind was chasing leaves along the sidewalk. The driver began to collect the bags. Vanessa was lying back against the blue velour seat, eyes closed.

"Vanessa, we're here," I said.

With an effort, she opened her eyes. "Where?"

"Boston. My apartment. You're spending the night with me."

She didn't answer. With Cathy on the other side, we helped Vanessa up the steps and into the old elevator, an open cage with grillwork on the sides.

"Should she still be so groggy?" I asked Cathy as we creaked up.

"Sure and those pills have knocked her out. I wouldn't give her any more."

"I certainly won't."

The stark apartment was uncomfortably warm. My housekeeper had come in, turned up the heat, and piled mail neatly on the hall table.

"Give me your coat," I said to Vanessa. "What about something to eat? Soup? Tea and toast? It won't take a minute." She shook her head and coughed. A hard, little cough, an ominous sound for a singer.

I looked at Cathy. "Maybe you'd better get her straight to bed. You know where to find her toothbrush and whatever she wears at night. The guest room's down this hall."

"Will the driver mind waiting?"

"He'll be pleased. He's being paid by the hour."

The two disappeared. I turned and tested the dirt in the potted cyclamens. It was soaking wet; nothing could convince the sweet Filipino housekeeper who came with the apartment that plants wouldn't survive the heavy watering.

Before leaving, I had activated the phone in the flat. The answering machine was blinking. The first call was from my son Jake: "Hi, Ma, missed you. I'll try again tomorrow." Nothing from his brother, Steve, a bad sign. I hadn't seen or heard from Steve since a family picnic in Manchester over Labor Day. Jake appeared to have accepted the loss of his father and home, but Steve was angry. With me.

"You should have told us what was going on last summer, Ma. That you were looking for Dad's killer and nearly got killed yourself."

Jake had advised patience: "He'll come around, Ma. Just give him space," but a cynical Oscar Wilde remark kept circling in my head: "Children begin by loving their parents.

[61]

After a time they judge them, Rarely, if ever, do they forgive them."

The second message was from Denise Daniels, the real estate agent. "A nice property has just come on the market. Call me as soon as you can."

"Tomorrow," I said aloud, and headed for the kitchen. Nothing in my house had been saved from the fire. Everything from sofas to saucepans was gone. Even thinking about starting from scratch was daunting. Worse, all the treasures that defined me as a person could never be replaced. The photographs. The tapes of my singing roles. The antiques I had collected over the years. The Grandma Moses painting in the hall.

Cathy was coming back. "She's in bed. I'll be going along."

"Thanks." I put my arm around her shoulders and hugged her; in the last two days I had come to love this girl. "We'll talk in the morning. I couldn't have managed without you."

"Ah, but weren't you the saint to come. Without you I'd have been destroyed entirely, the police and all."

"We were a team. We still are. I suppose that wretched man will be here first thing in the morning, beating down the door."

"He will, that."

"I'll try to talk to her early, before he comes, just on the chance she's been shocked out of that madness."

"And I'll be saying a prayer for miracles."

"Miracle or no miracle, he's in for a nasty surprise if he expects her to be up and running and able to leave. It'll be a good a test of how much he really cares about her."

"A good night's sleep may put her right."

"A good night's sleep is what we all need. I'll see you to the elevator. It shakes, but it's so slow it has to be safe."

Back in my room, I dropped my clothes on the floor and went to brush my teeth. Today, as we sat in the *campo* drinking

Bellinis, Seth Barzalon had come across as a sulky child of a larger size. An extreme egotist, a puzzle, but by pitting my brain against his I had managed to save Vanessa for one night. Not a great victory. From now on, I must think of myself as a safety net if—no, when—this ill-starred affair crashed and went up in flames.

Good mothers are programmed to wake at the sound of a wail in the night: the croupy cough, running footsteps in the hall—the dread preview to, "Ma, I'm going to be sick."

That mysterious sixth sense must have jolted me out of exhausted sleep. I turned my head and looked at the clock on my bedside table. Four thirty, the empty hour between night and morning.

With a groan, I got out of bed and stood there, shivering in my thin T-shirt. My standard remedy for sleeplessness was music on the all-night radio channel and a cup of chamomile tea.

There was no reason to check on Vanessa, but I hadn't liked the sound of that cough. Halfway on my way to the kitchen, I paused and turned on a light. Opened the guest room door a few inches and peered in. Stood still, my hand at my mouth. Vanessa was lying on the floor in a tangle of sheets.

"God. Oh my God." Without knowing I had moved, I was on my knees beside her, touching her forehead. It was burning hot. Her breathing was heavy and uneven.

"*Vanessa.*" I sat back on my heels, heart racing in staccato beats. Over the years I had learned to cope with various ailments. This was no ordinary illness. Not delayed shock. Not the aftereffect of tranquilizers. Vanessa was sick. Terribly, terribly sick.

Quickly I pulled blankets off the bed and covered her black

silk shift. One of Boston's best hospitals was nearby, just on the other side of Beacon Hill, but there was no way I could carry an inert Vanessa down to the street and get her into a taxi. It would have to be an ambulance.

"Keep your head," I said aloud. "Walk to the sitting room. Pick up the phone. Call nine-one-one."

In seconds, a woman's voice answered.

"My name is Emma Streat," I said, trying steady my voice. "I need an ambulance. I just found my niece lying on the bedroom floor. Unconscious."

"Is she injured?"

"No, but she's very sick. She's very sick and I can't move her."

Like the man who had answered my 911 call last June, this woman was brisk and competent. I gave her directions, then hurried back to the guest room.

Vanessa had turned on her side and thrown up. Luckily there hadn't been much in her stomach. I put a clean towel under her head, wiped her mouth and the front of the slithery black shift. Should I get her into something warm? No, better not to move her.

Vanessa coughed again—the wheezy, choking sound of lungs struggling for air. "Vanessa. I'm here," I whispered. "The ambulance is coming. It will be here in a minute."

Before leaving, Cathy had folded Vanessa's clothes neatly on a chair. The hospital would want identification. Insurance cards. They should be in her handbag—but suddenly I was back in the lobby of the Hotel Dordona. Just before the press interview, Vanessa had handed Cathy her handbag, standard procedure for a celebrity facing a microphone. Now it was stashed away in Cathy's big carryall. Over in the South End of Boston.

My own clothes still lay on the bedroom floor in a heap. I pulled off my T-shirt and tried to find a bra. Oh God, why was

I such a messy slob? Worse, why hadn't I seen last night that Vanessa was sick and taken her straight to the hospital?

Shoes. Sweater. My canvas travel bag was slung over the end of the bed. I picked it up, checked for money and credit cards, then raced back to Vanessa. She was alive, but breathing with an effort. Where in hell was the ambulance?

At last, the buzzer sounded. I ran to answer it.

"Third floor," I said into the box. "I'll be at the door."

With maddening slowness, the elevator creaked up. Two paramedics stepped out. A muscular young man and a woman with blond hair in a ponytail. They were carrying a portable stretcher.

"Ron and Tania," the man said. "Where's the trouble?"

"Down here." I led them along the hall and stood back as they bent over Vanessa.

After a moment, Ron straightened. "Off we go," he said cheerfully. "Tania, other side." In one quick motion they had Vanessa on the stretcher. Tania covered her with a blanket.

I followed them, hurrying to keep up. "Wait. I have to go with her. She's my niece. I have to identify her." For some reason, my mind was fixating on identification.

"Sure, no charge," Ron said. "Tania sweetheart, we'll have to use the stairs. Easy does it." It was clear that these two were used to working together.

In a moment we were on the street and the stretcher was in the ambulance. Tania climbed into the driver's seat. Ron motioned me to a narrow bench behind Vanessa's head. During the night the mass of red hair had lost its brightness.

As Ron hooked up his apparatus I concentrated on the overhead compartments for gloves. Large and extra large.

Finally Ron sat back. I looked at him. "How . . . how bad is she?"

Ron shook his head. "I have two rules, lady. We have fun—and no one dies." His standard joke, no doubt, but it was strangely comforting. When Lewis was struck down by a speeding car outside our place in Connecticut, I had followed the ambulance to the Newbury Clinic. I hadn't known that he was dead.

We were almost at the top of Beacon Hill. I glanced out at the familiar streets. It was still very dark outside, a sharp contrast to the gleaming steel interior of this fast-moving capsule. As we went down toward the river, I could hear Tania announcing our arrival. The ambulance slowed as we came into the narrow streets around the hospital. Stopped at the great white building. Slid into a low entrance with an unloading ramp.

Ron opened the doors. "Last stop," he said. "Should have made you ride up front with Tania, but you seemed to be in control."

"What happens now?"

"We check in with the T nurse on duty. Trauma nurse. He—she—decides whether we stay there or go to Triage."

With the precision of a dance troupe, Ron and Tania placed Vanessa on a gurney. I waited as Ron talked in a low voice to a nurse.

"Triage," Ron said to me, and I followed them into another hall lined with curtained bays.

"Relax, sweetheart; you've got a top crew here tonight," Ron said as Vanessa was shifted to a bed. "Take care, now."

For a few seconds I was alone with Vanessa. Her eyes were closed. The breathing seemed even more labored.

"Oh God," I said, and moved away as a nurse came in. Seconds later, the bay was filled with personnel. I went to stand outside in the hall.

Even at this hour, there was an air of focused activity. An overhead sign was indicating which bays were free. Two nurses passed, pushing another gurney, their shoes thumping along the floor as they ran. Above my head a voice was repeating, "Dr. Ryan. Stat ER. Dr. Ryan, stat ER." Under a thin veneer of control, this was a place of overwhelming fear and pain. Whatever happened, I musn't leave Vanessa alone.

A thin man in a rumpled white coat hurried into the bay. After a moment he came out.

"Are you with this patient?"

I stood straight. "Yes. Yes, I am."

"What can you tell me about her?"

I swallowed. "Her name is Vanessa Metcalf. She's my niece. She's a singer, a well-known singer. She had a recital in Venice three nights ago." He raised his hand, cutting me off.

"How long has she had this fever?"

"I . . . I'm not sure. We left Venice this morning. We got into Boston around six and went to my apartment. She slept all day on the plane. I was beginning to worry, but I thought it was just the pills."

"What pills?"

"She's been taking strong sedatives. An Italian doctor prescribed them. I don't know the name." It was important to speak slowly, not babble.

"Was she coughing on the plane?"

"I don't think so. The first cough I heard was just as she was going to bed. Something woke me. I went to look at her. She was unconscious, lying on the floor. I could see she was very sick. I called the ambulance."

"When did the vomiting start?"

"After I found her." I swallowed again. "What can you do?"

"Try to stabilize her. Move her to a bed as soon as one opens up."

"Wait." I pushed back my hair. Oh God, if I let Vanessa out of my sight, she would be nameless. A nameless person might not get attention. "She—my niece—doesn't have any identification with her. No insurance cards. She has them, but they aren't here."

"She's wearing a tag with her name and date of birth. That'll do for now, but you should go to the admitting office. Get her a blue card with an ID number." The doctor was turning.

I took a step forward. "I want her to have the best possible care. I'll be responsible for everything. Can I stay with her?"

"You may, but we need the space. I suggest you go to the admitting office. Down the hall."

"All right, but I'm not leaving the hospital. Not until I know what's wrong with her."

"There's a waiting room. Someone will contact you," and he went back into the bay. As the curtains opened, I could see Vanessa lying there, hooked up to steel poles, covered with a white blanket. A desperately sick person who now belonged to this hospital. These doctors.

The tired-looking woman in the admitting office looked resigned as I gave her information about Vanessa and said I would take care of expenses, however high. She sighed, shook her head, and began to work at the computer. Finally she turned.

"Vanessa Metcalf is in the system, but we need the insurance information as soon as possible."

"It'll be here in the morning. First thing. You've been very kind."

The waiting room was small, with groupings of utilitarian blue chairs. The television on the wall was showing a picture with no sound. I found a seat, leaned back, and closed my eyes. At the Newbury Clinic the chairs had been blue upholstery with gray specks. A doctor with gold-rimmed glasses had told me that Lewis was dead. I hadn't believed him. "My husband just went for a morning walk with O'Hara, our Jack Russell terrier. A hit-and-run driver ran him down on a little-used road. In broad daylight. Without warning."

After a while I opened my eyes. A fat man was sitting near me, stomach bulging like a football under a maroon velour shirt. He was talking on his cell phone, telling someone that his father's swollen legs were ready to burst. Another man in a navy T-shirt sat reading an old issue of *Yachting*. A young couple was holding hands, silent, staring into space. Five strangers, waiting for news, linked by pain and grief.

I must have drifted into exhausted sleep. I woke with a start as a nurse in a loose green uniform spoke to the young couple. They got up, still holding hands, and left. A dying baby? A much-loved parent? I looked at my watch again. Half past six. I was light-headed, in need of coffee, but if I left I might miss a doctor and news of Vanessa. And when someone finally came, I must be aggressive. Demand answers. Everyone knew that hospital mistakes were high on the list of causes of avoidable deaths.

"Mrs. Streat?" A man wearing a surgical cap had come in and was looking around.

I blinked and got to my feet. "I'm Mrs. Streat."

"You're a relative of Vanessa Metcalf?"

"I'm her aunt. I brought her in. I've been waiting to see her."

"Mrs. Streat, I'm afraid that's not possible. Your niece is still being evaluated."

I straightened. "Evaluated? How much longer will that take? I brought her here two hours ago."

The doctor cleared his throat. "I'm sorry, but I can't give you a definite answer at this time."

"What does that mean? I tell you, I'm not leaving until I see her."

"It means that it's too soon to give you any substantive news. I suggest you go home and wait there."

"Go home?" The accumulated distress of the past three days was surging up into my throat. I clenched my fists and stared at the doctor, the bright blue stare that used to send my boys sliding for the nearest door. "No. I will *not* go home and call in the morning."

"Very well, but I must tell you—"

"Yes, by all means tell me. You must know *something*," I said, aware that everyone in the waiting room was looking at me. "My niece is very sick. I want to know exactly what you're doing for her. I have a right to know and I intend to use that right."

"Go for it, lady," the man in the navy T-shirt muttered.

The doctor took off the surgical cap. "I suggest that we step into the hall, Mrs.—er—"

"Streat," I said, and followed him out of the room.

In the main hall, a MEDVAC team was bringing in a covered gurney. We moved to one side to let them pass. I folded my arms. I must ask more questions. Keep his feet to the fire.

The doctor cleared his throat again. "Mrs. Streat, you must understand that tests have to be run before there can be a diagnosis. Routine tests like tuberculosis. These tests take time."

"I understand, but I still want to see her. I'm the closest relative. Her parents are in Chile. There's no way I'm going to leave until I see her."

I waited. He rubbed his forehead, then put the sugical cap back on.

"You're her aunt. The parents are in Chile."

"Yes."

"In that case . . . I'm sorry to say that your niece presents with unusual symptoms. Because she could be highly contagious, she's been placed in a negative-pressure room. No one is allowed in except medical personnel."

"What's a negative-pressure room?"

"A negative-pressure room means that the air does not circulate in the usual way." He looked at his clipboard. "I understand that the two of you flew into Boston from Venice last night. What was the flight number?"

"The flight number? I don't remember. I must have it somewhere."

"While in Venice, were you in contact with anyone who was ill?"

"Not that I know of."

"Did the symptoms, the fever and cough, the nausea, come on suddenly?"

"The doctor in Triage asked me the same thing. Yes, they did. Yesterday she just seemed groggy. I thought it was the sedatives she'd been given for . . . stress. The fever and the cough and the nausea came on early this morning. I could see she was terribly sick. I called an ambulance."

He nodded, wrote on the clipboard, then put it under his arm. "I think that's all. Thank you for the information."

Unusual symptoms. Highly contagious. I opened my mouth to ask another question—then closed it. Instead of an adversary, I saw a middle-aged man with streaks of gray in his hair and dark circles under his eyes. A man who worked in a pressure cooker trying to save lives. Instead of yammering for information he couldn't give, I should be on my knees thanking God that this hadn't happened in Venice.

As he turned, I touched his arm. "I'm sorry," I said. "I know I'm being unreasonable. It's just that I'm frightened—and I *love* my niece. For all I know, she could be *dying*."

The doctor hesitated. His expression changed.

"I'll be frank with you. Your niece's condition is serious.

We're doing our best to stabilize her. On the bright side, she's young. She will have the best possible care. Here." He pulled out the clipboard again, tore off a piece of paper, and handed it to me. "The number for her special unit. I'll arrange it so that you can call at any time."

"Thank you. Thank you very much." I nodded, blinking back tears.

"I'm sorry. Now take my advice and go home. It's important to get some sleep. Keep yourself from becoming ill."

"Yes. I will."

"Good," and he went toward Triage, walking fast.

I leaned against the wall. A group of young people wearing the standard baggy cotton suits and sneakers passed me, talking and laughing. Maybe starting a new shift. The hospital world, so familiar to them, was closed and alien to me. It seemed like the height of desertion to leave Vanessa alone here. In limbo.

After a moment, I started down the hall, away from the emergency entrance. A security man went by. He was wearing a black shirt with a silver badge. Keys jingled from his heavy belt. I hurried after him.

"Excuse me, where can I find a taxi?"

"Straight ahead. Follow me. I'll take you."

"Will one be there this early or do I have to call?"

"Should be one or two in the rank, big place like this."

I followed, aware that my hands and feet were freezing. My brain seemed to be shutting down. Unfair that Vanessa was desperately sick. Unfair that I was forced to cope, with no one around to help. Lewis had possessed a quiet authority that always produced results. He was dead. Ned and Cassia were in Chile, thousands of miles away. Dear heaven, I must try to reach them.

". . . straight through the lobby, ma'am, and out through the revolving door."

I stumbled and looked at the guard. "Thank you. Thanks for your help." Three nights ago Vanessa had been standing in the gilded *salone* of a Venetian palazzo, enchanting the audience with her singing. I had worried about saving her career. Now I was agonizing about her *life.*

SIX

October 14

The ringing mobile beside my pillow woke me. I reached for it, fully awake, heart thudding. The hospital was calling. Vanessa was dead.

"Emma? Good morning, it's Denise Daniels. I hope you got my message."

"Denise. Yes." My sluggish brain circled—and fell into a slot. Denise Daniels. The real estate agent who wanted to show me upscale country houses.

"I know it's early, but I wanted to be in touch because this property would be perfect for you and your boys. Renovated barn. Tennis court. Swimming pool. Country, on a river, but not too far from Boston."

"Denise, it sounds great, but—"

"The thing is, if you're interested, we ought to get out there today. There's a young couple about to make an offer."

"Today? I can't. I've got a niece in intensive care. Her parents are in Chile and I'm in charge."

"In that case . . . I'm sorry." A long pause. "In that case, why don't you call me when you're free? There are always more listings. In fact, there's a lovely place in Dedham that might fit the bill." A hopeful note in the brisk voice. Denise was a single mother. A high-end sale would mean braces and ballet lessons for her two girls—or pay the rent.

"Let's leave it that I'll be in touch as soon as I can. Believe me, I really want to get settled."

"We'll talk soon, then."

"We will. Take care."

My eyes felt itchy and raw. I started to rub them, then looked at my watch. It was nine o'clock. I had overslept and there were important calls to make.

First the hospital. I reached for my handbag and dug through the litter for Vanessa's special unit number.

"It's Emma Streat, Vanessa Metcalf's aunt," I said to the voice at the other end. "I'd like to know how she is."

"One moment. I'll transfer you."

I waited, twisting the top sheet in my fingers, reminding myself that this was one of the world's great medical centers. Well able to deal with whatever nasty bug Vanessa had picked up in Venice.

"Good morning, Mrs. Streat." A woman with a pleasant voice. "Vanessa Metcalf's condition is listed as critical, but she's holding her own. I'm Dr. Reston's assistant. Dr. Samuel Reston, a specialist in infectious diseases. He's now in charge of the case."

"Holding her own, you say. Is she still in the . . . the negative-pressure room?"

"Mrs. Streat, Dr. Reston would like to talk to you as soon as possible. At the moment, he's doing rounds, but can you come to the hospital later this morning?"

"Of course. What time?"

"Eleven. He'll be free then."

"I'll be there, but how will I find him? That place is a jungle. A person could be lost for days."

"Come in at the main entrance and speak to the volunteer at the desk. Someone will come to meet you."

The mess of discarded clothes was still lying on the floor; in my next life I would be a paragon of neatness. Ignoring them, I got out of bed and headed for the shower. "One step at a time," a practical therapist once told me. After the shower, coffee. Then I must start trying to reach my brother, Ned, in Santiago. The call that every parent dreads.

The coffeemaker gurgled and dripped. I filled a mug, took it to the living room, and tried to get comfortable on the slippery leather sofa. With any luck, the converted barn would be available for a few more days and I could get out of this short lease.

Between gulps of coffee, I was beginning to realize that stress, jet lag, and two hours of sleep was having a negative effect on my organizational skills. To make matters worse, my brother's number in Chile was out of order. Finally I called his assistant at the State Street brokerage office. A bright young woman who promised to contact Ned.

Next, Cathy. She answered on the second ring.

"It's you," she said. "I was beginning to worry. How is she today?"

"I'm afraid I've got bad news. Really bad. She's at Boston General. I had to take her there at four thirty this morning. She's very sick."

"Holy Mother. Those pills. I gave her too many."

"No, nothing to do with the pills. She has a high fever. She's in some kind of isolation. It may be contagious."

"A disgrace, those canals, garbage and worse."

"Cathy, listen. She needs her insurance cards. I didn't have them with me. The admitting person was having a fit. Could you take them to the hospital this morning? As soon as possible?"

"I'll do that. Will I bring any of her things? Her slippers? Her teddy?"

"Not yet. Just go through the red tape and get a blue card. The bills are bound to be huge. One mercy, we got home just in time. God knows what would have happened in Venice."

I clicked off, took a deep breath, and flew into a frenzy of activity. Opened the windows in the guest room. Bundled up the sheets and hurled them into the washer. Back in my room, I put on designer slacks, a plum cashmere jacket, tied a silk scarf in an ascot. An attempt at confidence boosting.

In daylight, the famous hospital complex of medical centers had become busy and congested; a group of young people in white coats went by, carrying clipboards. Future doctors—the best learning their trade from the best. At the cul-de-sac entrance, a gleaming white concrete façade rose high above the twisted maze of old streets. On the left, a line of American Medical Response ambulances waited. After last night, I knew what they looked like inside.

"Thanks," I said to the taxi driver, and went into the big modern lobby. People of all shapes, sizes, and colors were hurrying by, following lines and signs. A fishbowl of humanity, swimming toward distant destinations.

Dr. Reston's office was small and compact. When I came in, he was sitting at a desk, talking on the phone. He smiled and motioned me to a chair. As he talked, I made a quick assessment: Gray hair. Late fifties or early sixties. A pleasant voice with authority. The line of framed certificates on the wall was impressive.

"I'll check with you later, Henry." He hung up, got to his feet, and leaned forward to shake my hand. "Mrs. Streat. Thank you for coming at such short notice."

"Believe me, I wanted to come. I'm terribly worried about my niece. No one seems to know what's wrong with her."

"Right." He looked down at his desk and moved a paper. "Mrs. Streat, I won't try to paint a rosy picture. Your niece is a very sick woman. We're doing a number of tests, but so far we haven't come up with any answers."

"Nothing at all?"

"Not as yet."

I swallowed. "It happened so *fast*. Is she—well, is she worse?"

"That's a difficult question. Last night your niece was put in what we call barrier nursing. She is being given a strong cocktail of antiviral medications."

"How long will they take to work?"

"Again, I can't give you a definitive answer. Fortunately, she's young. In excellent physical condition. Having said that, she has a very high fever. Her lungs are affected. The technical term is 'ARDS.' Acute respiratory distress syndrome."

"Oh God, no. Not her lungs." Suddenly I was sitting in another doctor's office. He was telling me that the retina and vocal cords were the two body tissues that never recovered from severe damage. It would come as a severe blow, but my voice would never regain volume. My operatic career was over.

Dr. Reston was looking at me with concern. I took a deep breath. "Sorry. Dr. Reston, you may not know, but Vanessa is a singer. A very talented singer. It would be a tragedy if she loses her voice—" I stopped. Singing was not what mattered now.

"Singer. I'll make a note." He wrote on a pad, then sat back, making a tent of his hands. "Now. It would be helpful to have more information about Miss Metcalf."

"I'll do my best."

The questions came thick and fast. How long had Vanessa been in Venice? Where had she stayed? Had we eaten the same food? Did her special water have a brand name? What were the first symptoms? When did they start?

For the next five minutes I tried to give Dr. Reston a concise version of the accompanist's sudden death. Vanessa's shock, the sleeping pills. Finding her on the floor at four thirty this morning. Like all good doctors he listened, giving me his full attention.

"Thank you. This is very useful," he said as I finished.

"I hope so." I sat back, feeling drained. "All the same, I can't forgive myself for not bringing her in sooner. I should have seen that she was so sick." I hesitated, then leaned forward. "I know this sounds stupid, but is there *anything* more you can do for Vanessa?"

"She's being given every antiviral drug in our arsenal. There are others in the testing stage, but not far enough along to be safe." He cleared his throat. "Tell me, Mrs. Streat. Are you, or have you been experiencing, any of these symptoms? Nausea? Cough? Fever?"

"No, I'm not. Aside from being tired and needing sleep, I'm fine."

"What about the assistant?"

"She was fine when I talked to her a while ago." I looked at him. "Are you saying we might come down with this—whatever it is?"

There was a long pause, as if he was trying to find the right words. He picked up the pad again and put it down.

"Tell me, Mrs. Streat. How much do you know about avian flu?"

"Avian flu?" I tried to concentrate as a montage of news reports flashed through my head. "Not a lot. Just what I've read in the papers about infected birds in the Far East. Once in a while there's talk about an epidemic."

" 'Global pandemic' would be a more accurate term. In my opinion, and that of others in this field, it's only a matter of time before this highly pathogenic virus finds a way to spread from human to human. An *efficient* way."

"Only a matter of time?"

"Let me explain. Killer pandemics come in cycles. They cannot be prevented. That leaves us with the question of *when,* not *if.* Unfortunately, avian flu—H five N one—is no longer found mainly in the Far East. Cases are cropping up in Europe."

"Many cases?"

"Not at high levels, but in this day and age microbes pass easily from country to country. Therefore, all transatlantic flights are a major concern. One cough and dozens of passengers are exposed. Within days there can be an outbreak. The threat is very real."

I touched my scarf. "Dr. Reston. Are you telling me that my niece has come down with avian flu?"

"I'm saying your niece's case is sending us warning signals. The first we have seen in this hospital. As a result, we are taking every precaution. Using every resource to identify this virus as quickly as possible."

Avian flu. Warning signals. I shook my head. "No. It doesn't make sense. Vanessa was in Paris and then Venice. She wouldn't have come near any birds—maybe pigeons in Venice. That's all. It can't possibly be avian flu."

Dr. Reston frowned. He took off his glasses and put them on

again. "I'm sorry. I know this is difficult to understand. To accept. On the other hand, the symptoms are there. It would be highly irresponsible—not to say dangerous—to ignore the possibility."

"But where—how—when will you know?"

"As I said, every resource is being used to identify this virus. We're now working with CDC in Atlanta—Centers for Disease Control. Unfortunately, matching rare viruses takes time."

"But . . . before that happens, will she die?"

Dr. Reston looked down at his pad. "As in any severe illness, no one can predict the outcome." He paused. "Our goal here is rapid detection and rapid intervention. The three key words are: *Identify. Isolate. Contain.* Therefore our best option is preparedness. There have been no reports of other cases in those particular areas, but the system of international surveillance has been alerted. WHO—the World Health Organization—is part of the UN. It has a global outbreak alert and a response network called GOARN. Operational support teams who fly to the affected site if needed. But as I say, it's unfortunate no vaccine has been developed enough to use. Even our present antivirals aren't nearly as effective as we'd like."

"I see." There was a pen-and-ink drawing of the Tree of Life on the wall behind Dr. Reston. I concentrated on the black lines of branches, trying to fasten my mind to a tangible object. Instead of office walls, I could see an Asian boy, bending over a dead chicken, thousands of miles away. Vanessa lying on the guest room floor, struggling to breathe.

"Mrs. Streat."

"Yes?"

"I realize that this is very distressing for you, but there's another problem that must be faced. The problem of secondary contacts. You say the cough didn't start until last night. With luck, that may have reduced the overall risk of exposure on the plane, but not to you, a person who has been close to her for days."

I stared. "You mean, I have to come here? Be put in isolation?"

He smiled. "Nothing as drastic as that. You strike me as a sensible, intelligent woman. Not likely to panic. I realize the inconvenience, but I'd like you to keep out of crowds. Not go to theaters, shopping malls. Stay in your home. See as few people as possible."

I closed my eyes, feeling dazed. "For how long?"

"We're talking about a voluntary quarantine. Enforcement is not an option at this time. As I understand it, your niece was well enough to sing in a recital four nights ago. So let's say four days. Of course, that may change. Do you think you can manage four days?"

"Yes."

"I want you to take your temperature three times a day. If it's over one hundred and one degrees, contact me immediately. Will you pass this request along to Miss Metcalf's assistant and anyone else who was close to Miss Metcalf?"

"Yes," I said. Barzalon. How to tell him?

"And last but not least, be extremely careful when you talk to family and friends. Any rumors about an outbreak of avian flu will bring the media out in force. The hospital would be bombarded with questions. There could be a general panic."

The telephone was ringing. I sat still as Dr. Reston talked about vital signs and how the patient presented. Was Dr. Reston overreacting, doing what doctors had to do to protect themselves from lawsuits? No, unless I was very wrong, this was a *good* doctor who put his patients first.

He put down the phone, I looked at him. "Dr. Reston, I *will* stay in my apartment, that's no problem, but I'll have to give a reason. And Vanessa's parents will have questions. What do I tell them?"

"The truth: Miss Metcalf is experiencing acute respiratory distress." He hesitated. "Frankly, Mrs. Streat, we're all on unfamiliar ground here. Feeling our way and hoping, very much hoping, for a good outcome. One moment." He picked up his pen, wrote a number on a card, and handed it to me. "My private number. Any questions, any concern about symptoms you might be feeling, don't hesitate to call me. Day or night. And keep in mind that your niece will be getting the best care that we can give."

"I know. Thank you." I took the card and put it in my bag. This was a *kind* man, as well as a good doctor. Had he been sleeping when he got the first alarm? Or shaving? Having breakfast? The caller's voice would have been controlled, hiding alarm: "Dr. Reston, a young woman was brought in by ambulance at four thirty. We'd like you to see her. We think she may present with H five N one."

A line of taxis waited outside the hospital entrance. Beyond them, the back side of Beacon Hill rose in a straight line of narrow brick houses. I began to walk toward them, needing to get air in my lungs. With no warning, the familiar world had taken on a new dimension. The threat of a pandemic was real—and Vanessa was the cause. And Emma Metcalf Streat, ordinary citizen, was a possible spreader of death and disease.

A bearded man was coming the other way, holding a small dog on a leash. What would he do if I ran after him, screaming, "You don't know it, but in ten days you may be dead"?

Sweat was running down my back. As I climbed, a scene

from the film *Outbreak* came flooding into my mind. Instead of a small-town setting, I could see a mob storming Boston General, pushing past security guards. Those endless halls were lined with desperate men, women, and children covered with sores, blood running from their mouths. At Logan Airport and the Hines Convention Center, people were staggering and collapsing on the floor.

Below me, an ambulance siren sounded. Down there, lying in a tangle of tubes, Vanessa was struggling for her life. Alone, with no family or friends around her. My mother had believed, deeply, in the comfort of the everlasting arms. When my husband was murdered and my house was blown up, I hadn't asked God for help; it hadn't seemed right to skip practice and expect the coach to put me into the game—but those were purely personal disasters. Nothing that would affect the man walking the dog—or the families that lived in these brick houses. Or people thousands of miles away.

I walked faster and a vague prayer began to form in my mind: Listen, God. Please listen. I'm not begging you to save Vanessa's lungs, or even her life. Just let her know that she's loved and that there are arms holding her up. And please, God, don't let *her* be the person who starts the next pandemic.

At the top of the hill, I slowed, then headed toward the neighborhood grocery. There was a fancy fall display of apples, cornstalks, and pumpkins in the windows. The annual pumpkins on my front step had been large and lopsided. My boys had carved grinning, toothy faces and filled the garbage cans with smelly pulp and seeds.

This year no pumpkins, but I was out of milk and yogurt and fruit. The cheerful Italian woman behind the counter waved when she saw me; in the past few weeks, she had become a good friend. I knew the names and ages of her six children. "Itsa fine day, Missa Streat," she said, smiling. "I havva fresh cider from big farm in the country."

I rocked back on my heels and turned. "Thanks, some other time," I said, and backed out. God forbid I should infect this woman and her swarm of little children.

Quickly I hurried along the uneven brick pavement. Somehow I would have to get food. Tell my little housekeeper that she couldn't come this week. I was almost at my entrance when I saw a black Alfa Romeo parked at the curb. The door opened and Seth Barzalon emerged. He was wearing the signature white linen trousers and a navy-and-white-striped pullover.

"Where were you?" A loud, belligerent voice. "I've been ringing your bell for ten minutes."

I stood still, needing to summon control. "Where was I? I'll tell you. I've just come back from Boston General. I took Vanessa there at four thirty this morning. She's very sick."

"Sick? Don't play games with me, Auntie." He folded his arms.

"Believe me, Vanessa is very sick. In a special unit. Maybe dying. You can check with the hospital if you don't believe me."

The expression on his face changed. He took a step forward. "What's the matter with her?"

"The doctors think it's some kind of virus, but they just don't know. I woke up early this morning and found her lying on the bedroom floor. I called an ambulance. I stayed at the hospital until after six. Went back again. They're still trying to stabilize her. All I can say is, you're lucky she's not in Sardinia."

He looked at me, as if weighing my words. "Jesus," he said, and hit the front of the car with his fist. "Hospitals. Death traps. Who's her primary doctor?"

I stared, startled by this physical reaction. "I don't know. Maybe she has one in New York. I've just seen a specialist, a Dr. Reston."

"Virus, you say. She needs someone with clout who can give me a personal report."

"Dr. Reston *has* clout," I said, clenching my fists.

"Never heard of him. I'll rev up my foundation, bunch of nerds hunched over their microscopes all day. High time they had their feet put to the fire." He pulled out his cell.

I took a step forward. "Wait. Are your people doctors?" The last thing Dr. Reston needed was this bullyboy throwing his weight around.

"My head honcho is supposed to be brilliant. I'll tell him to get his ass down there and ask questions. Not take no for an answer," and he punched in numbers.

"Barzalon here. Give me Dr. Atkins. Pronto." A pause. "Greg? Listen up. A friend of mine, a Vanessa Metcalf, is over at General. It's bad, some kind of virus. I want you to go down there and find out what's going on." A long pause.

"Jesus Christ, you know the situation. Deal with it. Right now I'm with this aunt on Beacon Hill. She's just back from the hospital. Says it happened last night. They're telling her it's some kind of virus; they don't know which one." He turned to me. "What are they testing for?"

"Last night they did routine tests. Now they're calling in the experts."

"Last night routine tests, now the experts. A Dr. Reston is in charge." Another pause. Seth Barzalon was listening, scowling. I watched him, trying to follow the body language. No doubt about it, he was upset. Badly.

"I read you," he said at last. "Yeah, yeah, I'll watch it. Just get down to General and get your foot in the door—yes, I know there's a board meeting. The accountants are there? . . . Already? . . . Tell the penny-pinchers I'll be with them later."

He clicked off and leaned against the car. Rubbed his head and stared down the street. After a moment, he looked at me as if seeing me for the first time.

"Not easy for you," he said in a different voice. "To be honest, I never expected anything like this to happen."

"No one could."

"Was she sick on the plane?"

"She was sleepy. Not sick. Not till early this morning."

"Bummer, but she's strong. She'll be all right."

I looked at him. If this was a truce, I had better take advantage. "We can't stand here in the street," I said. "Come up and have a cup of coffee. That is, if you're not in too much of a hurry."

"The accountants can cool their heels."

Once in the apartment, he began to pace again. I made more coffee and handed him a mug.

"Sit down, why don't you, and I'll tell you about last night." As he folded himself into a tubular chair, I replayed my story, leaving out any mention of avian flu. "It's a good hospital. They're doing their best," I finished. "Before I forget, Dr. Reston wants everyone close to Vanessa to stay out of crowds for four days. In case we're contagious."

He shrugged. "Crap. Doctors wanting to cover their asses."

"Maybe, but don't forget, you were close to her. Very close. If you begin to feel sick, you'd better check it out."

"Yes, Nurse." He grinned, an attempt, no doubt, to turn the interfering aunt into an ally, but for a short moment we were on the same page, sharing concern.

"When did you fly over?" I asked.

"Yesterday. Spent last night in New York, came up early. My pilot had to work overtime."

"The dashing Terry Gallagher. I think he's made a big impression on Vanessa's assistant."

"That Irish cow. I'd fire Gallagher tomorrow except that he's a damn good pilot."

"Then why fire him?

"Women. Can't leave them alone." He grinned again. "I know what you're thinking. The pot calling the kettle black."

"Perhaps." I put down my mug and shifted in my chair. In Venice, we had met in the open air. This was like being in a small space with an unpredictable animal—and for some reason, the sudden friendliness was more unnerving than extreme rudeness.

"More coffee before you go?" I asked, and stood up. Judging by the way he treated his associates, there might not be many places where he was welcome.

He yawned, stretched, then unwound himself from the chair. "Thanks, but I'd better get over to the foundation. Bad enough dealing with the accountants, Now my old man's decided to fly up from New York and make a nuisance of himself."

I glanced at him. "Your father? What kind of nuisance?"

"My grandfather put him on the board, a crumb to keep him quiet, but sometimes he gets ideas. Luckily, the trustees hold the purse strings."

"So what do *you* do?"

"Sign checks. Act like I'm on top of things. The truth is, I flunked every math course."

"Join the club. I never got beyond Algebra One. It used to drive my husband crazy."

We began to walk down the hall. As we reached the door, he

turned. "About my head honcho. His name is Greg Atkins, Dr. Atkins, and he talks the talk. He's going down to General this afternoon. Then he'll be in touch with you."

"Good." A Barzalon minion, but any link with the hospital could be useful. "Fine, but don't forget, if you feel sick, start to cough, you *have* to get yourself down to General. Unless you *want* to be deathly sick."

"Not going to happen."

I looked at him. "How can you be so sure?"

"Just telling you. Not going to happen."

"Well, I hope you're right," I said, keeping my smile in place. One good thing. This self-centered egotist wasn't likely to have much patience with illness; he was far too restless to stay in one place very long.

"See you," he said, and the door closed behind him. A moment later the black Alfa Romeo was roaring up the hill, breaking the strict speed limit.

Slowly, very slowly, the apartment contracted back to its normal size. I sat down and closed my eyes. Oh God, for a few hours of sleep—but first I must call Cathy and tell her about the quarantine. Four days locked together would send us both up the wall. If she couldn't stay on with her cousin, I'd have to think of something else.

There was no answer in the cousin's apartment. Cathy must be at the hospital. Next on the list, food. My housekeeper could buy it at the corner grocery and put it outside my door. During the fourteenth-century plague that had wiped out half of Europe, villages had paid to have food left at designated plague stones.

Yogurt. Bread. Milk. Fruit. Books ordered from the corner bookstore. The list was long. As I wrote, my mind kept coming back to Seth Barzalon. What sort of parents could have produced this combination of boorishness and sex appeal? There was one person who could shed light.

My godmother, Caroline Vogt, was seventy-four. She had a razor-sharp tongue, a voice like a tuba filled with gravel, and I adored her. Caroline had been divorced four times. She moved in the upper echelon of so-called East Coast society and was a walking encyclopedia of information about that shifting ladder. Caroline knew who was on the inside track and who was out. She knew what lay behind the deceptive surfaces of liaisons, marriages, and divorces. And if she didn't have the answer, she knew who did.

"Let her be at home," I muttered, and dialed her number in New York. One of her elderly maids answered the phone.

"Minnie? . . . It's Mrs. Streat. Is Mrs. Vogt in?" As Minnie went to find Caroline, I thought about this childless heiress from Chicago, my mother's roomate at Wellesley. My surrogate parent since my mother's death. Last summer I had tested Caroline's patience to the limit: "I am seriously angry, Emma. With good reason. I take you to a seminar in Cambridge and you leave after one day. One day, and not a word of explanation." In the end, I had been partially forgiven when it turned out that I was almost killed while exposing my husband's killer. Completely forgiven when I told her that I had gone off to Venice to recover. With a man.

"Darling girl," the tuba voice boomed in my ear. Caroline had called me darling girl from the day I was born. "Darling girl, it's been an age. How is Boston? Have you found a house?"

"Not yet," and I launched into a carefully edited account of the past few days. For once, Caroline didn't interrupt.

"I can't believe it," she said as I finished. "I can't believe you're deep in trouble again. So soon."

"I know, I know, but I love Vanessa. She's family and I care about her singing. But Caroline, she's so *sick*."

"Poor lamb. Is there anything I can do? You know how I hate illness, but I can get my usual suite at the Ritz."

"It's the Taj Boston now."

"Ritz to me. We'll go out to dinner. You can't sit in a hospital all day and night."

"That's kind of you, really kind, but no need. So far I'm coping."

"Well, give me Vanessa's room number. I'll send flowers. Grapes."

"Maybe later." A pause. "Look. There's one thing you *can* do. This Seth Barzalon. I can't figure him out. He's almost like a cartoon caricature of a playboy. Handsome, rich, not too bright, but he seems to think he has some God-given right to tank over people. I need to know what makes him tick—but it's not easy. Do you know the family?"

"Of course. Not my favorite people, but I know them."

"Tell, then. Everything you can."

"Let me think. There's a peculiar girl, a recluse who lives in Venice. The boy had trouble getting through school, some learning disability like dyslexia. Margaret, his mother, spoiled him rotten, but she died when Seth was about twelve. A sad creature. No looks, no style. James Barzalon married her for her money."

"Oh?"

"Classic case of homely rich daughter marries ambitious poor boy. James came from the Midwest—Akron, I think. He played a good game of golf, met Margaret at some country club and swept her off her feet."

"Were they happy?"

"Of course not. James had a roving eye and plenty of charm.

He figured on an easy ride for the rest of his life. She died and he hardly got a penny."

"Why not?"

"Because of her father, Charles Comstock. You know, Comstock Pharmaceuticals. The old man saw right through James. He sewed the money up tight."

"So what does James do now?"

"Backgammon. Bridge. Golf. Man-about-town. Escorts older ladies to events. God knows where he gets the money, but I see him eating at Le Cirque and places like that. Obviously he's managing—or else the bills are up to the ceiling."

"You don't like him, I take it."

"Understatement. If there's one thing I can't stand, it's that kind of practiced charm. He made a pass at me when Margaret was alive and I was on my second husband. I told him we were both jumped-up outsiders from the Midwest, never mind that his father-in-law had him taken into the Racquet and my mother-in-law got me into the Colony. Not what he wanted to hear."

I laughed. "I'm getting the dysfunctional picture. Boy with learning disabilities. A mother who spoiled him rotten, then died. Lightweight father who didn't get the money he was expecting."

"The irony there is that James is not stupid, not by a long shot. He might have done well in business if he hadn't had a compulsion to take a shortcut."

"What do you mean, shortcut?"

"Most of the world makes money by working for it, not looking for a quick fix. Like marrying money." A pause. "Darling girl, why this interrogation?"

"I told you. Seth Barzalon is my enemy. I need ammunition. Do you know anything about his foundation in Boston?"

"A bit. Old man Comstock started it for Seth, the only

grandson. His hope was to put him in the pharmaceutical world. Keep him out of trouble. Another classic case of wishful thinking."

"There *have* been troubles?"

"What do you think? It so happens my dear friend Maisie Dunlap is married to one of his trustees. According to Nick, it's like hitting a mule with a plank when it comes to making him cut back on his lifestyle. The race cars. The plane. The women."

"Women?"

"Spectacular affairs with celebrities. Last spring it was an Olympic skier. Tabloid heaven when he left her for a minor Greek royal. Darling girl, you must have read about it."

"I only read tabloids at the checkout counter."

"No need to be patronizing. There was a house party in Italy. A girl died. There were rumors that officials were paid off to avoid a scandal."

"Are you saying there's a dangerous streak under the bravado?"

"Darling girl, I don't know. I'm not an analyst."

"You've got sharp eyes—and ears—but do you and your friends really care about scandal?"

"You'd be surprised. In what's left of society, publicity is worse than the crime. You know, sin if you must, but don't frighten the horses. One more public scandal, Maisie says, and the trustees will cut off funds."

"Which would hurt," I said, remembering the confrontation in the *campo*. In the end, it was my warning about a scandal that had won the battle. Given me the lever to get Vanessa out of Venice without him.

"Of course." A pause. "Darling girl, keep me posted. Do you think Vanessa will go off with him when she leaves the hospital?"

"Not if I can help it. But it's hard to know what he's going to do."

"I'll keep my ear to the ground. How are the boys?"

"The boys are fine. You'll be glad to hear I haven't seen them for weeks."

"You're progressing. What about men?"

"None so far."

"I despair. A rich, good-looking widow with a great figure— what are you waiting for? After what you've been through, you're owed some fun."

"I am, but first I have to find a house. I can't stand this apartment much longer."

"Then leave. What's stopping you? Turn the key in the lock and leave. Which reminds me, I'm late for lunch with a museum director. He's after seed money for a new wing."

"Go, then. Love you."

For the rest of the afternoon, I scurried about as if preparing for a massive natural disaster. Arranged my bureau drawers and cleaned out the refrigerator. But as my hands worked, my mind was always on Vanessa. Had one of the drugs taken hold? Had the CDC found a match for the virus? When I called Vanessa's unit earlier there had been no change, but at five o'clock I was suddenly aware that my throat was sore and scratchy. Telling myself not to panic, I took my temperature for the second time. It was normal, but if I collapsed in the middle of the night, who would call 911? Get me to the hospital?

With a desperate need to keep moving, I worked faster. The kitchen shelves could be wiped down. I was taking clothes out of the dryer when the phone rang. I dropped the pile on the floor.

"Yes?"

"Anne Tremont from Transcontinental Artists. Vanessa Metcalf is one of my clients. The Hotel Dordona in Venice gave me your number. I need to speak to her. It's extremely urgent."

"Er . . . yes." I shifted the receiver and sat down. Vanessa's manager. A key person who should have been kept in the loop.

"And you are?"

"Emma Streat, Vanessa's aunt. I'm afraid there's bad news. Vanessa and I flew back yesterday from Venice. Last night she came down with a virus. Right now she's in Boston General's—um—intensive-care unit."

"That *is* bad news." The briskness was changing to concern. "What do the doctors say?"

"They're doing tests. She has a very high fever."

"Wait, I know who you are. I have a CD of your *Don Carlo*. Look here. Vanessa is expected in London next week for rehearsals. Can she make it?"

"No."

"Are you sure?"

"Positive."

"Well, as a singer, you can appreciate the upset of last-minute cancellations. Last-minute replacements. No one will be pleased, to put it mildly. Why wasn't I told sooner?"

"It was very sudden. I had to call an ambulance at four in the morning."

"I'm sorry. Extremely sorry." A pause. "You say you were in Venice with Vanessa. Is it true that Mark Dykstra committed suicide?"

I hesitated, needing to feel my way. Good managers would go the extra mile for their clients; they did endless mothering, hand-holding, but at some point their heads had to rule their hearts. How much more had Vanessa's manager heard? "Mark Dykstra is . . . dead," I said. "Actually, I think I'd better tell you what happened in Venice."

"I think you had. I also heard that Vanessa was sleeping with that race car driver Seth Barzalon. Ducked out of a reception in her honor. I hope that's just a rumor."

"I'm afraid not. On Tuesday, that was October eighth, Vanessa's assistant called me in Boston and told me about Barzalon. She was worried. She persuaded me to go over and see what I could do."

"And?"

"I didn't talk to Vanessa until after Mark Dykstra died. The assistant and I found him hanging in her hotel suite. The press had a field day—anyhow, one good thing. Instead of going to Sardinia with Barzalon, Vanessa flew back to Boston with me."

"Sardinia. Barzalon. I've been sent clippings. My God, what was she thinking? It's not like Vanessa to behave like a crazed teenager."

"Not like her at all. But at least the landscape has changed. The shock about Dykstra. This illness. There's no doubt in my mind that when she's better she'll see that her singing comes first." No need to mention stress or burnout. For Vanessa's sake, I must do my best to contain the damage.

"I most certainly hope so. Vanessa has great potential. I'm fond of her, I'm prepared to do my best, but it's an unforgiving world, as you know. The big opera houses aren't about to put up with last-minute cancellations. They don't like scandal. As I say, I'll do my best, but I should have been told sooner."

"I should have called you from Venice. I'm sorry."

"What's done is done. Keep in touch. Let me know how she is." The phone clicked off.

Slowly, I picked up the clothes and carried them into the bedroom. The frantic surge of energy was evaporating like the last drop of gas in the tank. There were choices: I could crawl under the covers and wake up at three in the morning. Or . . . I could take a hot shower and put on my blue bathrobe. Make scrambled eggs. Play a Jane Austen DVD and lose myself in a world where no one had ever heard of viruses.

The phone was ringing again. Seconds later, Seth Barzalon's voice reverberated through the room.

"Listen up, Auntie. My head honcho is down at General. He's going to stop by your place on his way back. Give you a first-hand report."

No blue bathrobe. No scrambled eggs. I sat down on the bed. "He could call me—no, never mind. I guess I'd better see him. Do you know when he'll get here?"

"Hell, no."

seven

The minion didn't arrive until after seven thirty, waking me out of exhausted sleep. Taking a deep breath, I arranged my lips in a cool smile and opened the door.

For some reason, I had expected a pudgy little man who talked as if he had stones in his mouth. A quick report and he would be on his way. The man standing there was slight and thin, with dark hair.

"Mrs. Streat? Greg Atkins. Sorry to be so late, but I had to wait to see your niece's doctor." A pleasant voice, slightly wary.

"Come in, won't you?"

"Thanks."

"What would you like to drink?" I asked as we went into the living room. "I've got white wine, red, pretty much every-thing except rum."

"Red would be fine."

"I'll have that, too. Would you mind opening the bottle?" I

had broken several corks using the rented bottle opener. Lewis had always opened bottles, carved chickens, laid fires. I could do these things, but not with the skill that comes from practice.

"I think I can manage," Dr. Atkins said with a smile. Two quick twists and the cork came out intact. He filled two glasses and handed one to me.

"That's more comfortable than it looks," I said, motioning him to a tubular chair. He sat down. I went to the sofa. For a moment, neither of us spoke.

"It was very kind of you to go to the hospital," I began. "To take time from your work—" I stopped. We both knew he'd had no choice.

"I only wish I could give you a more positive report. As you know, your niece is seriously ill."

"Is there any change?"

"The vitals are holding. That's the good news. In some of these severe viral outbreaks, Ebola or Marburg, for example, patients go downhill very fast."

I put my glass down with a thump. "Ebola. Marburg. My God, you'd think we were in Africa."

"If it's any comfort, your niece couldn't be in a better place."

"Even for avian flu?"

"Even that. General can reach out to other institutions and get a quick response. Get the best resources on board quickly."

"That's what I keep telling myself, but for most of us, hospitals are like another world. Dr. Reston talked about barrier nursing and I don't have a clue. I feel so cut off from Vanessa."

"Barrier nursing is just a way to keep disease from spreading. All personnel are suited up in protective clothing; even their eyes are protected. There are special exhaust fans to clean the air."

"Oh." I wrapped my hand around my glass and tried to

imagine Vanessa lying in a bubble, surrounded by people who looked like robots.

"Any other questions?"

I crossed my legs and looked at Dr. Atkins. "My head honcho is supposed to be brilliant," Seth had said. Maybe the last thing Atkins had needed was to be catapulted into Seth Barzalon's personal life. In any case, he was here, a captive expert. I had better get rid of any pre-antagonism and make use of him.

"Lots of questions. I'm just a layperson who gets confused about wild birds, infected chickens, and mutations. What's even worse, I don't know one virus from another."

"Not many people do. Are you asking for a course on viruses?"

"Maybe something simple. Just the basics."

"Basics, then. Ready?"

"Ready."

"Group A is avian. Group B is your classic winter flu. Group C is the common cold. Wild birds carry the Group A virus H five N one. It doesn't seem to affect them, but domestic birds are susceptible to their droppings. The virus may be passed on to humans."

"I thought it just had to be blood."

"Now imagine a tiny space capsule trying to invade a foreign body. The viral capsule is filled with a genetic code. It has little spikes sticking out of it. The spikes are filled with types of proteins that contain their own genetic codes. These spikes—invaders—will lock onto a living cell and try to enter and release their genetic material. Their RNA. Are you with me?"

"So far."

"A patient's own antibodies are the first line of defense, but let's say the virus capsule succeeds in breaking through. The patient becomes ill. Samples are taken to identfy the particular virus."

"What about this this mutation thing? The one that can cause a pandemic and kill millions of people?"

"A combination of bird virus plus a human virus. The combined RNAs form a new flu strain that could prove fatal to humans. Right now we're watching any changes to a protein that sits on the surface of the H five N one molecule and binds to receptor cells. These are like docking stations, allowing the virus to invade and infect—"

I held up my hand. "Stop. You've lost me. I haven't had much sleep, the last twenty-four hours. What about vaccines? I gather new flu vaccines are made every year. Why isn't there one for avian flu?"

"Good question. Vaccines are being manufactured by several major groups, but no one size fits all and making new vaccines takes time. Time and a great deal of money. You can't just throw in a few ingredients and stir the pot."

"Is that what you do at your foundation? Work on new vaccines?"

"Not vaccines. My research is about developing a new antiviral drug."

"I thought we already had those."

"There are several available, but again, it's not that simple. Once viruses mutate into the human population, it's hard to get rid of them. They adapt. They learn new tricks. The fear is that avian flu may become resistant to the leading antivirals."

"In other words, those lethal little capsules are trying to outwit us. And we have to outwit them."

"Exactly. It's a race against the clock to provide a new antiviral. One that's cheaper and more effective than anything we have at the moment."

"Are you close to finding it?"

"Close, but there are still major hurdles." He smiled. "It's complicated. Don't get me started."

"No, but I'm interested. I gather Vanessa is being given antiviral medication. If none of them work, could yours be used? I mean, is it far enough along?"

"Yes and no. The problem is, my project still needs testing on humans. Approval by the FDA. Even with new research techniques, there's a big time lag between lab use and use by the public. In the end, it's a safety issue."

"But what about a case of last resort? What if Vanessa's family agreed?"

"The people at General know about my antiviral, but the decision to use it is up to them. I'll do my best, but there's a risk."

"I see." I picked up my glass and put it down, aware that I had leaped to pre-judge. This was no Barzalon minion. Dr. Atkins was a man with a mission, doing important work. "Could you stand one more question?" I asked.

"Of course."

"Vanessa's virus. Do you know what they're doing to identify it?"

"I can tell you this. Her team is pulling out all the stops. The State Epidemiologist is on the job. A Dr. Nordberg from the Special Pathogens Branch at CDC will be here tomorrow with a Vickers mobile lab. The U.S. Army Medical Research Institute at Fort Detrick, Maryland, has been alerted. A lot of people are trying to find a matching virus. H five N one among others."

"So maybe there'll be an answer by tomorrow."

"Possibly, but in the meantime the hospital is taking every precaution. Like asking you to practice voluntary quarantine. Not easy. How are you managing?"

"I'm not sure. I've only just started. Dr. Reston told me to take my temperature three times a day."

"Have you?"

"Twice. It was normal. The trouble is, I saw what happened to Vanessa. It's—well, to be honest, I guess I'm terrified, waiting for the first cough." I hesitated. "By the way, aren't *you* taking a chance, coming here?"

"Possibly, but I've been exposed to viral shedding too many times to let it bother me. Besides, there's always the SWAG element."

"SWAG?"

"Scientific Wild Ass Guesses."

After a second, I laughed. "Do doctors actually say that?"

"Often. Look. It's not set in stone that your niece has avian flu. As Louis Pasteur once said, 'Chance favors the prepared mind.' That's what's happening at General. The reason for the precautions. We can't prevent disease. What we *can* do is prepare for it."

"Maybe, but it's horrible to think that a few bird droppings can throw the world into chaos. Make Vanessa so sick."

He held up his hand. "As I say, we can't be sure it's avian flu. You're under a lot of stress and the best thing you can do for yourself is concentrate on a good outcome. Protect your immune system. More wine?"

"Just a half." He refilled my glass and handed it to me. I took a sip and sat back. Slowly, the tension in my neck was beginning to loosen. "Enough of viruses," I said. "Tell me about the foundation. Have you been there long?"

"Six months. We're small. Independent. Funding comes from the pharmaceutical company that Seth Barzalon's grandfather started. There'd been a number of project failures in the past few years. I was brought in to turn things around with my antiviral concept. Try to hit the jackpot with a major break-through."

"It sounds as if you have a lot on your plate," I said, and shifted a magazine on the coffee table. "About Seth Barzalon. Isn't it unusual, to be a race car driver and run a foundation?"

"It is." A pause. "Tell me about your niece. I'd like to get a better sense of her, but not if it upsets you."

"It doesn't." He hadn't taken the hook I'd thrown out, but I had to respect his discretion. "Actually, it helps to pretend that nothing's wrong. First of all, she's beautiful. A talented singer. Her father, my brother, is a down-to-earth Bostonian. Her mother is Chilean, very volatile. That's where Vanessa gets her tempera-ment, but with her it's natural, not just a diva act."

"Are the two of you close?"

"We were. The Christmas she was twelve I went to her school play thinking I'd be bored out of my skull. It was *Amahl and the Night Visitors.* Vanessa was singing the part of the mother. The magic was there. I persuaded her parents to get good teachers for her."

"You were a singer?"

"Until I lost my voice. Years ago. Anyhow, I went to Venice to talk her out of going off with Seth Barzalon. I was afraid she'd be just another trophy to go with his racing cups. One more in his string of beautiful women. I gather there's a history."

He shook his head. "To be honest, I can't comment. I've never seen that side of his life. We just have a working relation-ship."

"I see."

For a moment we sat in silence. I glanced at Dr. Atkins as he studied his wineglass. A straight line of dark eyebrows defined a thin face and intense dark eyes. He was wearing a worn tweed coat with patches on the elbows, and his shoes needed a shine.

The look of a man who paid more attention to his work than to appearances.

One of my favorite CDs was playing in the background. Lorraine Hunt Lieberson singing Handel. He turned his head to listen.

"I don't know much about opera, but I like the Baroque, especially the old instruments. A colleague of mine is a cellist with the Boston Camerata. You may have heard of them."

"I haven't. I was born and raised in Cambridge, but that was a while ago. Anyhow, I'll be moving to the country as soon as I can find a place. My husband died last summer and my boys—they're both in college—they need open spaces, not this apartment."

"It can't be easy to make a new life."

"It isn't." The cell phone was buzzing. I picked it up.

"Emma." Rodale's voice. "I take it you're back in Boston."

"Yes." I closed my eyes. Oh God, I should have called earlier and told him about Vanessa.

"Are you alone?"

I pushed back my hair. Dr. Atkins already knew about Vanessa and avian flu. It should be safe to talk as long as I didn't identify the caller.

"I have a visitor, but he already knows the bad news."

"Bad news?"

"The flight was fine, but last night my niece got sick. A weird sort of virus. I had to take her to Boston General by ambulance. It's hard to believe, but they think it might be avian flu. Their first case. Maybe the first case in the country."

"Good God. Do they think she picked it up in Venice?"

"All they know is, she's terribly sick. Right now I'm in voluntary quarantine. Locked in my apartment for four days." I stopped and glanced at Dr. Atkins. "Actually, my visitor is a doctor who does research in antivirals at the Barzalon Foundation.

He's been at the hospital checking on her condition. He's been very helpful."

"Understood. I had a few details about Venice to pass on, but they can wait until tomorrow."

"Good." Somehow trouble in Venice seemed minuscule and far away.

"I'm extremely sorry about your niece. Extremely sorry. Take care of yourself." He hung up.

I put the phone back on the table and turned. "Sorry. That was a friend who helped us with the Venice problem."

"Venice problem?"

"Seth didn't tell you? Vanessa's accompanist killed himself after her recital. It looked like suicide, but then it turned out to be—" I stopped, my hand to my mouth. Dear God, what was I *thinking*?

"Turned out to be?"

"A mess. A total mess. Hotel manager in a flap. Police asking questions. Press camped out in the hotel lobby waiting for the next meal."

"Not what you needed."

"It wasn't." I had almost said "murder." Exhaustion must be affecting my brain. Dr. Atkins was looking at me. A concerned look.

"This friend. Is he likely to repeat what you told him? We don't want rumors spreading."

"No. No, I'm sure he won't. He's very . . . discreet," I said, aware that I was beginning to babble.

A close call, too close, but Dr. Atkins seemed to have bought the hasty cover-up. After a moment, he put down his glass and got to his feet.

"It's getting late. I have an early meeting and you've had a long day."

"And night." I stood up. Oh God, when the door closed be-hind Dr. Atkins I would be alone. A pariah. Incarcerated for the next four days.

As we walked to the door, he glanced at me, a questioning look. "Isolation can be very frightening. Particularly in this situa-tion. Here's a suggestion. If you should start to cough or feel ill, here's my cell number." He took out a card and handed it to me.

"Thank you," I said, aware that my hand was shaking.

"Let's hope you won't need it. About tomorrow. As soon as the board meeting is over I'll be going back to the hospital. Talk to the people I know there. Would you like me to stop on my way back? Give you an update?"

"Yes. Please. I know it's stupid, but every time the phone rings I think it's the hospital. Vanessa is so special. We all—her fami-ly—we love her so much." I swallowed, holding back the tears.

We had reached the door. He turned. "Tomorrow the out-look may be better. Play your CDs. Try to get some sleep."

"I will."

"Good night, then."

"Good night." I opened the door and watched him as he walked to the elevator. An hour ago, I had been fuming, expect-ing a nerdy Barzalon clone. Prepared to boot him out. This man was quiet. Courteous. He had answered endless questions. And, even more important, he had offered to be the lifeline I would need—badly—for the next four days.

eight

Day three. Vanessa was still alive. Yesterday, in the early after-noon, her temperature had gone up, straining her tenuous hold on life to the breaking point. My brother, Ned, back from Chile, had called: "I'm afraid we're going to lose her." A few hours later he called again: "It's still touch-and-go, but the fever is going down."

As for me, a slight sore throat disappeared with saltwater gargling. So far, I was symptom free. What's more, instead of being a prisoner in solitary, I was now command central, the operator who passed on the latest updates to worried family and friends. Years ago I would have been sitting at an old-fashioned switchboard plugging in wires.

Cathy and I talked twice a day. Luckily her cousin's qualms about infection had been soothed by my offer to pay hotel prices. But the cousin was out all day, working at a gift shop. It was up to me to keep Cathy in good spirits

Greg Atkins came in every evening on his way back from

the hospital. Last night he had brought another Hunt Lieberson CD along with the latest medical news: "She's holding her own, but this virus has got everyone puzzled. They're running out of tests and still no match."

I was up early, making my bed, when my older sister, Dolly, the consummate worrier, called for the daily report.

"Holding her own, no change," I said, pressing the cell to my cheek and pulling up the duvet.

"The problem is, she has no stamina. I always said she was going to burn herself out."

"Dolly, she has a virus. Nothing to do with burnout."

"Well, that's your opinion." A loud sniff. "By the way, why are you always in the apartment when I call? I thought you were supposed to be out looking for a house."

"I will; I am." The entry bell was buzzing. "Dolly, there's someone down at the door. I've got to run."

"Remember, you don't want to be too far out in the country where you can't get to—"

"You're right. Absolutely right, I'll call you back later," I said, and went to the window. The black Alfa Romeo was parked at the curb.

Moments later, like a gale-force wind, Barzalon came striding in. He was carrying a huge pot of green and white orchids, cypripediums in full bloom. Today he was wearing white canvas trousers and a blue-and-white-striped shirt. As always, he seemed to use up all the oxygen around him.

"For you," he said, and handed me the pot. "I've just taken a carload to the hospital. Had them sent up to Vanessa's floor. Nurses like orchids."

"Did you get what you wanted?"

"Tight asses wouldn't even give me a room number. Any coffee going?"

"There is." I carried the wildly expensive pot of orchids to the kitchen and put it in the sink. "Needs watering. By the way, thanks for putting me in touch with Dr. Atkins. He's been very helpful."

"Quiet sort of guy, all brains, not a barrel of fun, but hell, if he can make a breakthrough with his project, it'll be the miracle we need. The trustees and accountants will kiss his feet."

"He seems very dedicated."

"He'd better be, what he's paid." Barzalon glanced at me, picked up the coffee mug, and put it down. "Good news, Auntie. I'm off."

"Off?"

"Race in the south of France. Just heard about it today."

"I see," I said, keeping my face expressionless. Dear sweet God, let there be an accident, nothing fatal, but serious enough to keep him over there, out of Vanessa's life.

He grinned and shook his head. "Wishful thinking, Auntie. Greg has orders to keep me posted. Once she's on her feet, I'm taking her to this place in the Bahamas. Private island." He sat down on a kitchen stool and looked at me. "Hey. How're *you* doing? Ready to jump out of the window?"

"I'm fine," I said, annoyed that he had picked up on my vibes. "How about you?"

"Never better." He took a gulp of coffee.

"When are you leaving?"

"Today. Board meeting is over for another quarter. Have to go back and sign a few checks and I'm off." He hesitated, then began to drum with his fingers on the counter. "Something I've been meaning to ask you. Did the police ask questions about me before you left Venice?"

I stopped pouring water through the orchids. "Not that I remember. Why?"

"Because of what happened at the reception. The little poof dancing around, threatening to kill me."

"I know. I was there. You just brushed him off."

"Yeah, but then he goes and tops himself. Can't trust police. They might have figured I frightened him into it. Told him to drop dead."

"You had an alibi. You didn't see him again, did you?"

"Hell, no, but the fuzz could be looking for a way to cause trouble for me."

I straightened. Why this sudden concern about the police? There was no way he could have heard that Mark Dykstra's death was no suicide. "The police didn't ask about you. Not to me, anyhow. Why would they?"

"Never know with dagos." He finished the coffee and stood up. "Over and out, Auntie. Take care. See you," and he was gone.

I picked up his mug, rinsed it thoroughly, and put it out of sight in the dishwasher. Now to tell Cathy the good news.

To my surprise, the phone rang and rang. Finally, she was there.

"You sound out of breath," I said. "Are you all right?"

"I am. It's just that I had to run back from the door."

"I was worried. I thought for a moment you might be sick— no, never mind. Listen. Seth Barzalon just breezed in and out. He's leaving Boston. He's going racing. In France."

"I know. It'll be grand, not having him underfoot, causing trouble."

"Yes. It will." I took a deep breath. "Cathy, he just heard. How did *you* know?" No answer. I pushed back my hair. "Let's not beat around the bush. Was Terry there? Is that why the phone rang for so long just now?"

"He came to say good-bye and give me a lucky charm. To ward off bad spirits. Sure and there was no harm in that."

"All the same," I began, then bit my lip. Had Terry gone to the apartment more than once? It would explain why Cathy had been so surprisingly cheerful.

"Besides, he'd have been exposed going from Paris to Venice."

"I guess he was. Don't worry; we'll talk later," I said, and hung up. It made no sense for the dashing Terry to be so attentive to a naïve country girl. At some point, and soon, I would have to tell her that Terry Gallagher was bad news, that his boss, no novice in that field, had called Terry a womanizer given to playing games. Falling in love with Terry Gallagher was bound to end in tears.

At five thirty Greg Atkins appeared. From the moment he sat down, I could see that something was wrong. "You look very low," I said. "You'd better tell me. Is it Vanessa?"

"Vanessa? No. The nurses aren't dancing on tables, but you can feel a change in the atmosphere. It's almost day four and she's holding her own."

"Seth, then? He blew in with that monster orchid pot. He said he was on his way to the foundation and then off to France."

"Just the usual dysfunctional behavior. A waste of valuable time. No, this afternoon I got some updates on national security. Not good reading. This country is far too vulnerable to a pandemic."

"Vulnerable? In what way?"

"You name it. The public health system needs bolstering. Hospitals and clinics don't have enough surge capacity. You remember the flu vaccine shortage in 2003 and 2004? Now picture people dying in their houses. No vaccines, no reliable antivirals."

"But we're the most advanced country in the world in medicine."

"Only in certain fields. In my opinion, the government is putting too much emphasis on bioterrorism. Smallpox and anthrax are small change compared to an influenza pandemic. Hard enough to contain it here. Deadly if it starts in the poorer populations of Africa and India."

"But aren't the big pharmaceuticals working on the problem?"

"They are, but vaccines and antivirals aren't moneymakers. The big companies have to protect their patents. Lobby the government to prevent any legislation that would affect the bottom line."

"So what *can* small foundations do?"

"Try to develop a better, cheaper product. Sometimes I feel as if I'm just treading water." He shook his head. "Sorry. What else did Seth have to say?"

"He said you're supposed to send him reports about Vanessa. Just don't make them too cheery. I'm praying he'll lose patience. Find a replacement."

"Which may happen. I don't think he realizes how long it will take her to recover."

"I'm sure he doesn't. My godmother told me about his dyslexia. The mother who died young. The lightweight father. You know, under the bravado, I'm beginning to think Seth Barzalon is a very needy person, as they say."

"You have any suggestions?"

"None. Absolutely none. He and his pilot remind me of Mozart's *Don Giovanni.* Two macho cowboys roaming around, sweeping women off their feet, but there's nothing comic about Seth and Terry."

"You know Terry?"

"Not well, but he's too smooth by half. I wouldn't be surprised if he does something on the side. Like dealing drugs."

Greg put down his glass. "What makes you say that?"

"It's just a feeling I had in Venice."

"What happened?"

"I'm not sure. Terry was taking me to meet Seth. A gondolier came poling down a canal. Big reunion: 'Ho there, man.' 'Ho there, Fausto.' It surprised me that he and Terry were so close. Then Seth and I had our jousting match. As I left, those good buddies were yelling at each other in a bar."

"That makes Terry a criminal?"

"No, except that Seth did say Terry was always running off to do deals. Maybe that's what put it into my head. I know I shouldn't make statements like that, but I'm ticked—really ticked—because he's zeroing in on Vanessa's assistant."

"The Irish one who's staying with her cousin in South End?"

"I talked to her this morning. She admitted that he'd been to see her. She was very defensive, said there was no harm, he'd already been exposed, but I still don't like it. I've come to love this girl. I don't want her to get hurt. We went through a lot together in Venice."

"He's leaving."

"I wish it was the South Pole and the two of them were stranded on a melting ice floe. Anyhow, enough ranting. More wine? There's another bottle on the kitchen counter."

"I'll go open it," he said.

I sat back, listening as he moved around, still thinking about the odd couple. Terry and Fausto. As a cupboard door banged, I turned my head. It was taking him a long time to open that bottle.

"Isn't it there?" I called.

"It is, but I'm making a bad job of this cork."

"That gadget came with the apartment. I should get something better."

"Don't move; it's working," he said, and came back with the two glasses.

"Thanks." I took a sip and studied him as he sat at the other end of the white sofa. A dedicated, intense man. Attractive in a quiet way. At first I had treated him like a useful conduit of information. Tonight I was beginning to realize how much I looked forward to sitting down with him at the end of the day. Having a glass of wine. Talking. I missed having a man in my life.

"Nice, this red," he was saying. "Australian."

"I picked it up at that place on Charles Street. The man recommended it." I put my feet up on the sofa. Because of Vanessa, Greg and I had been able to bypass the usual exploratory chitchat. He knew about my marriage and my boys. I knew that he had been divorced nine years ago: "It was the classic story of a researcher who gets too wrapped up in his work. Melissa said I was married to my job and she was right. She married again, has two children."

"You're still worrying," I said now, breaking the silence.

He gave me a quick look. "You're right. Besides the pandemic, I worry that we're becoming an obese nation. Greedy. Soft. Spoiled."

"That's depressing."

"True. I should know by now that I'm always depressed after a board meeting. Dealing with Seth."

"I'm not surprised. It's funny, looking back, I almost told Seth I didn't want to see you. I thought you might be—well, abrasive."

"And now?"

"You've helped me keep my head above water."

"You've managed well. Extremely well."

"So far, but it's not over. I could still get sick. Vanessa could go downhill."

"True, but I'm going to go out on a limb and say that the worst may be over."

"You think?"

"I do." He sighed and put down his glass. "I'd better be off. These meetings always put me behind."

"And coming here has taken a lot of your time."

"Not a hardship." He looked at me. Then at his glass. He cleared his throat. "Once this is over, I'd like to take you to dinner. A concert. The Boston Symphony's doing a Mozart next week."

I hesitated. Greg Atkins had been too sensitive to make a move during the crisis, but tonight there were unmistakable signals that he would like to take our relationship to another level. From age fifteen I had divided men into groups. Those I could sleep with. Others who would never, in a million years, lay a finger on me. Greg Atkins fell into the first category, but one-night stands were out. Right now I needed permanence in my life. Greg might not light fires, but he was brilliant. Interesting. We *could* have a future—and as Caroline once said, "You're not cut out to be single."

"I'd like that," I said.

nine

October 17

At ten thirty the next morning, I was starting the dishwasher when Dolly made her daily check from Lake Forest, Illinois.

"Emma. I've just been talking to Ned. No need to get in a huff, he wasn't complaining, but it seems to me that you're not spending much time at the hospital."

"Well, there's so incredibly much—"

"Really. Is that fair? Ned needs support. We all know that Cassia's no good in a crisis. Too excitable."

"She's doing her best," I said firmly. Ned and I had agreed, from the start, not to tell Dolly about my quarantine—or the threat of avian flu.

"Still, I think I should come east, no matter what Ned says. I could stay in your apartment. Keep you company. Spell you both."

"Not right now. Maybe later—" I stopped. Another call was

coming in. "I'll have to put you on hold," I said, and pressed the Talk button.

"Mrs. Streat?" A man's voice.

"Yes."

"Dr. Reston. I've just seen your niece and the news is good. The last cocktail of drugs seems to have been effective."

"You mean—"

"There's always the chance of reversal, but as of this morning her fever is down. The lungs are clearing. Also, I think we can rule out avian flu."

"My God." I sat down on the white leather sofa. "My God. The relief. I can't begin to tell you."

"I understand. It's been a very worrying time. For all of us."

"This virus. Do you know what it was?"

"So far there's been no match. We'll keep testing stored viruses, but for the moment we're calling it atypical viral pneumonia."

"Pneumonia. Does that mean I'm not contagious? Out of quarantine?"

"So far, no other cases have been reported. As long as you're not experiencing any symptoms, you may resume your normal life. You'll be in touch, of course, if there's any change. And let me say here that I appreciate your cooperation. Not easy, but it seemed best to err on the side of caution."

"Of course. When can I see Vanessa?"

"If there are no setbacks in the next few days, she will be taken out of barrier nursing. Allowed to see her family. Do you have any more questions?"

"No . . . no. I'm just so— Thank you, thank you so much for all you've done, Dr. Reston. You and all the other people involved."

"It's been a team effort. It will take your niece time to get her strength back, but I believe the outcome will be positive."

"What about her voice?'

"Again, that will take time."

No pandemic. No mobs filling the streets, bleeding from nose and mouth. Feeling weightless, I went into the bathroom and threw the digital thermometer into a wastebasket. Picked up my fleece jacket and ran out of the apartment, out into the sunny street, and down the hill.

On Boston Common, the muted colors on the leaves looked brighter. Dogs were happily chasing balls. I zigzagged around them and went on into the Public Garden. The swan boats, a favorite childhood treat, had been put away for the winter, but a pink balloon was floating above the trees, soaring up into the sky.

On Newbury Street, people were carrying shopping bags from Burberry's and other upscale boutiques. Two boys in cargo pants and nose rings overtook two ladies dressed for lunch at the Taj Boston Café. Tomorrow, without fail, I would come back and buy a lot of new clothes. Colorful. Expensive.

There was a church halfway down the block. I stopped, then went to the door. It was open. I tiptoed in and slid into an empty seat. After a moment, I put my head in my hands. By now God and I were on daily speaking terms. Short, one-way conversations. I had asked him to give Vanessa comfort. Today he had come through with the gift of life.

High above, an organist began to play Bach's "Goldberg Variations," shifting from one key to another as if doing finger exercises.

As I sat in the dimness, my mind began to weave patterns through the music. I listened, remembering those thundering words in Handel's *Messiah*: "And we shall be changed." It was far too soon to know how the past few days had changed me, but once again I had been tested. Once again I had survived.

Did new strengths demand a new view of the world? New commitments? These were important concepts that required concentrated thought. But right now there was a mountain of catch-up work that needed to be done.

Back in the apartment, I opened all the windows and began to write a new list. Call Cathy. Somehow, without preaching, I must warn her not to take Terry Gallagher too seriously. Then my son Jake. Then try to reach the elusive Steve. He and Vanessa had always shared a cavalier approach to life; two summers ago Vanessa had taken her little cousin to a beach party. He had come home reeking of beer, a condition I had decided to ignore. Once.

My message to Steve was brief and to the point: "Vanessa's been very sick at General, but she's over the worst. Thought you'd want to know." No plans. No demands. Let him make the next move.

Next, my neglected real estate agent, Denise Daniels. She was out, probably showing high-end properties. I left a message: "Denise. Sorry not to get back to you sooner. It's been a bit crazy here, but I want to find a house as soon as possible. Call me."

After Denise, food. Breathing deeply, I did a quick dance step, then headed for the neighborhood grocery. The plump owner gave me a warm, welcoming smile.

"You well? Good. Your maid she talk so fast I no understand her."

"I'm fine now. I need some skim milk and hummus. And apples."

I was putting groceries away when the phone rang. It was Greg.

"Emma? I've just heard the news. This calls for a major celebration."

"It does."

"There's a new Italian restaurant on Exeter Street. Do you like Italian food?"

"Love it."

"What about tonight?"

I hesitated, aware that this was a crossroads moment. Go one way, and the relationship might end. Go another, and we would be in new territory.

"Sounds good," I said. "We could have a drink here first. What time?"

"I've got some work to finish. Is seven thirty too late for you?"

"No, fine. I'm rushing around playing catch-up."

"Seven thirty, then. I'll look forward to it."

"So will I." I clicked off and took a deep breath. "Throw out all your old nightgowns when you get a lover," Caroline had advised me last spring—but a woman with four divorces was no role model. There would be no jumping into bed, but now at least I would have something to tell Caroline: "He's a doctor. In research. Very brilliant and dedicated. I do seem to be attracted to these intense, dedicated men."

The phone was ringing. I picked it up.

"Emma. Are you alone?" Rodale's standard opening. I swallowed, annoyed that just hearing that voice could cause a stir.

"Yes, and I've just had good news. Vanessa's doctor called. She's out of danger and I'm out of quarantine."

"Excellent. Have they identified the virus?"

"Not yet, but it's not avian. They're calling it an atypical pneumonia. The doctor says—"

"Hold it. Something important has surfaced. We need to talk."

"Oh?" I put the hummus down on the counter with a thump.

"To be honest, whatever it is, I'm not into problems right now. These past few days have been utter hell."

"Granted, but this is serious. It may be connected to your niece."

"Oh God. What now?"

"To go back, there's been no progress on the Dykstra homicide. No fingerprints or signs of forced entry. Needless to say, the Questura isn't happy. They put a lot of stock into civic pride and face-saving."

"I can believe it."

"Commissario Filardi's superiors are giving him a hard time for letting you and your niece leave Venice. They want you both back to answer more questions. Find out if Dykstra had any history of drinking or drugs."

"I hope you told them we can't."

"I have, but it's not that simple."

"Why?"

"Because this case has taken on new dimensions. As I told you, we're doing a joint operation with the Questura. I can't give you details, but we've learned that live viruses are being transported from country to country."

"I know. By wild birds."

"Not birds. I'm talking about human viruses. Possibly stolen from old laboratories in the former Soviet Union. Illegally transported from country to country by human carriers. Venice may be a hub city for undercover transfers."

"That sounds bad."

"It is. Yesterday one of my agents on the case was murdered. Knifed, then thrown into the lagoon." There was no change in his voice, but I could sense raw anger under the tight control. Losing an agent would be a serious blow.

"I'm sorry," I said. "Very sorry."

"To sum up, two Englishmen have been murdered in Venice in the past few days. Your niece contracted a mysterious virus. It's possible that she may have been infected in Venice. It's essential to find out if there's any linkage with the illegal viruses. Terrorists, cells, networks—whoever is involved is proving to be elusive. Dangerous."

"I can see that."

"Good." He cleared his throat. "I told the Questura there was no way you would go back to Venice, but the questions remain. The need to know if there's a linkage. I know it's asking a great deal, but I'd like you to come to London. As soon as possible."

A truck went clanking up the street. I leaned against the counter and closed my eyes. Was this a replay of last summer when Andrew Rodale insisted that I return to England? I had gone, dragging my feet. We had succeeded in finding my husband's killer. Later, we had slept together. We knew each other on two very basic levels.

"You're right," I said. "It *is* asking a great deal. You wouldn't believe how much I have to do. Why can't we just talk on the phone?"

"Out of the question. Your line isn't secure. What's relevant is that you were in Venice the night Mark Dykstra was murdered. You've been involved with your niece's illness." A pause. "There's another reason."

"What?"

"We need your help. Last summer you proved that you have a rare ability to make critical connections. It gave our people quite a shock, the untrained American woman doing their work for them."

I dug my nails into the palms of my hands. This was standard Rodale method of persuasion: First the frighteners. Then the stroking. "Never mind this so-called rare ability," I said. "I just don't see that I can help."

"Not even to help find out what caused your niece's illness? I take it the doctors still haven't made a match?"

"No. They haven't."

"Well, then?"

I closed my eyes. Only one thing was clear: After a week of roller-coaster emotions, I felt battered. In fact, I was in no state to make instant decisions. Rodale knew exactly how to twist my arm, but no way was I going to jump when he said jump. Not again.

"The answer is, don't push me. I need to think."

"How much time?"

"How long would I be gone?"

"Not more than a few days."

"I'll call you back."

"When?"

"In a few hours."

Once again I put on my fleece jacket and headed down the hill to Charles Street and the familiar shops. A fancy 7-Eleven on the corner. The dry cleaner's. There were people sitting outside in the sunlight drinking coffee, eating pastries. Mothers pushed strollers over the uneven bricks; there seemed to be a surprising number of babies in this area.

The Charles Street post office had a discreet sign in gold letters and looked like an antique shop. Walking fast, I almost bumped into an elderly man coming out.

"Sorry," I said, and moved toward the curb. Instead of thrashing around, I must apply logic. Assemble facts. I had sent Rodale an SOS from Venice. Rodale had responded. I owed him. Now he had lost an agent. I had nearly lost my niece.

A maze of traffic circles marked the end of the shopping area. Turning right would bring me straight to Boston General. Somewhere in that labyrinth, Vanessa was still very, very sick— and none of the resources such as the CDC had been able to come up with an answer. According to Dr. Reston, there was no match to any available virus. Now, on the other side of the Atlantic, Rodale and his colleagues were trying to find the source of stolen viruses. Venice could be a hub city for illegal transport. But what did this have to do with Vanessa?

"Bloody hell," I said aloud. A young man carrying a briefcase glanced at me and quickened his pace. Pivoting on my heels, I began to walk back. I had no choice. If Vanessa's suffering had been caused by some criminal outfit, they must be found. And if going to London meant meeting Rodale again, so be it.

As I retraced my steps, I tried to be objective. A short affair between two unmarried adults was no big deal, but leaving him at Marco Polo Airport had hurt. This was a man with extraordinary powers, both physical and mental. A man who had made it painfully clear that his work came first.

A couple was walking ahead of me, arms around each other's waists. He bent his head and whispered something in her ear. I stopped and stared into a window filled with patisserie. The timing couldn't be worse. Going away now meant a hold on buying a house. Delaying a possible new relationship, one built on trust and a solid foundation.

The young couple was turning at the corner. He was rubbing her back. I walked faster. For Vanessa's sake, I had to blank out Venice. Put steel in my spine. Whatever happened next, Rodale must understand that this was a fact-finding mission.

The slightest move toward bed would be met with cool, firm rejection.

"Emma?" He must have been waiting for my call.

I took a deep breath. "You're a selfish bastard with a one-track mind. But I owe you for Venice. Without your help, Vanessa might have died there."

"You Americans are so provincial about falling ill away from home. Does this mean you'll come?"

"Yes."

"Tomorrow night?"

"Yes."

"Hold on." I could hear voices in the background. In a moment his personal assistant, Ian Trefusis, the computer wizard with a cherub face and a halo of curls, was on the line.

"Good to hear your voice, Mrs. Streat. Don't worry; we'll handle all the travel arrangements at this end. Here's Lord Rodale."

I took another deep breath. "One thing. I hope you realize this is the last thing in the world I want to do, but I have a responsibility toward my niece. A very great responsibility."

"Understood." A pause. "By the way."

"What?"

"It will be good, very good, to see you again."

part two

ten

October 19

England

The daytime British Airways flight from Logan to London's Heathrow was scheduled to land at 9:30 P.M. As always, the last half hour of the flight seemed like a conspiracy to keep prisoners trapped in the air.

As crisp-voiced First Class flight attendants removed hot towels, I unbuckled my seat belt and headed for the airline's excuse of a bathroom. Manipulated the flimsy folding doors. Studied my tired face in the mirror and applied blusher to my cheeks.

"Lord Rodale will meet you at Heathrow," Ian Trefusis had told me. There had been no mention of where I was to stay. It didn't matter. I would insist, from the start, on being treated like a professional who had come to work, not to indulge the senses. If Ian had arranged for a hotel suite, there would be meetings, but no way would Rodale set foot in my bedroom.

The great panoramic spread of London at night expanded. The lights of the runway came rushing up to meet us. There was a bump. A roar. People stirred, making the transition from one world to another.

Tonight there was no wait at the baggage carousel or at customs. I passed through the green line and on out to the exit; no matter how many times I did this, there was always a small, niggling fear that I wouldn't be met.

Andrew Rodale was there, facing the other way, a tall, dark-haired man who stood out and above the crowd. One of England's most eligible bachelors. A peer with a seat in the House of Lords. But I knew by now that the smooth outer trappings were deceptive. Under the impressive surface was a dedicated one-track mind that thrived on running down criminals.

He turned, saw me, came forward, and took my bag out of the cart. "Good flight?"

"The usual."

"Jenkins is waiting with the car. This way," and Rodale began to walk. In spite of a slight limp, the result of an ambush years ago in Ireland, he had a long stride. This was a take-charge man, always in a hurry.

By some official dispensation, the black sedan was drawn up at the curb. Rodale's driver was standing by the door; last summer I had learned that wiry little Jenkins wore a number of hats.

"Welcome back, Mrs. Streat. I'll put your bag in the boot."

"Thanks, Jenkins; it's good to see you again." The door closed and the car drew into a maelstrom of traffic.

"Place is worse than a zoo," Rodale said, stretching his legs. I glanced at him, remembering a night in July when Jenkins had driven us around London.

"It always is," I said, and moved a few inches away. Oxytocin levels and neurochemical ingredients couldn't explain this man's magnetic pull. The intensity under an impassive surface. A glint in gray eyes. A twist of the mouth. A deep voice that could change in a second from brusque to intimate. And—far more powerful—there was nothing contrived or practiced about Rodale. His power to attract was a true gift of nature.

As the maze of blinding overhead lights disappeared, I noticed that Jenkins had left the familiar highway. Rodale cleared his throat.

"Did Ian tell you? We're going down to my place in Wiltshire. I know how you feel about the London house."

"No. He didn't." I opened my mouth and shut it. It would be harder to keep a polite distance on Rodale's turf. "How do you know how I feel about your London house?" I asked, keeping my voice light. "I was there once. For half an hour."

"Dreary horror was written all over your face."

"I wasn't expecting curtains falling apart. Dog pee on the rugs."

He laughed. "No one's made any changes since my mother died. Even her old staff are there, eating their heads off."

"The butler wore a stiff collar," I said, remembering a conversation with Rodale's friend Lady Bellew. She had implied that a great many women would kill to get their hands on that house. Be the next Lady Rodale. "This place in Wiltshire," I said quickly. "Is it an ancient pile? A family seat?"

"Neither. It was built in 1751 for a king's mistress. I inherited it from my great-uncle who had an obsession with Palladian architecture. Couldn't stand turrets and acres of roofs. He knew I liked the spare classical look." A pause. "How did you leave your niece?"

"Still in the hospital. Very weak."

"Will she be able to sing again?"

"I think it all depends on how much she wants to work at it."

"What about the boyfriend?"

"He went racing. If he comes back, I hope to God she'll see him for what he is. She was so stressed out, people demanding so much of her—I think the idea of being swept off to Sardinia was just too much to resist."

"It didn't happen."

"No, but it still might." I coughed. My throat was dry from the air on the plane; my damaged voice was fading. There was no use trying to read Rodale's complex mind, but it was high time to establish the ground rules. "I thought I'd be in London," I said. "Aren't there other agencies involved?"

"There are. A very senior chap is coming down from London tomorrow to talk with you."

"Fine, but why bring him down from London?"

"Matter of security. Attracting less attention."

The car was gathering speed. Rodale shifted away toward his corner; over the years, we had both learned to cope with handicaps. My voice. His leg. He cleared his throat. "We've got a longish drive ahead," he said. "Lean back. Try to sleep."

I woke to the sound of gravel crunching under the wheels. The car stopped. I looked out. In the headlights, the tall, square house looked as white as polished marble. Rodale opened the door and got out.

"A good run," he said to Jenkins.

"Not much traffic. Will you be needing me tomorrow, sir?"

"Not as far as I know now."

"Right, then. I'll be off. Good night, sir."

"Good night." A pause. "Emma?"

I slid across the leather seat. Rodale picked up my bag and started toward a front door that was level with the ground. I followed, rubbing my arms, feeling cold and disoriented. He went in and began to turn on lights.

"Cold?"

"A little."

"I'll take you right up. Unless you want something to eat."

"No, I don't."

The low, square entrance room had the look of a small Roman atrium, with a marble floor and four central columns. Suddenly two black and white English setters appeared, their feathery tails waving frantically. Rodale leaned down to rub their heads.

"These are Chloe and her daughter Mandy."

"Chloe. Mandy," I said. O'Hara, my Jack Russell terrier, would have been leaping and clawing at my knees, howling of cruelty and desertion. These two had beautiful manners.

"Come along, then," Rodale said, leading the way up wide stairs that ended in a large, sparsely furnished hall. An early painting of Venice hung over the tall fireplace. He crossed the marble floor and opened a door. "The spare bedroom. I think you'll find everything you need." He put my bag on a chair. The dogs followed him out through the door, not letting him out of their sight.

I stood still. He hadn't even said good night. There had been no sign that he intended to repeat the Venice interlude. I had been deluding myself, creating a problem that never existed.

After a moment, I looked around. There was nothing spare or Palladian about this elegant room. Thick padded green and white chintz curtains were drawn over long windows. The large twin beds had quilted chintz covers. One had been turned down.

Shivering, I opened my bag and pulled out the white T-shirt I always wore at night. My godmother, Caroline Vogt, would have been appalled. I could hear her gravelly voice: "You should be wearing a wisp of black lace. Something to send him into orbit." Bad advice. What I needed now was a secure future, not another painful intermezzo—but memories of that first night in Venice kept surfacing. Rodale had made love with the same intensity that he brought to tracking down dangerous criminals. After a moment of guilt, I had matched passion for passion—a temporary fall from grace.

A hot shower warmed me. I dried myself with a large white towel from the heated rack and pulled on the boyish T-shirt. There was sure to be a woman in Rodale's life. Maybe several women. He must never guess that, like a dithering teenager, I had set myself up for humiliation.

I was untangling my wet hair when I heard the click of dogs' feet on the marble floor of the hall. The door opened. Rodale was standing there, a towel around his waist. He came over and took the brush out of my hand.

"We're wasting time. Your place or mine?"

The big bed was a private world, closed off with dark red damask curtains. I lay back on the pillows.

He raised himself on one elbow. "What are you thinking?"

"About men. Are they born with this kind of talent? Or does it come with practice?"

He laughed. "Loaded question."

"It's not—well, maybe it is."

"You're not happy?"

"Oh, I am. That was very nice."

"Nice?"

"All right. It was good. The best."

eleven

I woke to bright daylight. After a moment I stretched and looked over at the rumpled pillows. The bed was empty, the red damask curtains pulled back. Last night belonged to warmth and darkness. Today would require a different kind of concentration.

One of my best singing roles had been Adina in Donizetti's *L'elisir d'amore.* An improbable farce about a love potion, but making love with Rodale seemed to have the same effect as a magic drug. All my resolutions, my willpower, had evaporated into the ether. Did it matter? We were both consenting adults, hurting no one.

Stretching again, I reached over and touched the pillow. My strict New England ancestors believed that sleeping with a man should lead to procreation, not pure pleasure, but after the angst of the past two weeks I was *owed*. Had the king and his mistress slept in this bed? I should be preparing my mind for today's meeting, but all I wanted was to stay where I was. An addict craving the next fix.

After a while, I sat up and looked around. This was a man's room, with heavy Jacobean furniture and crimson flocked wallpaper. The house itself was strangely silent. I should stop this aimless meandering. Go back to my room and get dressed. Was one of those heavy English breakfasts waiting on a sideboard?

"You're awake." Rodale was coming through the door, carrying a large tray. Today he was wearing tan corduroys, a checked shirt, and a tweed jacket with patches at the elbows. The dogs followed, a dignified pair with noble, domed heads. They sat down politely and looked at me with soft dark eyes. By now O'Hara would have been up burrowing under the covers. Rodale put the tray down on my lap and touched my neck.

"Good morning."

"I didn't hear you get up."

"I didn't want to wake you. Here's your breakfast."

"Thanks." I studied the tray. There was a coffeepot. A boiled egg in a holder. A rack of toast. A bowl of oatmeal, enough for three people. Rodale couldn't have cooked all this himself; there must be unseen hands at work somewhere in the silent house.

"That do you?" he asked.

"No bacon and sausage and kippers?"

"Americans don't appreciate fatty fry-ups. Tuck in. It's after nine, and the Colonel will be here at eleven."

I poured coffee into a large porcelain cup painted with hunting scenes. It was clear that last night's melding was on the back burner. The one-track mind had taken over.

"I'll be ready. Does he have a last name?"

"He does, but just call him Colonel."

"Colonel." Another clear signal that I was about to enter the shadowy world of espionage.

The coffee was strong and hot. Rodale walked over to a window. He stood there, rubbing his chin.

"Emma."

"Yes?"

"Two things. First. Don't start having regrets about last night."

I put down the cup. "I don't plan to."

"Second point. This talk with the Colonel. For God's sake, don't underestimate yourself."

I leaned back on the pillows. "What's *that* supposed to mean?"

"I've said it before and I'll say it again. Last summer you connected a number of dots. You put a name to a hired killer. You talked Joanna Estes into a confession. In the end, you were the one who smoked out Robina Lausch. An unlikely criminal if ever there was one."

"You were there. We were working together."

"True, but in the process you established yourself as a person who has an unusual ability to see new angles. A rare commodity. You have a track record with people who count. Why the Colonel is coming down from London."

"I just hope it's not a waste of his time." At our first meeting, Rodale had ordered me to leave detecting to the professionals. I had reacted like a head-tossing teenager. Now he was singing a different song, but bringing back this untrained American woman must have taken some doing.

He shook his head. "There you go, proving my point. How can I get this through your head? You're here because you have the ability to see the playing field with a fresh eye. In this situation, getting a new perspective is important. It could be very important."

"All I can say is, I'll do my best."

"And your best is very good indeed. Eleven, then, in the library." He walked over and picked up the large bowl of oatmeal. "Not on, Emma. Putting this down the drain could clog the entire system."

At quarter of eleven, I tied a Hermès scarf over my blue cashmere sweater and tried to focus on the upcoming meeting with the Colonel. "Getting a new perspective is important," Rodale had said. I would listen, answer questions, and once the ordeal was over there would be a long, uninterrupted day. Together in the red damask bed.

Pushing back my hair, I went to the long windows that looked out on a stretch of rough lawn that sloped down to a stream. There were clumps of trees, but no fountains. Not a flower in sight.

A rabbit ran across the lawn, paused, ears raised, then disappeared into the taller grass. I watched, as a compelling What If scenario began to take shape. True, Rodale's aristocratic world was a far cry from mine, but there was no reason I couldn't adapt to his. I had been born and brought up with every advantage. I had been a successful singer, then American industrial royalty.

Standing there, l let the scenario run ahead. Rodale and I pleased each other in bed. We respected each other's abilities. More than other women, I could accept the fact that Rodale's work came first. And . . . once in a lifetime a person should be allowed to ride the wind. Take risks. Years ago I had visited an old woman in a nursing home. Her nightgown had slipped and I had been horrified by the hanging folds of skin, the withered breasts.

Five of eleven. I turned back to the dressing table, retied the scarf, and went out, carefully shutting the door behind me, a British habit that now came naturally.

The house was still silent as I went down the wide stairs. There was no sign of a cook or maid, but someone must have turned down the spare-room bed last night. Cooked the breakfast. As I reached the entrance hall, a door opened and Rodale came out.

"We're in the library. Ready?"

"Ready."

The library was small and cluttered, a contrast from stark Palladian classicism. There were large cushioned beds for the dogs. A leather hearth fender, high enough for sitting. Magazines scattered on tables and walls lined with books. Rodale took my elbow and led me forward.

"Colonel, this is Mrs. Streat."

The Colonel was standing in front of the fireplace, hands behind his back in the stiff parade ground posture. A compact man with grizzled gray hair. One eyelid drooped. He came forward and shook my hand.

"Very good of you to cross the pond, Mrs. Streat. I gather you've been going through a bad patch."

"Yes. I have," I said, and tried not to look at the drooping eyelid.

Rodale motioned me to a worn leather chair and went to stand by a large desk. It was obvious that he was deferring to the senior man.

The Colonel returned to the fireplace. He straightened his shoulders. "My thought is to begin by giving you the larger picture, Mrs. Streat. Set the parameters, so to speak."

"I'd appreciate that. Very much."

"Right. In this line of work, as you may know, it often happens that one break leads to another. Last August a major drug dealer was picked up in Leeds, an industrial city in the English Midlands. During—ah—interrogations, he tipped us off to the fact that a new and profitable underworld market is developing. This market involves the illegal sale and transport of live viruses."

I nodded. "Lord Rodale has told me a little about the . . . problem."

"Good. To go on, the dealer couldn't—or wouldn't—give details, but it appears that these viruses are being stolen from badly guarded stockpiles in Russia and neighboring countries. Transported to various European cities and on to the end buyers. The dealer told us that he himself had been approached, but he wanted no part of this profitable but risky game."

"I see."

The Colonel paused. He gave me a quick look. "Knowing the dealer's history, this sent us a most disturbing message. Who is the mastermind behind a widespread and highly dangerous illegal activity? Outfits like Al Qaeda often rent and lease operatives to other outfits. Criminal affiliations are formed to obtain needed expertise. We find that terrorist networks may have fuzzy lines and mixed ideologies, but their common goal is to cause severe disruption. Create a vacuum that they can fill. Unfortunately, they thrive on chaos."

He stopped, as if waiting for a response, then went on. "It's my view that biological weapons are the poor man's atomic bomb. For example, it takes very little expertise to contaminate reservoirs and large bodies of water. A few bad actors can do enormous damage. If you follow."

"Yes."

"Try to compare this market to the arms trade. A commingling of business, crime syndicates, governments. In any case, we must anticipate that relatively cheap and effective ways to cause chaos may be used to create a black hole." He paused.

"Which brings us to the threat of worldwide contagious infection. Our health systems are alert to the possible spread of the H five N one virus from human to human, but present preparations will be woefully inadequate if millions are suddenly stricken. Stores and banks will close. Communication systems will break down. Hospitals will be overwhelmed as the infrastructure collapses. Not a pleasant prognosis."

I stared at the small fire burning in the grate. A cold chill was creeping up my spine. The Colonel's voice had been dry and matter-of-fact as he described a global catastrophe that might kill us all. A mild-looking man, but I had the feeling that a criminal who took him for a pussycat might find the prison doors clanking shut. He gave me an assessing look.

"So much for background. About your niece's illness. I gather she's recovering and there were no further cases."

"As far as I know. The hospital isolated her right away."

"I'm also told that the virus has not been identified." He paused. "Unfortunately, there have been several similar cases recently, mostly in Europe. We think they may be linked to this illegal network, but we have no evidence. No proof. As Lord Rodale has told you, last week one of our best agents was taken out in Venice."

"Taken out?"

"Killed. For us, a flawed operation. As well, a signal that Venice may be part of this underground transport network. Possibly a jumping-off place to Libya or France." The Colonel turned. "Your pigeon, Rodale. Carry on."

"Very well, sir." Rodale came forward. "This particular agent was a British national. His cover was to act as undersecretary to the British consulate in Venice. We think he may have infiltrated the network and was eliminated before he could get any farther."

I nodded without speaking. I could tell by his overly tight control that Rodale was taking this death as a personal failure.

"What's more, it was very cleverly done. He was pushed off the quay in front of the Hotel Dordona just as he was getting onto a vaporetto. At first the people around him thought he had tried to make a last-minute leap to board and had fallen into the water. They were calling him a drunk fool, shouting for the police. The examination showed that he had been stabbed in the neck."

Rodale moved back. I sat still. The morning after the recital I had looked down at a floating quay filled with jostling people. Watching as a crowded vaporetto moved slowly into the lagoon.

The Colonel folded his arms. "Right. Now to your niece's situation. The possibility that she might have been infected in Venice. There are questions, which is why Commissario Filardi is taking heat for letting you leave."

"I told him all I know."

"That may be, but you can appreciate the Questura's concern. Two British nationals are murdered in the heart of the city. No suspects, no evidence. They think we may be keeping information from them. Playing our own game, which, of course, we are. But it works both ways. We think they may have found papers in the accompanist's room at the Europa." He paused. "This chap Dykstra. Do you see him connected to criminal activities?"

"I didn't meet him, just saw him at the reception. It's hard to imagine how Mark Dykstra could get his hands on a stolen virus—or know how to use it. He was a good accompanist who wore a funny little wig. He was concerned about his health." I hesitated. "Before we go on, I have a question. When my niece was so sick, virus samples were being rushed back and forth between Boston and Atlanta by plane and special courier. Time was key. So how could a live virus be transported from the old Russia, say, to Venice?"

"A good question. We know that a virus can be kept alive in a viral transport solution. It would be packed in dry ice. The actual container could be fairly small, something that could fit into a knapsack or a briefcase. Nothing that would draw attention."

"So the carrier would look like an ordinary traveler."

"Not easy to spot, which leads to more questions. What type of transport? What routes? Couriers, known as mules, probably wouldn't risk carrying this material through airports. Therefore they could be using trains. Boats. There are any number of possibilities. As well, we're trying to trace unexplained funds. Find out who pays the operatives who steal from security-lax laboratories or stockpiles. Pays the human mules."

"I see."

The Colonel was looking at me, as if waiting for more. After a moment he squared his shoulders. "Another question, Mrs. Streat. Because there's been no widespread outbreak, the signs point to contamination by water rather than an airborne virus. Did your niece carry her own water with her?"

"Always. Most singers do, to keep from upsetting their systems when they're on tour."

"And who would have had access to that water?"

"A lot of people. The crew on Barzalon's plane. Staff at the hotel. My niece's assistant could make a list. It was part of her job to make sure there was a supply handy."

For the next half hour I answered the familiar questions about Vanessa. Where she had been. What she ate and drank. "You have to remember, I wasn't there until the night of the recital," I said at last.

"Granted, but were you aware of any quarrels? Any incidents that might point to a person who wished her harm?"

"I've heard of singers who'll do anything to get another singer's part. It's the classic way to make a name for yourself, but Vanessa was doing a recital. Alone."

"Anything else?"

"Yes. As a matter of fact, there is." I hesitated, feeling my way. "Vanessa and Mark Dykstra had words after the recital. She told him she wouldn't be singing again. Fired him. He was terribly upset. That's why we assumed that he had gone to the hotel and hung himself. Besides losing his job, he was in love with her."

"Interesting. Difficult to see where the man fits into the picture, but he can't be ruled out completely. He had access to her suite. Someone wanted him dead. He might have had valuable information. On the other hand, it could be a simple case of being in the wrong place at the wrong time."

"Like interrupting a robbery? Nothing was taken."

"And most thieves in that situation would take to their heels. The killing was done with skill. No prints. No sign of an entrance or exit."

"The clerk at the front desk let Dykstra in. Maybe he's involved."

"The Questura has questioned him. With no results."

A log fell in the grate with a small crash. The dogs raised their heads from their baskets. These two men were working against time. Under the controlled professional manner, I could sense urgency. An accompanist had been murdered. An agent had been stabbed and thrown into the lagoon. A singer might have been fatally poisoned. Mrs. Streat had been brought here to connect the dots—but so far she had contributed nothing.

"I'm sorry," I said. "I'm afraid I haven't been any help."

The Colonel frowned. "These things aren't easy. Perhaps something may come to mind later."

"It may." I closed my eyes, remembering a statement that Sergeant Johnson had made last summer: "One little lead can get the case rolling. People remember something that didn't seem right, but wasn't important at the time."

"If it does, you'll be in touch with Lord Rodale?"

"Of course," I said. Human mules. Briefcases. Trains. Boats. Boats. I leaned forward. "One thing. It may be nothing, but it puzzled me at the time."

"Yes?"

"The morning after Dykstra hanged himself, I was desperate to talk Seth Barzalon out of taking my niece to Sardinia. His head pilot, Terry Gallagher, met me at the Dordona. Walked me to a trattoria away from the hotels and the press."

"Go on."

"On the way, a young gondolier came poling down a canal. He asked Terry if they were going to meet in the usual place. They seemed to know each other surprisingly well."

"Did you get the gondolier's name?"

"Fausto. It was Fausto."

"An unusual name."

"One reason I paid attention. When we got to the trattoria, I sat down with Barzalon. Terry went into the bar. After our talk, Barzalon asked where his pilot had gone. Said he was a womanizer, always running off making deals. When I looked around, these good buddies, Terry and Fausto, were in the bar having an argument, fists waving. I had to wonder what was going on."

"This pilot. Tell me about him."

"He's Irish, breezy, a devil-take-the-hindmost sort of man. A womanizer like his boss, but they don't seem to get on too well. On the way to the trattoria he told me he'd gone to the beach the night of the recital. Said he doesn't like the dirty water in Venice. He was expecting to fly to Sardinia, so he came back early that morning for routine checks."

"Indeed." The Colonel was still frowning.

I stared at the drooping eyelid. "Actually, I'm not suggesting that Terry is a criminal. You asked me to think of anything that made an impression. That's all it was, really. An impression."

A dog yawned. From outside came the sound of a car pulling onto the gravel drive. The Colonel looked at his watch, then at Rodale.

"My driver. He's a bit early, but I believe we've covered the ground." The colonel paused, then came toward me, holding out his hand. "Thank you again for making the trip, Mrs. Streat. Very much appreciated. Good luck to you." Suddenly he seemed to be in a hurry to leave.

I stood up. "Thank you, sir. I wish I could have been more help."

"Not at all. Have a safe journey home. A word with you, Rodale," and the two men walked toward the door, followed by the dogs.

The room was growing cold. I went to the fireplace and stood there, feeling drained. Al Qaeda. Terrorist networks. Biological weapons. Was this the world my boys would be facing? I shivered and folded my arms over my chest, willing Rodale to come back. Take me upstairs to the big Jacobean bed. Keep fear at bay behind the red damask curtains.

At last the door opened and he was there. "Sorry to be so long."

"I'm afraid I wasted the Colonel's time."

"No. You did well. Maybe too well. Shall we walk? There'll be a coat in the cloakroom."

The cloakroom was on the far side of the house. Barbour jackets and tweed caps hung on pegs; Wellington boots in different sizes were lined neatly against the wall. The usual trappings of British country life, as opposed to lacrosse sticks and Frisbees.

A side door opened to the rough lawn. The dogs ran ahead, quartering, noses to the ground.

"Next week they'll be in training for national field trials," Rodale said. "Chloe is apt to go wide, wants to hunt the next county."

"I thought you had horses."

"In Newmarket. With my ex-mother-in-law."

I walked faster. Field trials. Hunt the next county. Racehorses.

The lawn continued past the clump of beeches. "There don't seem to be any flower gardens," I said.

"Not Palladian enough for my great-uncle, but we have a grotto. Built later. Very fashionable at one time. This way," and we started down an overgrown path. After a moment, he cleared his throat. "Bad news. There's been a change in plans. I have to go back to London. Now. Jenkins is on his way."

"Go back? Why?"

"The Colonel wants more information about Gallagher and the gondolier. He wants it by tomorrow. That means driving back this afternoon."

"Oh." I stumbled over a loose stone, trying to take in his words. Oh God, by bringing up Terry and the gondolier had I shot myself in the foot? Now, instead of being here with me, Rodale was going off like a rocket to London.

"What I said about Terry was just a . . . an impression. Nothing more."

"Even so, it's a lead that has to be followed. Unfortunately, they're thin on the ground."

"Still, I can't believe—"

"Emma." He turned to face me. "Think. Pilots of privately owned planes fly in and out of airports. They have their own security procedures with loopholes. Frankly, until now we hadn't put pilots of private jets into the equation, but it bears looking into."

"Are you suggesting that Terry put a virus into Vanessa's special water? He was up in front flying the plane from Paris to Venice. He never was close to her—or her water—again."

"Perhaps not, but there's this. Let's say he got into the suite and was tampering with her water. Dykstra comes in and catches him in the act."

"Terry told me that he was at the beach that night."

"We have no proof, as yet. He could be lying. Covering his tracks."

"True. The man is an operator. For some reason, he's amusing himself with Vanessa's naïve assistant. I wouldn't put it past him to be doing something on the side like smuggling drugs, but to deliberately poison Vanessa—" I stumbled again.

Rodale took my arm. "We'll run some data on him. It may be a blank, but as the Colonel said, one break can lead to another. Like hounds following a line. Sometimes they're thrown off the scent, but the good ones keep their noses to the ground."

"I still think you're overreacting."

"You heard the Colonel. You saw what happened to your niece. These people must be found before they can do more harm." He stopped and pointed to a cave, half-hidden by overgrown vines. "The resident grotto. Do you want to go in and explore?"

Grotesque stone gargoyles had been carved around the entrance, mouths open, as if waiting for the next meal. "Certainly not," I said. "God knows what's been dragged in over the years."

"Probably nothing but dead leaves." He looked at his watch. "It's getting on. We'd better start back."

As we turned, I kept my eyes on the path. This morning, in a weak moment, I had let myself imagine what it would be like to live with him in this house. In fairness, I had always known that I would take second place behind his work, but once again, it was painfully clear where I stood in his life. The outsider.

He took my arm again. "I'd hoped we could have some time together. We still can. I could put you up at a hotel. I'll be working around the clock at the mausoleum on Upper Brook Street, but with any luck, I could get free for a few hours tomorrow. Maybe the next day. What do you want to do?"

"I'm not sure. Let me think."

We were coming out onto the lawn. I picked up a small stone and rolled it around in my hand. Did I want to go back to London and see him for a few hours? Did I want to be a backstreet mistress, convenient for bed? Live on his terms, not mine?

We were coming closer to the house. Cold and white and classic. He put his arm around my shoulder. "What's it to be?"

I dropped the stone. "Actually, I really need to get home. There was the mad dash to Venice. Then the quarantine. You wouldn't believe the mess that has to be dealt with."

"You're sure?"

"I'm sure." What mattered now was to hide my humiliating lapse into delusion. It would hurt, really hurt, to walk away from this man again, but the cord must be cut. And the cut must be sharp.

He let go of my shoulder and took my face in his hands. "Emma. Are you cutting me out of your life?"

I turned my head away. Reading my mind was one of his many skills. "What if I am?"

He took my hand and turned it over. "I told you once that you're a remarkable woman with the most beautiful eyes. It was the morning after you were nearly killed in the company flat. Do you remember?"

"I remember."

"Take that up a notch. If I had to be stranded on a desert island tomorrow, you'd be the one woman I'd want with me."

"Not much of a risk. It won't happen."

"Don't be too sure. There's this island in the British Virgins. An old cane plantation. The owners rent it out. Once this case is sorted out—"

"You *bastard*." The words came out like gunfire. Over the years I had been forced to overcome a childhood temper, but sometimes it detonated out of control.

"Emma."

Using all my strength, I pulled away. "I mean it. You're a one-track-minded bastard and some night some woman is going to stab you through the heart in that big bed."

He took a step back and looked down at me. For once, there was surprise on that impassive face. "Strong words," he said in a low voice.

"Not strong enough. I could have talked to the Colonel in London, but oh no, you wanted to combine business and pleasure. Two for the price of one. I should have known better."

"I thought we understood each other."

"All I understand is, I'm being jerked around. Again." I stopped. My throat was closing, holding back tears. I was be-having like an angry child, a humiliated child, not like a grown woman with steel in her spine.

The dogs were out of sight. He whistled for them, then

turned. "Let's get this straight. You say I'm using you. I'd prefer to think that we're working together for a common goal. I respect your abilities. I enjoy your company, in and out of bed. An unusual relationship, but it's one I value. A great deal. I'm sorry, extremely sorry, that your visit had to end like this."

Silence. I stared at the clump of beeches, the peaceful slope of land leading to the stream. "All right," I said at last. "I still think you're a one-track-minded bastard, but it's always in a good cause. To be fair, you never misled me. I got into your bed with my eyes wide open."

"So why the temper tantrum?"

"I don't know. I don't know. Maybe it's because you're a complication in my life. I don't need complications."

"Nor do I. That's what I meant by understanding each other. I was wrong."

There was nothing more to say. The dogs were returning, running in circles, noses to the ground. "Mandy. Chloe," he called. Obediently, they lifted their heads and came toward us. He cleared his throat and looked at me. "Back to business. Will you be seeing Seth Barzalon again?"

"I suppose it depends on Vanessa. Why?"

"Barzalon is sure to have information about his own pilot. We can put Gallagher through the databases, but we need boots on the ground over there. In other words, we still need your help."

"Oh?" The sleeves of the Barbour jacket were too long. I put my hands behind my back, telling myself not to overreact. "Let's get this straight. If you're asking me to be one of the agents you're running, the answer is no. I don't want to end up in a lagoon."

"Keep your shirt on. I'm only asking you to keep your eyes

open. Do a little discreet probing. Come up with another connection."

"These connections. I'm tired of hearing about them."

"And I'm tired of hearing you belittle your abilities. As I said last summer, you will never be thanked officially, but it's why the Colonel took time to make this trip. And went away with a valid lead."

"Which may or may not be useful."

"That's not the point. The question is this: Are you willing to take part in this investigation? Be part of the team?"

"All I know is, for the past few months I've been bounced from crisis to crisis. I want to move ahead with my life, not be involved in any more trouble."

"Not even to help your niece?"

I kicked at a pile of leaves. "That's right. Aim for the vulnerable soft spot. Of course I want to know if my niece was deliberately infected. Of course I don't want a bunch of thugs starting a pandemic. On the other hand, I don't see Terry Gallagher as a big player."

"Which may be exactly what he wants, to mislead you. Everyone."

"Please, no lecture on the dangers of taking people at face value. I'm not happy about this, but I love my niece. I'll go back and ask a few questions. Will that do?"

"That'll do."

At last we were reaching the tall white house. Suddenly I could hardly wait to leave. The dogs sat down, panting, waiting. Rodale opened the door and motioned me ahead.

"I'll go and pack," I said. "How much time do I have?"

"Half an hour. Here, I'll hang up that jacket for you." His hands were on my shoulders. I moved quickly toward the hall.

Right now I must concentrate on leaving with my pride intact.

He followed.

"Emma. About that desert island."

"What about it?"

"The offer still stands."

I laughed. "In your dreams."

twelve

October 21

Boston

When I arrived the next evening, the streets of Boston were gray and dull with rain, not a welcoming warmth. The apartment seemed smaller and more alien than ever. There was an odd chemical smell in the sitting room—a faint residue of something I couldn't quite identify. Had someone come in? Not a workman. Not my little housekeeper. The plants were dry, needing water.

After dumping my bags in the bedroom, I went to the kitchen for a glass of milk. After one taste, I spit it into the sink. The milk had gone sour.

"Shit," I said, and poured myself a glass of wine. Sat down on the slippery white sofa and tried to block out images of a Palladian house with a wide sweep of open field. A Jacobean bed. One night—and then the abrupt departure. I should have known better than to put my head on the block.

If asked, Caroline, veteran of four marriages and numerous

affairs, would give astringent advice. I could almost hear that tuba voice: "Darling girl, don't pine. Think of him as a very expensive spa that specializes in rejuvenation. Go when you feel the need."

"The offer still stands," Rodale had said, but no one could live forever at a spa. In fact, it didn't take Caroline—or a therapist— to tell me that I should concentrate on making a solid new life, one that didn't depend on addiction to one larger-than-life Brit. High-octane moments of physical and mental passion.

There was a pile of books on the coffee table, ones that I had ordered last week and never read. Absently, I wiped a thin layer of dust from a book jacket, and remembered an article I had read several months ago. It had stated that the key to wisdom was to be resilient in the face of adversity. "Resiliency." A good word.

The muscles in my legs were stiff from hours of sitting. I got up and leaned against the refrigerator, stretching out the tight hamstrings According to Rodale, all I had to do was keep my eyes open. Try to get in touch with Seth Barzalon and ask a few questions about Terry. Easier said than done. Even trickier, no one must have the slightest suspicion that I was part of an ongoing police investigation. There had been one close call in front of Greg Atkins. Then this sudden trip. My excuse had been that someone must deal with Dykstra's sister, an unreasonable woman who was threatening to make trouble for Vanessa.

Resiliency. My new mantra to combat depression. After a while I straightened, rotated my shoulders, and picked up a pad of paper. The list of priorities was long. Call Cathy. Jake and Steve. Denise Daniels, the real estate agent. Doris Gates, the caretaker at the remains of my place in Hardwick. Greg Atkins.

But calling my brother couldn't wait until tomorrow. Vanessa was my first priority, the reason for this cat's cradle of intrigue. In the past few days I had come to realize how much I loved Vanessa. Partly because she had taken the place of the daughter who had died at birth. Partly because she had carried the torch for my lost voice, partly for herself.

My brother, Ned, lived in a rambling shingled house in Manchester-by-the-Sea. His wife, Cassia, answered the phone.

"Emma. You're back."

"Just got in. How's Vanessa?"

"Terribly weak, but improving. She's in a private room. Ned's there now. We can't believe we still have her."

"I know. Have they found out about the virus?"

"If they have, they haven't told us. What about the accompanist's sister? Did you see her?"

"I talked to her. I told her that Vanessa wanted to make a significant contribution." Not quite a lie. I *had* called the sister from Heathrow. "Look, I'll tell you more tomorrow. Right now I'm too jet-lagged to think straight."

"Poor lamb. It's so good to have you back. Vanessa's been asking where you are."

"I long to see her. Touch her. I'll be there first thing tomorrow."

By now I was becoming familiar with the size of Boston General. Like a seasoned traveler, I found the right wing, rode elevators, and trekked down corridors. The smell was the same, the nurses and aides moved with purpose, but in this area there was no sense of life-threatening emergency.

At room 711, I slowed and stopped at the half-open door.

Vanessa was lying on her back, eyes closed. Her face was very thin. Her hair had lost its lustre. A heart-wrenching change, but I must keep the dismay from showing.

"Vanessa?"

Her eyes opened. She moved her head and smiled. "Emma. They said you were away."

"Not for long." I leaned down and kissed her cheek. "Here's some light reading," I said, and put two magazines on the end of the bed. "My God, what a scare you gave me. Don't ever do that again."

"They said you had to call an ambulance."

I pulled a chair closer to the bed and sat down. "I did. I was terrified. Do you remember anything at all?"

"Just feeling sick on the plane. Going to bed in your apartment. After that a blur. Faces wavering in and out." She hesitated. "This may sound weird, but sometimes I had the feeling that you were there with me. Holding on to me."

I leaned forward. "Believe it or not, I was. I've never been deep into religion, but I prayed like I've never prayed before, not even when Lewis died. I prayed that you would know that you weren't alone. That you knew you were loved. When Dr. Reston called and said you were going to be all right, I went down to that church on Newbury Street and did some *very* major thanking."

"You did?"

"Of course." I sat back. "How are you feeling now?"

"Spacy. Bored." Her hand plucked at the sheet. "I've been lying here thinking. It's about all I *can* do."

"Thinking about what?"

"The doctors say I may not lose my voice."

"That's good news. The best."

"Is it? I know I should be glad, but oh my God, it would

mean starting over. From scratch. All that work, and then there might not be the same sound."

"You'll never know unless you try."

"I know how to find out." She turned her head and grinned, a shadow of the tomboy with pigtails. "The world according to Emma: Discipline. Build a foundation. Don't take shortcuts."

"My burned-child syndrome. The truth is, you have a great gift. Far greater than mine ever was."

"And you came to Venice because you were afraid I would throw it away. It may happen anyhow. No matter what I do."

"What makes you say that?"

"Because no one will tell me what made me so sick. It's as if I have some rare disease and no one dares tell me."

I shook my head. "Not true. As far as anyone knows, it's still an unidentified virus. When the white coats get a match, they'll have to tell you and your family. Patient's rights. Your job now is to get strong. Not lie there and worry."

"I know. I'll try." She turned her head and looked at me. "I'm glad you're here, Emma. I have an announcement. I want you to be the first to know."

I opened my mouth and closed it. "An announcement?"

"Brace yourself. I never want to see Seth Barzalon again. It's over. Finished. Now do me a huge favor and wipe that revolting smile off your face."

"Sorry. I mean, sorry about the smile. What changed your mind?"

"It was when I heard he brought orchids to the nurses. Great expensive pots of orchids. As if that would buy me better care."

"I got one, too. A great expensive pot."

"He left a note. Three scrawled lines to say he was off to some race in Europe. I mean, I was *dying*. Did *you* see him?"

"Twice. Once the day after you got sick. He arrived at the

door ready to sling you over his shoulder. I had to tell him I'd taken you to the hospital. To be fair, he was pretty upset."

"Upset because he didn't know when I'd be well enough to fly off with him."

"He's not used to waiting for what he wants."

"Neither are two-year-olds. It began to dawn on me that there had never been one *word* about what *I* was giving up for him. I mean, he could have his racing, but *I* had to give up my singing."

She was plucking at the sheet again. I took her hand. "Stop. It's over."

"Yes, but it nearly happened. That's what's so scary. I can't believe what I almost did."

"Don't be hard on yourself. It's not easy to be a celebrity— maybe 'commodity' is a better word. Cut off from the real world by people who expect too much of you."

"Excuses, excuses. I should have been able to cope." She moved her head as if it was hurting.

I looked at my watch. "I should go," I said. "By the way, does Cathy know you're through with Barzalon?"

"Not yet. I'm not allowed a phone. Right now she's in New York sorting things out there. Is it true the two of you had to go into quarantine?"

"As in staying in my apartment. It wasn't too bad. Cathy's a treasure, the way she took care of you in Venice," I said, and put the thin hand back on the sheet.

"Wait." Vanessa reached out. "Can you stand one more favor?"

"Of course."

"Barzalon. I never want to see him again. I don't want the parents to know about him. Ever."

"They don't have to."

"It was partly my fault. I was looking for a painkiller and I let it happen. All the same, I want to be rid of him without a fuss. Or a ghastly bedside scene with him shouting and nurses running."

"We know what he's like. It won't be easy to keep him away."

"Maybe there's some kind of court order, like 'do not let this man come within a hundred feet of room seven-eleven. If only we knew when he might come back."

I hesitated. Here, out of the blue, was a valid reason to track down Seth Barzalon. And through him, Terry Gallagher.

"Relax," I said. "There may be a way through the Barzalon Foundation. I got to know one of the researchers there. Quite well."

"Can you do it soon?"

"I'll call the foundation today. When I get in touch, I'll say that you're very weak. That you're sorry, but you haven't the strength to see him."

"Anything." She closed her eyes. "It seems as if you're always having to bail me out."

"No problem. Grab the freebies while they last. Right now we'd all crawl to New York for you. Has anyone said how long you'll be here?"

"You know what doctors are like, but they may let me go home next week. Ma's been hovering. She can't wait to start me on soy milk and tofu."

"You'll be lucky if she doesn't put a baby monitor in your room." I leaned over and touched her hair. "Love you. Take care. I'll be back tomorrow."

A cart was rattling down the hall. A seriously overweight young woman came in with a food tray. She cranked up the bed, swung the bed table around, and plunked the tray down.

"Enjoy," she said, and left.

Vanessa lifted the steel cover and made a face. "Dog's dinner."

"Eat the applesauce. Drink the milk. I'll bring you some treats from Whole Foods."

"Emma." She reached out and caught the end of my scarf in her hand.

"What now?"

"Just thank you. For everything."

I tried to smile. "You're a keeper. Flighty, but sound at the core."

As I went out into the hall, I almost collided with a fast-moving bed. A man lay there, covered with a white blanket and connected to hanging tubes. I hurried by. If I never set foot in a hospital again, it would be too soon.

The weather was turning cold. Instead of heading up the back side of Beacon Hill, I turned and made my way through busy traffic patterns to the Esplanade, the long promenade that bordered the Charles River.

There were no crews bending to their oars, skimming the surface of the water. Somewhere on the opposite side of the river, Harvard's colonial brick buildings stood solid and serene. My elusive son, Steve, lived in one of those buildings. He hadn't been in touch with me since Labor Day. "Give him space," his brother, Jake, had advised. "He may be having a delayed reaction. Cut him some slack."

Back in the apartment, I pulled out my new Rolodex and flipped to Vanessa Metcalf's number in New York.

"Cathy? It's Emma," I said "I got back last night."

"Holy Mother. I wanted to call you, but I was afraid you were still away." There was no mistaking the distress in Cathy's voice.

"What's wrong? You sound worried."

"I am, and that's the truth of it."

"Tell me what happened."

"I will. I was sitting here; it was late yesterday afternoon. I was making myself a cup of tea. The phone rang. It was Terry Gallagher."

I straightened. "So they're back. I just saw Vanessa. She never wants to see Seth Barzalon again. I promised to head him off. Do you know where they are now? Where they're going next?"

"No, and I never want to lay eyes on that Terry again."

"Sorry. I didn't mean to interrupt. Go on."

"At first it was grand. He took me to a Chinese place, very fancy red and gold. I ate with chopsticks, all except the rice. Then he asked if he could come back to the apartment. I didn't see the harm in it."

"I see." Whatever was coming, I mustn't lecture.

"Vanessa . . . has a table for drinks in the front room. Glasses and bottles and such. He helped himself to the whiskey. He wanted me to drink with him, but I've no use for the hard stuff. I've seen me father and brother the worse for drink. It's a terrible trial to their wives."

"So what you need is a nice American who likes one beer with his dinner. Was Terry difficult?"

"At first he was on about Barzalon, how the man treated him like a piece of dirt. Then it was a stream of questions about Mark Dykstra."

"What kind of questions?"

"What we had seen when we came back to the suite. What we said to the police. What the police said to us and did they think it was a suicide. He even asked questions about you, did

I know the name of your friend in the police that got us out of Venice. He was ranting on and on, as if he could shake it out of me."

"Was he violent?"

"He never laid a hand on me, but he was halfway through the bottle. I had the fear of what was coming. There's body-guards laid on for the actor who lives on the sixth floor. I told Terry if if he didn't go, I'd call security. He slammed down the glass. It broke on the floor. He went crashing out in a state. What did he want of me?" Her voice wavered. I could tell that she was crying.

"Nasty. Really nasty."

"It was. I'd never see the man again, not after the way he acted last night."

"No, you shouldn't." I hesitated. This was serious. Cathy must be warned, but first I would have to call Rodale. "Cathy, there's something not right about the man. Don't let him near you."

"Ah, I won't, but what did it mean, those questions?"

"I don't know, but we need to talk. As soon as possible. Are you almost done in New York?"

"Vanessa's manager is doing her best with the broken contracts, but it will be weeks before she has it straight. I could finish up today and take the train tomorrow."

"Will your cousin have you to stay again?"

"She will, now that I'm not going to die on her hands. It gives her a little extra coming in and she likes to gossip about the family."

"Then here's a plan. You take the train tomorrow. Go to your cousin. Come to my apartment the next day. That's Thursday. We'll have lunch, go over everything that happened in Venice.

Everything we know about Terry. Then we'll decide what to do. Whether we should bring in . . . other people."

"Other people? Holy Mother, you're not talking about the police?"

"No, no, not police. More like a . . . a private detective."

"Ah, I should never have let him set foot in this place."

"It happened. Don't take on blame; we'll get it sorted. After we've talked, we'll go see Vanessa."

"That would be grand."

"I've told her you're a treasure. Take care," and I clicked off. One small mercy. Terry had lost his hold on Cathy. She wasn't going to see him again. Both he and his boss were history.

Rodale wasn't answering his cell. I left a message, telling him that Terry had been in New York last night. That he had tried to extract information from Cathy Riordan about the Dykstra suicide. That Cathy and I were going to meet on Thursday to talk and I would try to get a clearer picture.

The day was flying away. I rubbed my neck, trying to relieve the tension. There was a message on the answering machine from Greg Atkins: "Let's have dinner. Call me when you get back." I hesitated, then tapped his number.

"Emma. You're back. Good trip?"

"Not too bad. Dykstra's sister didn't give me too much trouble. Her bark was worse than her bite."

"There's that new Italian place on Exeter. We were going to try it, but then you rushed off to England."

"Tonight?"

"I've missed you."

"I haven't been gone very long." I hesitated. It was too soon after Rodale to go forward with Greg. "Not tonight," I said. "To be honest, I'm really tired. I might topple into the soup."

"Maybe tomorrow, then. I should work late at the lab. It's not for publication, but there are two new confirmed cases of avian in Europe. If this keeps up, the public will be advised to buy masks and get in a ten-day supply of food and water."

"That's . . . bad." Was Rodale involved in these cases? "I'll tell you one thing. I'm not staying alone in this place, not knowing if my boys are alive or dead. We'll make a dash for my grandmother's old house in New Hampshire."

"The roads may be blocked."

"Maybe it'll be like the millennium, everyone getting ready for disaster." A pause. "By the way, I saw Vanessa today. She's still very weak, but she says she's finished with Seth Barzalon. The thing is, she can't face seeing him and I'm supposed to tell him. Do you know where he is at the moment?"

"I don't, but I'll let you know if he gets in touch. About the pandemic. I'm sorry if I frightened you, especially when you're dead on your feet. What you need is a good night's sleep."

"You're right. I do."

"Good night, then. I'll call you first thing in the morning."

"Good. Don't work too late," I said as the line went dead. With Greg, there would never be the intoxication of a Rodale, but being with Rodale demanded a level of physical and mental excitement that was unsustainable. Greg would be there for me. Supportive. I would have to move cautiously with the boys; they would resent anyone trying to take their father's place. On the other hand, they were old enough to appreciate Greg's work. What he was trying to do.

After a moment, I went to the window. Across the street, a young woman emerged from her black-painted door. She was carrying a pail and trowel. Standing on the steps, she reached into the window box and began to replace last summer's geraniums' stems with shiny holly branches. I watched, suddenly aware that in a few weeks the holidays would be upon us. Thanksgiving. Christmas. Family bonding. There was a saying that children are on loan to us. For a short time.

Quickly I pushed in numbers for Jake's cell. For once, he was reachable. "Hi, Ma. What's going on?"

"Not too much. How about you?"

"Trying to get through my science requirement. How's Vanessa doing?"

"I saw her today. She may be going home next week."

"Say hi. Tell her I'm glad she's okay."

"I will. Miss you," I said, then wished I hadn't.

"Miss you, too." A pause. "There's a soccer game this weekend, a home game, if you feel like coming down. One thing, though. No jumping around and yelling."

"*Jake*. You *know* I never yell."

"Just kidding. You used to get pretty mad at mothers who did."

"Only at the loudmouth who tried to out-coach the coach."

"Two o'clock. I'll let you know what field. Don't forget the brownies."

"Very funny." I took a deep breath. "Have you heard from Steve lately?"

"No. Have you?"

"Not since we were all in Manchester over Labor Day." I hesitated. "I know he thinks I should have been open with him about last summer. He's angry, and I'm doing my best to be hands-off, I really am, but he's just across the river. And he has a cell."

"It's his first year. There's a lot going on."

"I don't expect him to come here; I know he hates this apartment. So do I. In fact, it's beginning to give me the creeps."

"It was always stopgap."

"I'm about to start looking for a place near Boston with plenty of land. Or I could rebuild in Hardwick. What do you think?"

"I think you should go back there and have a fresh look. Then do what feels right for you. About Steve. Maybe you could leave him a message about Vanessa. Nothing heavy."

"I will. Thanks. Let me know about the game." Jake was born kind, growing more and more like Lewis. As for Steve—at eighteen, all I cared about was my social life, my new car, my clothes. Singing had forced me to change.

It was now the middle of the afternoon. Before making more calls, I must force myself to sit down and pay the now overdue bills. When we were first married, Lewis and I had made a pact: He would put up with my messiness about clothes. I would pay bills promptly. In Lewis's working-class family, never owing money was a matter of pride. Over the years, I had worked out a system. Put the biggest bill on top and work down.

An ominously thick pile lay on the shiny black desk. Before leaving for London, I had done a quick sorting. The Visa bill with all the Venice expenses had been by far the largest. I had put it on top, making a mental note to shift money into my checking account. But the paper facing me was the September statement from the rental agency on Boylston Street.

I sat still, staring at the agency figures. The little housekeeper hadn't been in since the quarantine began. No one else had a key. There had been no sign of a break-in—nothing wrong except last night's uneasiness when I first opened the door.

After a moment, I lay down on the floor and began my neglected push-ups. Maybe stress could cause lapses into absentmindedness. It was time for a change. A day away from this apartment.

As every mother knows, being locked into a car is a time-tested way to loosen a child's tongue. The message I left on Steve's cell phone was short and undemanding: "Vanessa improving. Driving down to Hardwick tomorrow for a few hours. Need to decide whether to rebuild or look for a new place. It would be great if you're free and could drive me."

thirteen

I hadn't been in Hardwick since the long August heat wave. To-day, on the Massachusetts Turnpike, the fall coloring was reaching its zenith, a last gasp of brilliance before winter's monotones. My five-year-old Volvo station wagon had been sitting for weeks in a garage on Brimmer Street. Now, with Steve at the wheel, it forged ahead like a racehorse let out of the starting gate.

I glanced at my son, amazed, once again, at the sheer size of him. The arms that once looked like pieces of macaroni now bunched with muscle. On the other hand, he had lost his summer tan and looked thin. Was he binge drinking? Did he have a girl? I was in no position to ask questions, not when *I* had so much to hide. There was no way to tell a son that I had slept with a man since his father died. And . . . I was still hiding trouble from Steve. A new and very complicated trouble.

It was eleven thirty when we left the highway and headed toward the wide river where Pequot Indians once paddled around the sweeping curves. Steve slowed as we passed the general store and the white church with the cut-off steeple. The church where Lewis's service had been held.

"Not much change," Steve said quickly.

"No," I said, bracing myself against the moment when he would turn into the dirt road. Pass the place where I had found Lewis lying dead on the grass verge. Go through the white gates and down the winding drive that once led to a yellow clapboard house.

The Sterling house had been built in 1780 as an "ordinary"— a designated inn for travelers. The Streats, newcomers, had added a new wing, a long terrace, but it was always known as the Sterling place. Now two stone chimneys rose from a mass of rubble and a bedraggled crop of weeds.

Steve pulled into the circle and stopped. We sat, confronting the visual marks of loss. Somewhere in the debris were the ashes of my treasures: the round kitchen table, the Grandma Moses painting that hung in the hall. The photos. My singing tapes. The remains of the home I had created with so much love.

"Goodness me. There you are." Our caretaker, Mrs. Gates, was coming from the nearby barn we had used as a garage with an apartment above. Mrs. Gates was a round, cheerful woman; for years she had been my unfailing support and my friend.

I opened the door and got out. "We made good time. Steve drove me."

"He's a good boy. Here's someone who's glad to see you," she said as O'Hara, my Jack Russell terrier, dashed forward, barking shrilly. He stopped, looked at me for a few seconds, then flung himself at my knees, whining and quivering: Lady, lady, why did you leave me? I leaned down and scratched his ears. He was putting on weight; his back was broader; his belly drooped from too many treats. Did dogs have any long-term memory?

"Enough of the helpless-victim act," I said to him.

Steve was giving Mrs. Gates a hug. "Hey, Mrs. G." She had been his other caregiver, purveyor of brownies and unjudgmental affection.

She hugged him back. "Taller than ever. Behaving yourself?"

"When don't I?"

"When did you? I could tell a few stories."

I gave O'Hara a final pat and straightened. "I'm afraid we can't stay long. Anything special I need to do?"

"There's mail, mostly those dratted catalogues. Two real estate men came by last week, smooth talkers, wanted to know if the place would be coming on the market. I told them I didn't know. I didn't give them your number. Was that right?"

"Absolutely right. I have to start making plans, not put it off any longer. Having my niece so sick put everything on hold."

"Must have been a real fright. You look tired."

"I am, but I wanted to come down and see you. Is O'Hara being a nuisance? Can you keep him a little longer?"

"He's company. No trouble. My sister is after me to come live with her, but there's no rush."

I touched her shoulder. "You're the best. I don't know what I'd have done without you."

She patted my hand. "You're a brave girl. You'd have managed. I've made soup and sandwiches. There's fresh cider from the farm market."

"Steve will like that," I said. For years there had always been a hungry gang at our house. Boys needing help with homework. Games to watch. Steve had turned away and was walking toward the river. I looked at Mrs. Gates.

"I'd stay longer, but Steve has to get back. You know how it is. I was just glad he could drive me."

"Nice for you. How's he liking college?"

"We haven't talked about it. To be honest, he's . . . been a little remote. I think he maybe was more upset about . . . everything . . . than Jake. Funny, I thought it would be the other way around."

"Loss takes people different ways."

"It does." I looked at my watch. "Lewis's grave. I've been wanting to see the new stone. When did it finally come?"

"Three weeks ago. I put some chrysanthemums in front."

"Bless you."

Steve was standing on the path that led to the shore. Farther along, a weeping willow stood sentinel over the place where Lewis was buried. Last June we had put his ashes in a tin box he had used for fishing tackle and marked it with a makeshift board.

The new stone was large, a heavy granite rock from a nearby field. The inscription was simple:

LEWIS PATRICK STREAT
MAY 29, 1954, TO JUNE 11, 2004

I took a deep breath. Strange, that a life could be reduced to a name and two dates. Lewis and I had met in a wine bar a few months after I had lost my voice. For twenty-two years, he had been my rock, my foundation, a rare combination of brilliance and integrity and good judgment, destroyed, not by sickness but by greed. A senseless loss for his sons. For the world.

"You all right, Ma?" Steve put his arm around my shoulder.

"All right, just wishing he was still here. He loved you and Jake so much. He wanted to spend more time with you, but being a CEO can eat you up. The responsibility. So many people depending on you."

"We had some good times. Those fishing trips. Besides, you were always there for us. You never missed a game. We could always bring friends home. A lot of guys don't have that."

"It was fun. Now I need to decide whether to find a place near Boston and Providence. A place where you and Jake could bring friends, I mean, when you have time. Or I could rebuild here. What do you think?"

"I guess you have to do what your gut tells you. This was a great place, but you can't turn back the clock." He scuffed at the rough grass. "I wonder if the sculls are still there."

"We'll go and see," I said, aware that he needed space.

The banks of mountain laurel were growing over the path. We pushed our way down to the shore and came out on the narrow beach. For years the boys had sculled up and down the river, shouting at the top of their lungs, getting in the way of larger boats.

Steve began to walk along the shore. I didn't follow. No way did I want to re-visit the place where the SWAT team from New London had shot Tom Myers dead. Tom, my nemesis, the hired gun who had killed Lewis in front of the white gates. Tried four times to kill me. Blown up my house.

In a moment Steve was back. "Nothing there. Some shits have taken the sculls."

"I should have brought them up to the barn after graduation."

"No sweat." He bent down, picked up a stone, and threw it into the water. "Wasn't it right along here that the guy came in on a raft and torched the house? The guy who killed Dad?"

I kept my eyes on the river. "He came in near the sculls, but he was killed closer to the house." I hesitated. "I always imagined that the man would be a stranger. Not someone I met in Cambridge."

"Bummer."

"It was." I turned. "I know you thought I wasn't being straight with you. Hiding the truth. The problem was, it wasn't my story to tell. The Brits were involved, then the FBI. It was a matter of security."

"You could have trusted me."

"This had nothing to do with trust."

"All the same, it was pretty weird to hear that my father had been murdered. Hear it months later."

"I didn't know it myself for a while. After Lewis's service, you and Jake went back to your summer jobs. Those first few weeks I was in a daze. Then I began to have a feeling there was something wrong about the way he died."

"The police here should have done more."

"They tried, but there was no evidence. Then I talked to the English physicist Lewis was working with and *he* was killed. That got attention, but there was still no suspect. The worst, for me, was when I thought your uncle Hank was behind it."

"I remember when his wife came with him for Dad's service. Tall. Dark, sort of a cold fish. Hard to believe she tried to burn you alive."

"We were friends. Until the last moment I never saw her as *evil.*" I pushed back my hair. "Looking back, there were so many things I didn't see. I guess there always are."

Steve was frowning, scuffing sand. "Uncle Hank. How's he doing?"

"Not too well. He's left London. Dad's company is falling apart."

"Tough. When you think how hard Dad worked—" He stopped. "I think I left some CDs in the pool house."

"Mrs. Gates made sandwiches. I'll meet you at the barn," I said. The barrier between us was coming down, but I mustn't push.

An hour later, we were back in the car, heading toward the Mass Pike. "I needed that," I said. "I needed to get away, see the river again. Maybe it's better just to remember the good things, not try to revive them. On the other hand, good things do repeat themselves. Like you being at Harvard. Your grandfather would have been pleased."

"He was an English professor, right? We never talked much. Then he died and it was too late."

"American history. Advanced. For nerds. I wanted him to bring home hockey players and preppies."

Steve laughed. "We have some preppies in our entry, but there's a guy from South Dakota next door. On a full scholarship. One day we got to talking. He told me about his family, what they were giving up to send him here. I remembered what Dad used to say: 'You're being handed the best education money can buy. Don't throw it away.'"

"Lewis had to work his way through MIT. He was always afraid of making things too easy for you."

Steve gave me a sideways look. "So were you. I know what's been going through your mind. Binge drinking. Up before the Dean. I have to admit, those first few weeks were pretty wild, but I made the JV soccer team."

"You did? Congratulations; I mean, that's great. I guess all those after-school practices weren't wasted."

We were in the fast lane, passing a BMW at high speed. I folded my hands tightly in my lap.

Steve laughed. "Chill, Ma, but it's time to get rid of this relic. Trade up."

"To what? A Hummer?"

"Hybrid. What do you hear from Jake? How's he doing?"

For the rest of the ride, we went over the Thanksgiving options. Manchester with Ned and Cassia or maybe at Vanessa's apartment in New York, always a drawing card. At the corner of Massachusetts Avenue, Steve pulled over and we switched places, holding up traffic. Horns began to honk.

"Hang in, Ma. Be in touch," and he was gone, loping off to his private life. No doubt there was a lot he hadn't told me, but it worked both ways. At last I was on the right track with Steve. Jake had asked me to watch a game.

It was five o'clock by the time I left the Volvo in the Pinckney Street garage. Charles Street was filled with young people, enjoying the late-fall warmth. I walked along slowly, feeling at peace for the first time in months. It had been a productive day; a number of loose ends were now securely in place. I would sell the Hardwick place, find a new home. Rather than replace antiques, it might be fun to create an Asian look. Once that was underway, I would start looking for volunteer work. There were so many needs—and my family's unwritten ethic of giving back was still a priority. And before moving out, I would learn more about this historic area. One-thirty-seven Charles Street had been the home of Annie Fields, the leading Boston hostess who had entertained Charles Dickens. Oliver Wendell Holmes had lived on Beacon Street.

As I reached the entrance to my building, the young couple who lived on the fifth floor came down the steps, jostling and laughing. I hardly ever saw them; they seemed to work all day and go out in the evening, free of responsibility and children.

"Hi," the woman said to me.

The man was looking across the street. "There's that guy again," he said. "That's the third time I've seen him standing there. Now he's walking away."

The woman shook her head. "Maybe he's waiting for some-one. Come on, sug; we're late."

The elevator creaked up. I took out my key and let myself in. Picked up my cell. Needing one day of peace, I had left it behind on the desk.

There was a message from Cathy. "Emma? There's something about Terry you should know. It's too complicated to text, but it's bad. Call me as soon as you can."

"Damn," I said aloud. Quickly I tried Cathy's cell and then her cousin's number in the South End. No answer. I must try again in an hour.

Yawning, I went into the bedroom, took off my shoes, and unfastened the silver and turquoise pendant my sister-in-law, Cassia, had brought me from New Mexico. Except for a few pieces at the bank, all my jewelry had melted in the fire. Now for a shower. Scrambled eggs. Start a list of what I would need in a new place, ranging from sofas to saucepans.

As a minor concession to security, I was keeping my new pieces of jewelry in a small square china dish in the second bureau drawer, hidden behind my bras. I made a circle of the pendant chain. Opened the drawer—and closed it as if it held a live grenade. This morning I had left the box fitted tightly into the far left-hand corner. It had been moved several inches to the right.

For a few seconds I stood still, my hand at my throat. Panic welled up like a cut that wouldn't stop bleeding. Shifted papers on my desk could have have been written off as carelessness under stress. Not this.

Back in the sitting room, I sat down on the sofa and put my head in my hands. Someone *had* been in this apartment. Twice. I could call the police and make a report, but I knew what they would say: "Sorry, ma'am, unless something was taken we can't investigate." I could send an SOS to my boys—and open a Pandora's box of questions. I could demand that the rental agency change the locks, maybe break the lease—but nothing could be done until tomorrow.

The light outside was changing. Soon it would be dark. Moving fast, I went back to the bedroom. Picked up a small chair, carried it to the hall, and wedged it under the front door. No need to undress. I could sleep on the sofa in my clothes. Keep the cell on the floor beside me, the conduit to 911 if someone tried to open the door. On the other hand, it would be minutes before help arrived.

I needed a weapon. Breathing fast, I went into the kitchen. Knives were neatly arranged in a wooden block. There was a carving knife—but even in the grip of primal fear I could never stab a knife into human flesh.

"Think," I said aloud. *"Think."* There would be a few seconds of warning as the intruder opened the door. Time to give him a crack on the head—but what could I use? A lamp?

Finally I went to a cabinet and pulled out a heavy iron frying pan. As he came through, I would raise the pan with both hands, then bring it down with a stunning blow. With luck, I wouldn't kill him.

fourteen

October 24

I dozed and waked and dozed again, turning restlessly on the slippery leather sofa. The slacks and shirt I had worn in Hardwick were too tight for comfort, but wearing them made me feel less vulnerable.

At five in the morning, it was still dark outside. Sleep was impossible, so I slid off of the sofa and went to make a pot of coffee. While it brewed, I would take a shower. Face the day with clean hair and clean clothes. At nine, I would call the rental agency. Demand a locksmith. Warn them I might have to break the lease.

The cell I had left on the sofa began to buzz. I looked at it, hesitated, then forced myself to pick it up. A call at this hour spelled trouble. Big trouble.

"Is this 617-555-9021?" A man's voice.

"It— Who's calling?"

"Sergeant Thomas, Boston police. I'm sorry if I woke you,

ma'am." My heart leaped sideways in my chest. Steve. Jake. An accident.

"What happened?"

"Excuse me, ma'am, but do you have a daughter? Or a sister?"

My stiff fingers relaxed. Not Steve. Not Jake. But was this man really police? "I think you have a wrong number," I said sharply. "What's more, it's much too early in the morning to be calling people."

"Please hold, ma'am."

In a few seconds, a woman was on the line. "Officer Sutton. Boston police patrol unit. We realize a call at this hour can be very upsetting, ma'am, but we're trying to identify a young woman. This number was found in her possession."

"A young woman? You're trying to identify her? I don't understand."

"Let me give you a description. She appears to be in her early twenties. Five feet four, weight about a hundred and forty pounds. Dark brown hair. Curly. Freckles on her skin. Gray eyes."

Freckles. Curly brown hair. Gray eyes. I could feel the blood going from my head.

"Where is she?"

"I'm afraid I can't give you that information over the telephone."

"Does she have thick black eyelashes? Very short and thick?"

"Yes."

"Is she wearing a little silver cross around her neck?"

"No."

"Then it can't be the person I was . . . thinking of."

"But other than that, does this description fit anyone you know?"

"Wait," I said, and sat down on a tubular chair. No silver cross, but so few people knew my number.

"Are you there, ma'am?"

"Yes, but I'm not going to say another word until I know what's going on."

"Just a moment." A pause. Voices in the background.

Then the man was back on the line. "I'm sorry to have to tell you this, ma'am, but there's been a death. We need to establish an identification and all we have is your number."

"This person is *dead*?"

"Yes, ma'am."

Leaning back, I closed my eyes. This would be a valid reason for a call at five in the morning—but Cathy always wore that silver cross around her neck. It couldn't be Cathy.

"Look," I said, trying to keep my voice steady. "I need to know what happened. This is very— I mean, it might be a friend, but I don't think so."

"Ma'am, we know this is asking a great deal of you, but it would be helpful if you could come and see if this is your friend."

"Where are you?"

"At the Hotel Franklin. That's in downtown Boston. If you'll give us your name and an address, a cruiser will come and pick you up."

"It's— Beacon Hill." I hesitated and decided not to give my name. Hard to fake a police cruiser, but a taxi would be safer. "Don't send a cruiser. I'll take a taxi. I'll be there as soon as I can," I said, and hung up.

The number for Boston Taxi was written at the top of my address book. Would they be closed at this hour? After a few seconds, a man answered.

"I need a taxi," I said, and gave him my address. "How soon can somone be here?"

"Three minutes, ma'am."

Three minutes. No time to change or even brush my hair. I picked up a fleece jacket, snatched my handbag from the hall table, threw in the cell, and made for the elevator.

The street was still dark. I waited on the sidewalk, shivering, an easy target for anyone lurking in a doorway. What had the policewoman actually told me? A dead woman had curly brown hair and freckles, nothing unusual—except for the telephone number. Oh God, I should have brought Cathy's cousin's number along with me. Woken her and asked if Cathy was there.

A brown and white taxi came slowly down the street. It stopped. I opened the door and got in. The light was dim, but I could see that the young driver was wearing glasses and a baseball cap.

"Hotel Franklin, downtown Boston," I said. "Do you know it?"

"Sure."

"Go as fast as you can. It's an emergency."

"Gotcha," and he swooped down the deserted street and into the brighter lights of Charles Street.

The police had made a mistake. Everything could be explained. I sat back as the young driver gunned the taxi down Arlington Street. "There can't be many calls at this hour," I said, wanting distraction.

"Why I like this shift. Gives me a chance to study."

"Study where?" I held on to the strap as we hurtled down Boylston Street.

"Northeastern. Political science." He turned a corner, tires squealing, then slowed and stopped in front of an old building, squashed between tall office structures. Two police cruisers were blocking the entrance, lights flashing. I pulled out the fare plus a big tip.

"Keep the change. Good luck."

"Hey, thanks. Same to you."

The lobby of the Hotel Franklin smelled of stale smoke and cheap perfume. The floor was grimy, gray fake marble. A heavy man of Middle East extraction was standing behind the counter. I went up to him.

"The police are expecting me," I said.

He picked up the phone on the counter and dialed. "Woman here for the police." He turned to me. His stubby hands were shaking. "Third floor. Room three-seventeen." His heavy-lidded drugged eyes moved past me to the police cars.

"Thank you." If this hotel catered to sordid sex and drug dealers, no wonder the unsavory clerk was nervous.

The elevator smelled of discarded cigarette butts. Room 317 was toward the end of a long, dimly lit hall. I stood outside the door for a few seconds, then knocked. Whatever happened now, I must be calm. Stay in control.

A policewoman wearing a long-sleeved shirt and trousers came out. She had short dark hair and a round face.

"Officer Tobin," she said. "I wasn't sure you'd come."

"I'm here. I'm Emma Streat."

"I should warn you, the young woman is dead, but there's no visible trauma. Are you ready to go in?"

"Yes."

The room was small. The overhead lights were harsh after the badly lit hall. Two men in dark suits, one short, one tall, were standing by the window, talking in low voices.

A body covered by a sheet lay on one of the two beds. Officer Tobin pulled the sheet down to the waist. Cathy was wearing a red wool dress. Her gray eyes, fringed with dark lashes, stared at the ceiling. I put my hand to my mouth. The policewoman pulled the sheet back up.

"You know her?"

I nodded, pressing my stomach with both hands.

The policewoman took my arm. "You want the bathroom?"

"Yes. No." Not Cathy. Not Cathy.

"Sit." With a hand on my arm, Officer Tobin led me to a chair by a round table. "Keep your head down." I put my head between my knees. It wasn't a stranger who looked like Cathy. A stranger lying there under a sheet.

After a moment, Officer Tobin cleared her throat. "I'm sorry." A pause. "Can you give me a name?"

"Cathy. Cathy Riordan." A whisper.

"Relative?"

"Friend."

The policewoman touched my shoulder. "Sorry for your loss. When you're ready, we'll talk. Take your time."

After a moment I straightened. I had never felt so sick. The cheap ersatz-wood table was scarred with cigarette burns. I stared at a crumpled brochure with a map of Boston. Swallowed, then wiped my face with my sleeve.

"I talked to her two days ago and she was fine. We were going to have lunch today."

The taller of the two men coughed and turned. He was wearing a raincoat and seemed to have a bad cold.

"Inspector Graves. District Detective Unit. Thank you for coming, Mrs.—er—"

"Streat."

"A friend, you say."

"Yes. What happened?"

"Pills. An empty bottle." He pointed to the bedside table. "It appears to be a case of suicide."

"*Suicide?*" My head jerked up. I could see Cathy's horrified face at the sight of Mark Dykstra dangling from a cord. "A mortal sin," she had whispered, crossing herself. " 'Tis a mortal sin."

"No," I said loudly. "Not suicide. She wouldn't have."

The Inspector looked at me. He blew his nose, then sat down on the edge of the second bed. "I'm sorry. These deaths are hard to accept. Very hard. Can you tell me what you know about her?"

I closed my eyes. His voice seemed to be coming from a great distance. He was trying to be kind. I must pull myself together.

"We were friends. Not for long, but we had become very close. She came here from Ireland a few months ago to be my niece's assistant. My niece is a well-known singer, Vanessa Metcalf. Cathy lived with her. Traveled with her. Who . . . who found her?"

He hesitated, as if trying to decide how much to say, then nodded, as if re-assured that I wasn't about to collapse.

"There was a fire alarm around one in the morning. The night watchman who checked the rooms found the body. The manager called nine-one-one. The nearest cruiser responded. As I said, it appears to be an overdose—"

I raised my hand. "No. My friend was a very devout Catholic. Believe me, there's no way in this world she would kill herself."

The Inspector coughed again. "It's natural for you to feel that way, Mrs.—er—Streat. The truth is, people do unpredictable things. Now we need to notify the next of kin. Can you give us a name?"

"She has a cousin over here. In Boston."

"Address?"

"M. Riordan, South Boston."

"Do you know this cousin? We've found that this kind of news comes better from a friend."

I nodded. "I can talk to the cousin. She knows who I am."

"That would be helpful." He pulled out a pad and began to write.

I sat still, holding tightly to the arms of the chair. I seemed to be having trouble breathing. For the police, this was just another routine job, a suicide in a sordid little hotel. The process must move ahead, but they were wrong—very wrong. I touched my throat.

"There's something I don't understand," I said to the Inspector.

He lifted his head. "Yes?"

"Her cross. She always wore a little silver cross around her neck."

"There was no jewelry. No handbag. Just the clothes she was wearing." He stood up. "Thank you for coming, Mrs.—er—Streat. Officer Tobin will see that you get home."

I didn't move. I must act for Cathy. They must listen. If I hadn't come, they'd still be looking for identification.

"Just a minute," I said. "I gather she wrote down my number on a pad by the bed. There was no other identification."

"Correct."

"I don't see how—but there's this. How did she pay for this room? She must have had a handbag or a wallet when she came in."

A long pause. Officer Tobin frowned. "I checked that with the clerk. She came in with a man, Mrs. Streat. He paid for the room in cash, probably happens a lot in this hotel. I asked the clerk for a description. He wasn't able to give one."

I sat straight. Suddenly my head was clear. "I guess that's not surprising," I said, keeping my voice steady. "That clerk looks as if he's high on something. What happened to the man? Where did he go?"

Inspector Graves coughed, then put a lozenge in his mouth; he should have been home in bed. "We're looking for him," he said, then nodded at Officer Tobin. I could read his mind: She's getting to be a nuisance. Take her away.

I stood up. Oh God, I should have warned Cathy that Terry was being investigated. I had failed her in the worst possible way. Now, somehow, I must keep the police from labeling her a suicide, a disgrace to her family. The police were finished with me. In a moment it would be too late.

"I'm sorry," I said. "I know I'm asking too many questions, it's a bad habit of mine, but what happened to the silver cross she always wore? Her handbag? Someone must have taken them away. Maybe when the fire alarm went off. If there hadn't been that fire alarm, she might not have been found for hours. Days."

"This will be looked into."

I swallowed. Desperate circumstances called for desperate measures. Barefaced lies. "There's something else you should know," I said. "Cathy Riordan had a boyfriend. A very serious boyfriend."

The Inspector gave me a sharp look. "Name?"

I hesitated. Rodale had made me his surrogate over here. Before I gave the Boston police sensitive information, he must be put in the picture. "His name? To be honest, I don't know. I never met him. She was very secretive about him. In fact, I was beginning to wonder if he was mixed up in something like drug dealing. Which could be why the clerk didn't give you a description."

"What else can you tell us about him?"

"Let me think. Last week she showed me a . . . a bracelet he gave her. It must have cost thousands. I mean, *thousands*." I stopped. If the lie boomeranged, I could get my gold and diamond bangle out of the bank safety-deposit box.

"That isn't much to go on. When did you last see your friend?"

"A few days ago. We were going to have lunch today. She was happy. She had a good job. She was in love—maybe with the wrong person."

"As I say, that's not much to go on."

"No, but there's this. Cathy Riordan wasn't long out of a little town in Ireland. She wasn't street-smart about men. Maybe she found out too much about him. Maybe he decided she was a threat. One thing is for sure. She would *never* come to a place like this on her own. Not unless she was forced to."

The officers looked at each other again. "Is that all, ma'am?" the shorter man asked.

"Yes." I stopped. Studied the floral pattern in the carpet, dulled with ground-in dirt. My whole body felt battered, as if invaded by a toxic poison.

"Right." Inspector Graves blew his nose. "We have your telephone number, Mrs. Streat. Thank you again for your help. We'll be in touch." Officer Tobin opened the door. I went out, keeping my eyes away from the bed.

"These things are never easy," she said as we started down the hall toward the elevator.

"I still can't take it in," I said. "Were you the first to get there?"

"My partner and I were in a cruiser on Dartmouth Street. We responded."

"But why were the other two there?"

"District detectives are called for any unattended death."

"What if it had been a homicide?"

"Then they would hand over to the homicide detectives."

"What does that mean? I'm sorry, I have this awful habit of asking questions, and this is . . . such a blow."

"Well, there's a process. A crime scene is established. The room is sealed off and checked for fingerprints. DNA. Evidence. After that, the body is released to the Medical Examiner's Office. Before issuing a death certificate, the ME has to come up with the manner of death, whether natural, accidental, suicidal, or homicidal. His office may conduct an autopsy to determine cause of death."

In the lobby, the clerk was still behind the counter, gazing into space. "Wait here while I alert a cruiser," Officer Tobin said, and went out into the street.

At seven o'clock in the morning, it was light outside. The empty streets were moving into the rhythm of a new day. Two girls in very high heels walked by, holding Starbucks cups.

I stood beside a fake ficus tree, seeing Terry in that room. He was forcing pills down Cathy's throat. When the fire alarm went off, he must have taken to his heels. Headed for the airport—or stayed to see what would happen.

A man carrying a briefcase hurried by. I watched, trying to put myself in Terry's shoes. Bad news when the police cruisers arrived so soon. Very bad news when Mrs. Streat stepped out of a taxi. If Cathy had told her about his behavior Monday night, this woman was bound to cause trouble. Start an investigation.

I touched a dusty ficus leaf. Was Terry desperate enough to kill again in order to contain the damage? Was he waiting outside the apartment?

A cruiser was pulling up. Officer Tobin got out and came through the door.

"Where do you want to go?" she asked.

I took a deep breath. "The Taj Boston on Arlington Street. No, first to the CVS on Boylston Street. There's something I have to get there."

"If you're sure."

"I'm sure," I said, and got in. With luck, the CVS would be open and I could pick up some kind of bag. Essential, because a woman coming off the street with no luggage would never get past the receptionist at the elegant Taj Boston.

fifteen

At this hour, the lobby of the Taj Boston was almost empty. I stood still, breathing fast, the hunted animal darting into a place of safety, then looked around. There had been consternation when the Ritz changed hands, but the new management had been wise enough to keep the old ambiance. The dark wood paneling outlined with gilded ropes. Ceilings with fancy plaster, and subdued lights set in ornate iron frames. The air smelled like expensive—and subtle—perfume.

The elderly receptionist was wearing a dark suit and striped vest. I ran a hand over my face, and smoothed my hair, seeing myself in his eyes. The crumpled slacks and worn fleece jacket. The cheap duffel bag. Somehow I would have to convince him that I could afford to stay here.

With head held high, I marched across the Oriental carpet. "Good morning. I'm Mrs. Lewis Streat. I have a problem."

"Yes, madam?"

"A disaster, really. I live on Beacon Hill. The woman on the floor above left her bathwater running and now my ceilings are crashing down." I took a deep breath. Today my lies were flowing out like an ersatz flood.

The receptionist looked concerned. "Very upsetting, madam."

"It is. Very. I need a room. This was the first place I thought of. My family often comes here. So does my godmother, Mrs. Vogt."

"I'll see what I can do, Mrs. Streat. How long will you be staying?"

"I guess it depends on how much damage is done. I'll take anything that's available," I said, reaching into my bag. "I have my credit cards, my driver's license, all that."

"One moment, please." He took the Platinum Plus Visa card and disappeared into the office to check my credit rating or whatever hotels did to make sure guests could pay.

A young woman in a black apron appeared from a side door. She placed a large vase of exotic flowers on a gilded table stand and disappeared. As I waited, the tightness in my chest began to ease. Over the years I had often dashed in from Newbury Street and used the ladies' room upstairs, a marble haven with linen towels and gold bolts on the doors. According to my mother, the Ritz bar had been a gathering place during the war; there had once been a roof garden with dancing and what was known as a society singer.

The elderly receptionist was back.

"We're booked rather full, but I can give you a corner suite on the ninth floor. One that looks out over the Public Garden."

"Thank you." A corner suite overlooking the Public Garden would cost the earth, but this was no time to think about money. A young uniformed porter appeared, standing as if a steel rod had been strapped to his spine.

"Take Mrs. Streat up to suite nine-fifty-four," the receptionist said. And to me: "Please call on us if we can be of service in any way."

"Thank you. I will."

As we went up in the elevator, I stared at the design in the beige, black, and white marble floor. My mind seemed to be fixated on small details, a way to ward off anguish. Cathy. Not Cathy.

The suite door opened into a little entry with the bath on the right. The porter led the way past a bedroom and into a sitting room. It was small, with soft yellow walls and fitted diamond-patterned carpets. The porter bustled around, determined to show me every unique function, including a working fireplace.

"Thanks, that's fine," I said, almost pushing him to the door.

After a moment, I went to the window. Below was the Lagoon, the graceful little bridge, the 9/11 Memorial—and, beyond the Common, a panorama of Boston buildings. This corner of the Public Garden was almost as familiar as my childhood home.

I stared out, seeing the pattern of a grimy rug in a sordid bedroom, and tried to wrap my mind around the unthinkable. Cathy was dead and I was partly to blame. I had committed a terrible, unforgivable sin of omission. The pain, when it took hold, would be consuming.

Slowly, I went into the shiny marble bathroom and picked up a bar of scented soap. Before telephoning, I must scrub away the smell of the Hotel Franklin. My head was swimming, my stomach was on the edge of nausea, but collapse would have to wait.

The porter had put my cheap duffel on a luggage rack in the bedroom. I sat down on the bed, opened a bedside table drawer, and found a telephone directory. There was a listing for

M. Riordan on St. Botolph Street, the number I had used to reach Cathy.

Over the years, I had learned, the hard way, that there is a process for breaking bad news. First the warning, then the blow. "Do it. Just do it," I said aloud, but my fingers were shaking too much to function. Pulling off the bedspread, I crawled under the down duvet.

After a moment I tried again. The phone began to ring. I held my breath. It was still very early to call.

"Billy, is that you?" A woman's voice.

"Is this Mrs. Riordan?"

"It is."

"I'm— This is Emma Streat. Vanessa Metcalf's aunt."

A pause. "Cathy's friend Mrs. Streat?"

"Yes." I closed my eyes. "Mrs. Riordan. I'm calling about Cathy. I'm sorry, but I'm afraid I have very bad news."

A radio was playing loudly in the background, a choir chanting a hymn. Cathy had told me her cousin was a widow and very religious.

"Let me turn this down," the woman said. In a moment she was back. "Bad news, you say? About Cathy?"

"Very bad news. The worst. I'm afraid she's dead."

"That can't be. There must be some mistake."

"I'm afraid it's true."

"Ah no. Was it an accident, then?"

"Not an accident. Mrs. Riordan, I don't know how to tell you. I know this will come as a terrible shock, but she swallowed a bottle of pills early this morning. She died."

"Ah no." A smothered gasp. "Holy Mother, she'd never do such a thing. Not Cathy. Who told you?"

"The police called me early this morning. I went to the hotel and identified her."

"A hotel? Ah, God, I can't take it in at all." A brogue thicker than Cathy's.

"I'm so sorry, Mrs. Riordan. I loved Cathy. We all did."

"I don't understand it at all. She'd never—not Cathy. I'll not believe it."

"Mrs. Riordan, I'm afraid it's true. The police were there. It was at the Hotel Franklin, a small hotel in downtown Boston."

"But why would she do such a thing? She never acted as if there was any trouble. No trouble at all. There was the virus, but that was only a scare. Nothing came of it."

"I know. I talked to her on Tuesday, and she was fine. She told me she was coming back to you on Wednesday. Did you see her?"

"Ah, let me think. She called from New York asking could she come. I said fine, but I'd be off to Foxwoods with the girls. Once a month we go down in a bus. We play the slots, a limit of twenty-five dollars, have a nice dinner, and come back."

"Did she come?"

"Her suitcase was in the spare room. She'd started to unpack."

"Yes, but was there—did she leave a note? Say where she was going?"

"No, and that's not like her. She always leaves a message on the hall table if she's going out. Just to say if she'll be late coming in. I didn't pay much heed, she comes and goes as she likes, but maybe if I'd been there, if I'd seen her, we would have talked. I would have found out what . . . what would—" Mrs. Riordan was sobbing.

"You musn't blame yourself. You were very good to her. She often said how good—"

"Holy Mother, the poor parents. Nell and Patrick. This'll

take the heart clean out of them, they were that proud of her. To kill herself, and so far away." The sobs were changing to wails.

"It's terrible for them. Terrible. Mrs. Riordan, will you let them know? I mean, the news would come better from you, not from a stranger." Tears were beginning to run down my cheeks, wetting the pillow. Right now, far across the ocean, Cathy's parents would be doing whatever they did on Thursdays. There was no warning that they were about to get the most heartbreaking call in the world.

"I will, so. They'll be destroyed entirely."

My throat tightened. This was not the time to ask if Cathy had taken a coat or if there was a sign that someone had come into the apartment. "Mrs. Riordan, I'm so sorry. I want to help any way I can." I wiped my face with the back of my hand. No matter how cruel, I had to press on. "One more thing. It seems dreadful to bother you with details, but you're her next of kin. Decisions need to be made."

"Decisions?"

"I think she'll be taken to the morgue."

"The morgue, is it? That's not right. Not at all."

"I believe it's the law. I've known Cathy only a few weeks, but I loved her. I realize how hard this is for you. I just wish there was some way to make it easier. After the . . . morgue, where do you want her to go?"

"Go? My head's in a whirl. There's a funeral home a few blocks away, my neighbor's nephew's place. But her father will want her back."

"You mean, back to Ireland?"

"He will, so, but he'll want to keep it quiet, how it happened. It's very religious they are in that village. The priest might make trouble—ah, ye never know. When the phone rang, I thought it was my son in the Navy. He calls me early. I worry about him. Ye never know." The brogue was getting thicker.

"No. We don't. I'll be in touch as soon as I hear anything more. We'll keep in touch," I said, and laid the cell down.

Under the down duvet, I was shivering. The muscles in my legs were jerking in spasms, but Rodale must be told. I looked at my watch. Right now it was early afternoon in England.

There was a long pause between rings. I bit my lip. Please, God, don't let him be out of the country on some secret mission. Unreachable. Then, after an agonizing pause, his voice.

"Rodale."

"Thank God. Thank God you're there." I pulled my knees to my chest and burrowed farther into the bed. "Something terrible has happened."

"I can't hear you. Can you talk a little louder?"

"It's my niece's assistant. Cathy Riordan. She's dead. I think Terry Gallagher killed her."

"Steady on. When?"

"Early this morning. In a seedy little hotel—oh God, oh God, it never should have happened, it's all my fault, but she said she wasn't going to see him again. If I'd warned her, told her he was being investigated—"

"Emma. Get a grip. Start at the beginning."

"The beginning? It started Monday night in New York. My head's gone, but I'm sure I sent you a message about Terry being back. Going to Vanessa's apartment. Drinking. Pounding Cathy with questions about Dykstra."

"You did. I passed it on to the Colonel."

"She called me. I told her to come here. We were going to have lunch today. She called on her way to Boston, saying there was something I should know about Terry."

"You didn't follow up?"

"I tried, but . . . it didn't happen. The police called me at five this morning from the hotel. There was no identification except my phone number. She wrote it down on one of those little pads by the bed. She could have been dying, but she wrote it down." I coughed. My voice was fading.

"Steady. What was the cause of death?"

"They're calling it suicide; there was an empty bottle of pills. They're wrong. She would never kill herself."

" 'Never' is a strong word—"

"Wait. *Wait.* A man paid for the room, there was a fire alarm, and he disappeared. Andrew, all her things were gone. Except for my number she might not have been identified for days. How could he do it to her? How could *anyone* be so cruel?"

"A man, you say. Any description?"

"None. I . . . lied. I *tried* to convince the police that she had a boyfriend and he did it. Terry must have done it. She would never have gone to that hotel on her own. Taken pills."

"Did you give the police Gallagher's name?"

"No. I wanted to tell you first, but he did it and I know why. He didn't want us to meet, but why kill her? Why did he have to *kill* her?"

"Hold on. Will there be an autopsy?"

"I don't *know.* I don't know if the police believed me, that she would never have killed herself."

"Where are you now?"

"At the Taj Boston. I ran in here like . . . like someone seeking sanctuary in a church. I couldn't go back to my apartment. Someone has been breaking in. Going through my things."

"Are you sure?"

"I'm sure," and I poured out the story of the jewelry box that had been moved. The man lurking across the street.

"You didn't recognize him?"

"I looked, but he was gone. Oh God, she was so *young*. She was dying and she was trying to reach me. It's the worst thing that's ever happened to me. The worst—"

"Emma. Stop. Be quiet. That's an order." A voice like a whip.

I gasped as if he had slapped me in the face. "What—"

"You've had a shock. You're frightened. Understandable, but tearing yourself into strips isn't going to help that girl."

"But it's the worst—"

"Quiet. I'm going to tell you a story. Are you listening?"

"Yes."

"Right. It was in the late eighties. I was in charge of a patrol near Derry. One of those peaceful Irish country roads. We'd had word that an IRA leader was hiding in a house nearby. I should have double-checked the intelligence. Instead, I took my lorry straight into a road mine. Three men were killed. The young driver's head was blown into my lap. His brains were all over me."

"Andrew."

"I survived with a game leg. I tried to drink myself into oblivion. In the end, a man I respected took me by the scruff of the neck and raked me over the coals. Made me see that the only way to go on was to turn my personal pain into work. The work I do now." A pause. "I'm telling you this story for a reason. You have two choices. You can blame yourself, wallow in guilt, or you can help to find the assistant's killer. And the decision has to be made now, while we're talking. Either you're on board, on the team, or we move ahead without you."

"Wait." I pushed myself up from under the duvet and sat there, my head in my hands. This death was the most terrible thing that had ever happened to me, but no one was going to hold my hand. In his ruthless way, Rodale had just doused me with a verbal bucket of cold water. "Either you're on board, on the team, or we move ahead without you." He meant what he said. If I didn't pull myself together—now, at once—I would be cut out of the loop. The process would go forward without me.

"Well?"

I reached for a tissue and wiped my nose. "All right. You've made your point. I'm on board, but what do I do now? If he saw me come out of that hotel with the police, he'll know he's made a terrible mistake. He may be watching the apartment. If he's a killer, or driven to be a killer, he may be waiting for his chance."

"You did the right thing, going to the hotel. I'll see that you get protection." A pause. "Back to Gallagher. So far the background check shows nothing but a possible connection with the IRA fifteen years ago."

"That's all?"

"Yes. To go back. Let's say he wasn't away from Venice that night. He's in the Dordona suite. He strings Dykstra up and hopes to fool the police. He finds out they know it's a homicide. He grills Vanessa's assistant. Now she's a threat that has to be removed. The question is, why was he in the suite? Who was giving him orders? To kill shows us the stakes are very high. Murder means taking on serious risk."

"I'm not sure the Boston police are going to treat this case as a homicide. It can't be very high on their list."

"That will change after I pull some strings. It's called furnishing assistance. I'll make it clear that we're putting a high priority on finding Gallagher. The Yanks have their FBI and TRAC—that's the FBI's Terrorist Research and Analytical Center. We have our Holmes database. I'll also make it clear that you've been involved in the case and must be kept informed. Protected."

"I'm not setting a foot outside this door until I'm sure it's safe. The police may have a problem understanding where I fit in. I mean, it's not exactly in the rule book."

"They will have a good deal of trouble. You don't fit into any category. They will be very reluctant to share information. Which is natural."

"What's more, they didn't like me not accepting the suicide verdict. Asking so many questions."

"Stands to reason." A pause. "See here, Emma. You're convinced Gallagher is a killer. You may be right, but hold your fire or it will seem as if you're trying to teach them their job. You'll get nowhere with them."

"I know. I'll try, but I'm angry, very angry."

"Anger has a way of focusing the mind, but it can be misused. What's needed now is evidence."

"I know."

"Just remember this. There will be bad moments, just as there are for me, but you're a strong woman. You've been through the fire before and survived."

He was gone. I put the cell down and lay back on the pillows. My hands were still shaking, but Rodale's astringent methods had worked. And—in a strange way—any remaining physical addiction had disappeared. The professional half of our relationship was in play again.

After a moment, I pulled up the duvet and rolled onto my side; the cotton shirt, now on its second day, felt pasted to my skin. I was cold to the marrow, but the muscle spasms had stopped. "You've been through the fire before and survived," Rodale had said. True, but I had been powerless to prevent the other deaths. Losing Cathy was a horror that would strike, retreat, then strike again, as long as I lived.

For a few merciful moments, talking to Rodale had submerged the pain. Now, lying there, I could see Cathy holding the Paddington bear the night we met in Vanessa's dressing room. I could see the sordid little room where she died. Frightened. Alone. Without her little silver cross.

sixteen

It was midafternoon when I woke up, stiff and thirsty. A few hours of sleep had given me space from the morning's trauma, but I still felt disoriented, as if gripped in a feverish dream.

Moving slowly, I got up, went into the sitting room, and looked around. The portrait of a nineteenth-century lady in black lace looked down from a carved mantel. At three thirty, the light coming through the long windows was still bright. On the Common, once a cow pasture, a man was raking leaves; children with backpacks were going home from school. The ordinary world was going about its business, but I was a virtual prisoner. Safe, but only as long as I stayed behind a locked door. Rodale had promised protection. What kind of person would come?

Back in the bedroom, I paused and took stock. All I had in my handbag was a wallet, mints, a receipt for gas, a pen that didn't work. No toothbrush, not even a comb. My unbrushed hair looked as if I'd been standing in a high wind. My clothes were all on their second day.

With a sudden burst of energy, I went into the bathroom and washed myself from head to toe, making use of every expensive lotion. Washed my clothes in the bathtub and hung them over the railings; instead of marble ambiance, the bathroom now had the look of a cheap motel. Later, I would call the housekeeper, tell her about the flood, and arrange for a few necessities. But first, food.

Room service was almost too prompt. Pulling on the complimentary terry cloth robe, I hurried into the foyer, looked through the peephole, then stood back to let the waiter wheel in a round table covered with a pink linen cloth.

"Lovely fall day, madam," he said as he arranged soup, a club sandwich, and fruit salad, my compromise between lunch and dinner and breakfast.

"Yes. Lovely." If I had to stay here for very long, the staff would begin to wonder about the woman in the terry cloth robe who never left the suite.

Pulling up a Louis XVI chair, I poured coffee from a silver pot, then picked up the newspaper and skimmed through it. There was nothing about a suicide at the Hotel Franklin. Did Cathy's death have no news value?

"I could kill you with my bare hands," I said aloud. "I'm going to find you if it's the last thing I do." But how? Rodale had his extensive resources. I had none. Once again it was time to apply Sergeant Johnson's lesson: "Most of the time it's slog and slog and nothing fits. Then one little lead can get the case rolling. People remember something that didn't seem right, but wasn't important at the time." My job now was to stop agonizing about atonement and start to slog. Look for more little discrepancies—like Fausto.

The minestrone soup was hot and satisfying. I was finishing the sandwich, wishing I had ordered something rich and chocolaty for dessert, when my cell rang.

"Is this Mrs. Streat?" A man's voice.

"Who's calling?"

"Superintendent McNulty from Homicide. Mrs. Streat?"

"Oh. Yes. I'm Mrs. Streat." A superintendent, no less. It hadn't taken Rodale long to pull strings.

"I can be with you in half an hour, if that's convenient."

"I'll be expecting you." An abrupt manner, but now, thank God, I was connected into a system. No longer in limbo.

The Superintendent was fifteen minutes late. When a knock came at the door, I went to open it. The man standing outside was large, heavily built, with short brown hair. A brown suit and tie. I glanced at the card he was holding out and handed it back, ignoring the fine print.

"Come in," I said, and led the way into the living room. "Sit down, won't you?"

"Thanks, I'll stand. This won't take long," and he placed himself in front of the fireplace, a busy man with authority. Not a hand-holder.

"All right." I went to the love seat, hoping I wouldn't leave a damp patch on the pale green brocade. Rather than meet him in a robe, I had pulled on my wet clothes, and a clammy chill was creeping up my spine.

He cleared his throat. "London has given us a briefing. Asked us to provide assistance wherever feasible. I'll go straight to the point. We were informed that there may have been an intruder in your apartment on Beacon Hill. Acting on instructions, our people went in this morning and made a thorough search." He paused and gave me a quick look, as if waiting for my reaction.

I nodded. "There *was* an intruder. I would have called the police, but nothing was taken."

He cleared his throat again. "Mrs. Streat, I'm sorry to tell you that two small listening devices were found in your apartment. One in the kitchen under the sink. One in the living room on a wall."

My hand went to my throat. "Oh God," I said. "Not *again*."

"This has happened before?"

"Last summer. In Connecticut." Suddenly I was back in my house. Bill, the FBI agent, was telling me about the listeners in the broom closet. I closed my eyes. "This is really hard to believe. I mean, I never thought it would happen again. Not twice."

"Not unusual. People refuse to believe that entrance without keys is child's play. Easy to do and it gets results." A pause. "It would be helpful to know who had access. Permission to go in and out."

"Very few. There's my Filipino housekeeper; she's been with me since I came at the end of August. She goes with the rental, but I can't see her dealing with high tech. She'd be more likely to take something."

"Unless she had a partner. There will be a background check. Who else?"

"I'm trying to think. An electrician replaced a gear on the dishwasher. He came from the rental agency. I don't remember his name."

"Again, we'll check. What about guests?"

"Practically none. My boys, once in September. Ten days ago I was in quarantine for four days."

"We were told of your niece's illness. The possibility of H five N one."

"That's right. Dr. Greg Atkins, the head virologist at the

Barzalon Foundation, came every evening to tell me about my niece's condition. The quarantine didn't seem to bother him."

"He came every evening?"

"He was my only visitor. It kept me from climbing the wall."

"He had a key?"

"No key. He would come for an hour or so around six. I don't think he ever left the living room. Maybe into the kitchen to open a bottle of wine." I hesitated. There *had* been that time when he couldn't find the corkscrew. Time enough to install listeners? "Oh, and Seth Barzalon. Twice. The day after we came back from Venice and before he left for France."

"There were no moments when either of those two men were alone? Perhaps when you were in the bathroom? I ask because there was no device in the bedroom, the usual place for a bug."

"I don't think they were ever alone long enough, certainly not Barzalon."

"To go back, what made you suspect an intruder?"

"When I got back from England I went to my desk to pay bills. I have a system. A paper had been shifted. Then the jewelry box in my bureau was moved. That was last night. I slept in my clothes. At five in the morning I had the call from the police."

"And you're sure nothing was taken?"

"Positive. And he wasn't enough of a pro to cover his tracks."

"Which leaves us with the fact that the intruder was looking for something of value. Electronically, and in your things. Possibly information. Do you remember any telephone conversations of particular significance? With Lord Rodale, for instance?"

"I talked to him several times, but I was always very careful not to mention his name." I hesitated. No need to tell the Superintendent I had almost slipped once, in front of Dr. Atkins, but managed to cover the slip.

The Superintendent was looking at his watch. I noticed that

he was wearing what looked like a Naval Academy ring. In fact, his whole bearing was that of a military man. Upright. Competent. His questions had been efficient and to the point—but giving nothing away. I could hear him talking to his subordinates after Rodale's call: "Sounds a bit tricky. I'd better handle this myself."

". . . is there anything you would like to add to this report?" he was saying.

"Not at the moment." I folded my hands with a growing sense of dismay. In a moment he would be gone, and there had been no mention of Cathy. No sense that I would be included in any investigation.

"About your protection, Mrs. Streat. The head of security at the hotel will be alerted, but it would be difficult to provide police personnel around the clock. My advice is to use the peephole, even for waiters and housekeepers. Above all, and this is key, never leave the suite without contacting me first."

"Yes, but if this goes on very long, people—family and friends—will begin to ask questions."

"I believe you told the receptionist there was a flood in your apartment. Use that." He looked at his watch again. "Anything else?"

I shifted on the damp love seat and took a deep breath. "Yes. Officer Tobin told me Cathy Riordan would be taken to the morgue. Do you know if there's going to be an autopsy?"

"There is."

"How long will it take to get results?"

I was pushing the envelope. He frowned. "That would depend on the schedule. The amount of paperwork. A death must be classified as natural, accidental, suicidal, or homicidal. It can take up to two weeks to get the material collated."

"That long." I swallowed and stood up. "The thing is, I was

very close to Miss Riordan. I'm very sure she didn't commit suicide. It's important to me to hear about the autopsy."

"Right." Another of those quick looks. "I'll keep you informed. In the meantime, here's a number where you can reach me." He held out a card, this large, impassive man who was keeping me at arm's length. Somehow I must break through the official wall of silence before he walked out the door.

"Thanks," I said, taking the card. "Thanks for coming and thank you for your patience. I realize that you're a very busy man and I'm asking too many questions. In fact, I was told not to be a nuisance."

A slight smile. He touched the tie again. "It's been a difficult day. The news about the intruder in your apartment. The death of your friend."

"It was a shock." I paused. "I should keep my mouth shut, but for me it all comes back to finding the man who took her to the hotel. I think it was Seth Barzalon's pilot. His name is Terry Gallagher. He was close to Cathy Riordan. Very close. I think he killed her because she knew something about him. I think he wants to kill me for the same reason. Why I'm here."

"I can tell you that an extensive search for him is under way."

"I'm glad. Cathy was so young, just over from Ireland, with all her life ahead of her."

The Superintendent rocked back on his heels, then straightened. "I'll say this, Mrs. Streat. Justice should be evenhanded, but I'm second-generation Irish here. I don't like this happening to a young Irish girl. I'll get back to you with the autopsy results. We appreciated your help this morning with the identification." With an abrupt nod, he marched to the door and was gone.

Water was dripping onto the carpet. I hurried into the bathroom, pulled off my clothes, and wrapped myself in the terry cloth robe. Being humble and playing the Irish card had opened the door a crack. The Superintendent had admitted that a search for Terry was under way, but I needed more leverage to be a real player. Maybe I should try to reach Chet, the pilot who used to fly our Gulfstream. Find out if he had ever seen Terry in places where pilots met. But first I needed to talk to Greg.

Back in the sitting room, I sat down on a dry chair and punched in Greg's cell phone number.

"Emma." The familiar pleasant voice. "I've been thinking about you. Any chance of dinner tonight?"

"Not tonight, I'm afraid. The most frustrating thing has happened. The woman who lives above me went out for the night and left water running. My ceilings came crashing down."

"Good Lord. Where are you now?"

"At the Taj Boston. In a very grand suite. Very expensive. It better not be for long, but look, I need your help. It's about my niece, Vanessa. I think I told you that she's through with Barzalon. That's the good news. The bad is that I have to tell him to leave her alone."

"I don't envy you. How is she?"

"Still in the hospital, working herself up for fear he may come barging in. Have you heard anything from him?"

"As a matter of fact, I have. He'll be in Boston tomorrow. We seem to be in crisis mode again. The Barzalons have demanded a meeting. Want to know why my antiviral isn't ready for marketing."

"Both Barzalons? My godmother says the father is a man-about-town who spends his time playing golf and bridge. I got the feeling from Seth they're not close, so why does he keep coming to meetings?"

"He's on the board." A pause, as if Greg was choosing his words carefully. "Once in a while he puts his oar in and muddies the water. Has attacks of thinking he's a man of business. A waste of time, but I have to show respect. Needless to say, Seth is fuming."

"Too bad." I shifted the receiver. "I suppose he'll be coming in the Gulfstream."

"As far as I know. After our meeting, I'll take the Barzalons to lunch. Then, with any luck, they'll be off."

"Which doesn't leave me much time. Maybe I should try to reach Seth at the foundation. I really do need to talk to him."

"You could call. I'll try to fix a time—but here's a thought. James insists on going to the Taj for lunch. It used to be the old dining room, now it's The Café. He likes women, particularly beautiful women. It would be a godsend if you could join us. Ease the tension."

"Join you and the Barzalons for lunch? I'm not sure that's a good idea."

"Why not? I know Seth Barzalon isn't high in your book, but looking at you would take the the old man's mind off of clinical testing. And that way you'll be able to put in a word about your niece."

"True." I hesitated. Even though I wouldn't be leaving the hotel, the Superintendent must be told. "What time?" I asked.

"I've made reservations for one o'clock. With luck we can wrap up the business before we sit down."

Two long-drawn-out hours of dealing with Seth? "I have a better idea. Why don't I join you for coffee? I mean, that way you'll be done with your business. Seth isn't too crazy about me, but he can't object to giving me coffee. And I can still get in a word about Vanessa."

"Point taken."

"So, unless you hear from me, I'll make my entrance around two. And Greg—we *will* have that dinner. Soon."

"Very soon. I've missed you."

"Good luck with the meeting." I clicked off and stood up. Suddenly, out of the blue, here was a possible breakthrough. And . . . a way to improve my credit rating with the Superintendent.

To reach him, I was passed through a chain of command. At last he was on the line.

"It's Emma Streat," I said. "I'm sorry to bother you so soon, but something just came up. I told you about the head of research at the Barzalon Foundation who helped me through the quarantine. A Dr. Atkins. Anyhow, he's asked me to have lunch with Seth Barzalon and his father tomorrow. Here at The Café, at two. It could be a way to locate Terry Gallagher."

"We thought we had that plane covered, but let me get this straight. You're to meet these three men tomorrow. In The Café at two."

"For coffee. If you agree."

"It can't hurt. An agent will be in your suite at one thirty. Follow you down. Stay nearby and take you back."

"That would be—oh God," I said, and pushed back my hair. "I can't. I can't do it. I don't have any clothes. I don't even have makeup."

There was a short pause. The Superintendent laughed. "Not a problem. One of our people can bring your things over from your apartment. We'll use a plumber's truck in case there's a watcher nearby."

"Watcher?"

"Someone who might try to get in and remove those listening devices. We're doing round-the-clock surveillance. Now give me your list. Not too long."

"I'll be quick," I said, and went to the desk. Surveillance around the clock must mean that the Boston Police Department was starting to put resources into this case.

The list was unexpectedly long. After reading it to the Superintendent, I went back to the bedroom. I lay down, hands under my head, and tried to focus on the listeners. What information could they have picked up? There had been talk with Greg. With Dr. Reston and family. I had been careful not to mention Rodale by name; there was only the near slip with Greg that Dykstra's suicide had, in fact, been murder.

Nothing of importance to Terry—until it came to Cathy. First there was the fact that he had visited her during quarantine. Then the very damaging description of his behavior in New York. My suggestion that after talking we might bring in a detective. This would have set off alarms. Yesterday Cathy had used her cell: "There's something about Terry you should know. . . . It's bad." But after one attempt to reach her, I had gone into my bedroom and found that my apartment had been searched. The shock had rocked my brain, but I would never forgive myself.

So now—was Terry acting on his own, or had a higher-up given him orders to remove two women who knew too much? A case of frenzied overkill?

I rubbed my eyes and stared up at the ceiling, willing the inert white plaster to help me. The role of Euridice in Gluck's *Orfeo* had never been in my repertoire, but I knew the story, how Orfeo had wandered sorrowfully through the underworld. *"Misero giovane, che vuoi, che mediti."* Like Orfeo, I was wandering in a mysterious labyrinth with subterranean passages. An underworld where every step could be fatal.

seventeen

October 25

The Superintendent was as good as his word. At noon, just as I was beginning to panic, there was a knock on the door. A young woman was standing there, holding two duffels. Her hair was long and blond, cut in the latest layered style. She was wearing a gray wool miniskirt and a starched white blouse.

"Hi," she said. "Mrs. Streat? I'm Sally Rudnick. Your security agent. I'm afraid the plumber types in your apartment didn't do a very good job of packing; I just hope they didn't leave out anything important like shoes."

"I hope not. Come in." I hesitated. "You're from security?"

"Don't go by appearances. I have a black-belt certificate. Nothing I like better than flattening creeps. Stomping on groins. I also have a boyfriend who's a backup guitarist in a band called The Killers."

I laughed. "No groins to stomp on today. Sorry."

"Shucks. Here's the plan. I'll be back at quarter of two. I'll follow you down. I'll be sitting at a nearby table. Just ignore me unless there's a problem. Then I'll see you home." And she disappeared.

There was comfort in little things. I began to arrange the motley assortment. My natural-bristle hairbrush. My fleecy blue bathrobe. The black suede pants suit—but no black shoes. The Hermès scarf would have to divert attention from tan loafers.

I was giving my hair a good brushing when the phone rang.

"Superintendent McNulty here. Did you get your clothes?"

"Yes, I did. Thanks very much."

"I'm calling because the autopsy on Miss Riordan was performed early this morning. Given high priority." A pause. "The report now lists homicide as cause of death."

I put down the brush. Willed myself to calm. "I'm not surprised. I had a feeling she would never have killed herself." My best effort at diplomacy.

"A certificate will be issued."

"One thing. The police at the hotel asked me about next of kin. I gave them the cousin's name. Has she been told it was . . . a homicide?"

"She has. Also that the body can be moved to a funeral home."

"I see." Another blow for poor Mrs. Riordan, but maybe this would hurt less than suicide. "Superintendent, I realize you can't give away the store, but can you tell me anything more? I mean, anything about how it was done?"

"Under the circumstances, I think you have a right to know. There was a needle mark on her inner arm. Further lab work will help to determine the exact cause of death. That will take a few days, but preliminary findings indicate that the assailant used a codeine-based substance. It would have been slow acting; the victim would have gradually lost consciousness."

"So after the fire alarm, after the man had gone, she would have had time to write down my number. Would there have been . . . pain?"

"My guess is, no. She wouldn't have felt pain."

"What about fingerprints? DNA? I mean, she wouldn't just stand still and let him stick her with a needle."

"For DNA, we need a match. Fingerprints solve more crimes, but none were found at the scene. There was no sign of a struggle. No evidence of intercourse."

"So, no evidence at all."

"Except that it appears her assailant may not have had much medical training. There was a large dark bruise and swelling around the injection."

My hand went to my mouth. Terry holding a needle. Cathy fighting him, realizing that she was in danger.

"Any more questions, Mrs. Streat?"

"You say 'assailant,' but it had to be someone close to her, to get her into that hotel. Like Gallagher. Even so, how did he manage? She said she was through with him. She *never* would have gone there willingly."

"The assailant could have had a gun or a knife at her back. Neighbors are being questioned."

"I see." In other words, more evidence was needed before Terry could be named a suspect. I must accept that and behave like a professional.

The Superintendent cleared his throat. "If anything develops from your lunch date, you'll let me know."

"Of course."

I put down the phone and looked at the clock. It was only one o'clock. There was time to call Cathy's cousin.

Mrs. Riordan answered the phone. "It's Emma Streat," I said. "Vanessa Metcalf's aunt. The police have told me about the autopsy."

"Ah, I can't take it in. Holy Mother, who in the world would want to murther a poor child who never hurt a soul? The world's a terrible place."

"I'm sure the police will find whoever did it. I just wanted to tell you again how sorry I am. And I was wondering if you've had time to make any arrangements."

"Ah, there'll be a viewing tomorrow night at my neighbor's nephew's place. O'Reilly and Sons Funeral Home. A cremation. I've talked to the parents. They want the ashes taken back to their village. They want Cathy to have a proper mass and a wake."

"She would have wanted that."

"I'll take time from my job and fly over on the twenty-eighth; that's three days from now. There's an Aer Lingus flight to Shannon. I can't stay long, but I can tell them about Cathy. How she was happy over here. Ease their minds as best I can."

"That's really good of you. About the viewing. I seem to have a horrible cold, Vanessa's still in the hospital, but my brother and sister-in-law will want to send flowers. They'll try to be there themselves."

"Ah, that would be kind."

"It's the least we can do," I said, and put down the phone. It was time to dress—and prepare my mind for what was bound to be an unpleasant half hour.

The Café looked directly onto the sidewalks of Newbury Street, an elegant, civilized setting with white paneling and a green patterned carpet.

I paused at the gold railing at the top of marble steps. A

number of tables were occupied, but the talk was hushed. The three men were sitting at the far end of the room. According to Caroline, James Barzalon had married for money and never got it. A man who had periodic fits of interfering in the Barzalon Foundation's business. His son was a boorish, self-centered race car driver who was saddled with a research foundation he never wanted. Their employee Greg Atkins was a brilliant virologist, harassed by the two Barzalons. And in the background there was a pilot, Terry Gallagher, possibly a cold-blooded murderer.

"Good afternoon, madam." The sleek-haired maître d' was coming forward.

"Good afternoon," I said. "I'm expected at that table over there."

"Very good, madam," and he led the way forward.

My timing was exactly right; a waiter was just taking away the remains of dessert. Greg was the first to see me. He stood up. He was wearing a dark suit, not the usual tweed coat with patches at the elbows.

"I hope I'm not too late," I said, hiding concern. Greg looked as if he'd been put through the proverbial wringer. The intelligent, sensitive face was white. There were dark circles under his eyes.

"We're about to have coffee," he said. "James, I'd like you to meet Emma Streat."

The older man was getting to his feet. How had Greg explained my presence here? "I'm very glad to meet you, young lady."

"I'm very glad to meet you, Mr. Barzalon," I said. James Barzalon was a tall man with a full head of white hair; his navy pinstripe suit had a silk handkerchief showing in the pocket. He gave a courtly bow and registered the Hermès scarf.

"Another chair, please," he said to the waiter.

Seth Barzalon hadn't moved. He had knotted a token tie

over a canvas jacket. Now he raised his hand in a casual half salute, not a welcoming gesture.

"Hey, Emma," he muttered.

"Seth. How are you?" It was clear that he was having a violent attack of the sulks. Out of the corner of my eye, I could see the maître d' seating Sally at the next table.

"Don't ask. Greg says Vanessa is still in the hospital. Just so you know, I'm not going back there."

"Perhaps that's just as well. She can't see anyone but family. I'm afraid getting back on her feet is going to take a long time, a very long time."

"I get the message. Get out of her life."

James Barzalon cleared his throat. "I gather this has been a very trying time for you, young lady. Have the doctors been able to find the cause of this illness?"

"Not yet, but they're still testing."

The waiter was bringing another cup. He filled it with coffee. "Cream and sugar, madam?"

"Nothing, thanks." I took a sip of coffee. "I haven't been here for ages," I said, trying to break the silence. "Not much has changed."

Seth grunted. "Same lousy food and service."

James Barzalon frowned, ignoring him. "Tell me, Mrs. Streat. Do you live in Boston?"

"I'm renting an apartment on Beacon Hill while I look for a house. Two nights ago I had a flood. Right now the place is filled with huge drying machines; it sounds like a dozen jet planes taking off. Why I'm staying at the Taj."

"My favorite hotel," and he was off on a rambling account of coming-out parties in the old Ritz. People he knew in Boston. I listened, head tilted, the model of a fascinated audience, aware that I was being slotted into a place on his social ladder. It was all too clear why Caroline disliked him: "Can't stand that kind of practiced charm."

The waiter was hovering, but no one wanted more coffee. I twisted my hands under the table. In a moment I would be leaving empty-handed. A frontal attack might have consequences, but it was the only way to produce for the Superintendent. Taking a deep breath, I turned to Seth.

"I hope your race went well."

"Washout."

"Sorry. When did you get back?"

"Why?"

"No reason, except I want to get a message to your pilot Terry. Do you know where I can reach him?" I waited, noticing that both Greg and James Barzalon had straightened in their chairs.

Seth's eyes shifted from his coffee cup to my face. "Jesus. What's the bastard done now?"

"Nothing to me. It's just that he was seeing a lot of Vanessa's assistant. Cathy Riordan."

"That Irish girl. Not much of a looker."

"Maybe not, but she died a couple of nights ago. According to her cousin, she committed suicide. Sleeping pills. I thought Terry might want to know."

No one spoke. The other two were staring at Seth, as if waiting for some kind of explosion. Seth pulled at his tie. He seemed to be struggling for words. After a few seconds, he shrugged his shoulders.

"None of your business, but Gallagher is history. I don't know where he is and I don't give a shit. I fired him as soon as we got back to New York."

"Oh? I thought he was supposed to be a good pilot."

"Good pilot, bad trouble. That's all I need, to get arrested for carting drugs around in my plane."

I picked up a fork and put it down. Here, at last, was some sort of breakthrough. I must feel my way inch by inch.

"That's bad. It's lucky you found out."

"There's a guy who services the plane at Teterboro. He took me aside after we landed. Figured the information was worth a big reward—which it was. I gave Gallagher a check for a month's salary and told him to get lost. Said if he ever caused any trouble I'd have the police on him so fast he wouldn't know what hit him. I think he got the message. Now the plane is sitting there until I get a replacement. Had to take the bloody shuttle to get here."

"I'm sorry," I said, keeping my voice even. First the hesitation, then the uncharacteristic flood of words. Unless I was very wrong, Seth had been taken off guard. What was he hiding?

"Sure you are." He pushed back his chair and looked at Greg. "Are we done here?"

"There's nothing more on my agenda," Greg said tightly.

"Then let's pack it up."

I put down my cup and turned to James Barzalon.

"It's been nice to meet you, Mr. Barzalon."

"A pleasure—that is, a great pleasure to meet you, young lady." The practiced courtier putting the best face on his son's atrocious behavior.

Seth was still slouched in his chair, staring out at Newbury Street. "Thank you for the coffee," I said. "All I can say is, better luck from now on." There was no point in parting on bad terms when I might need to be in touch later. The Superintendent could start to check the mechanics at Teterboro.

No answer. Greg got to his feet. "I'll see you to the elevator, Emma."

It seemed a long way to the entrance. As we passed, Sally was reading a pamphlet. Two elderly ladies were talking with their heads close together. A foursome of businessmen were ordering drinks. As we reached the main hall, Greg ran a hand over his drawn face.

"Sorry about that."

"Not your fault. I guess I hit a raw nerve, asking Seth about his pilot."

"Don't worry. Being with his father always brings out the worst in him."

"I was surprised, though, how much he let his father take charge. I thought it would be the other way around."

"Well, it usually is. It's just that today—"

"No need to explain, but now I can understand why my godmother can't stand James Barzalon. That kind of charm sends her up the wall."

"Does she know him well?"

"From way back. It's rather a pathetic story, the man who didn't get the money he was expecting—" I stopped. Days ago, when I grilled Caroline about the Barzalons, she had mentioned a death at a house party in Italy. Rumors that officials were paid off to avoid a scandal. Until now I had been annoyed by Seth's rudeness. Today there had been aggressiveness that bordered on the violent. And . . . the morning he came to my apartment, why had he wanted to know if the police in Venice had asked questions about him?

We were reaching the elevator. I turned and put a hand on Greg's arm. "You look terrible. I don't know why you put up with those two."

"They've heard that a big competitor is breathing down our necks. They can't seem to understand that there aren't any shortcuts in research. That's only one problem—" He stopped. Shook his head as if to clear it. "I need to get the taste of them out of my mouth. What about dinner tonight?"

I hesitated, anticipating the Superintendent's negative reaction. "Tonight? I'd like to, I really would, but I'm beat. At the end of my rope."

"The flood?"

"Not the flood. It's losing Cathy. Everyone's upset."

"I never met her, but I know she was close to you."

"She was. And to Vanessa."

"It's hard, wondering what you could have done. I was hoping that tonight we might get away from our problems. Be together again."

We were at the elevator. I pushed the button, my mind racing. Greg was a friend and he was hurting. Also, he was my one link to the Barzalons. Unless I was very wrong, Seth had lied through his teeth. The other two had been braced for trouble. This needed to be probed.

"Here's a thought," I said. "I really don't want to go out, but why not come here for a drink around six? I've got this suite that's costing the earth. I only hope my insurance will pay."

For a few seconds, Greg didn't anwer. He ran his hand over his face again. It was shaking slightly. Then he nodded. "Six it is. By the way, thanks for turning up."

"I wasn't much help, but I owe you. It was the least I could do."

"You owe me nothing. I'd better get back to the table and take care of the bill. James insists on the Taj, but he's too cheap to pay."

"I can believe it. Take care. See you later. I'll order a bottle of decent red."

Back in the suite, I took off my shoes, splashed water over my face, then put in a call to the Superintendent. Somewhere up the chain of command I was informed that the Superintendent was unavailable and would I leave a message.

As concisely as possible, I tried to sum up the findings at lunch. No doubt the Superintendent hadn't expected any results, but this had to be useful information. No need to tell him about the drinks with Greg. I wouldn't be leaving the suite.

Caroline was my next call. After a short wait, she was on the line.

"Emma." The deep gravelly voice. "Darling girl, I was just thinking about you. How's Vanessa? Have you found a house?"

"A house? Not yet, but I've decided not to go back to Hardwick."

"Start fresh is my motto. Places *and* men. In fact, I have a new walker."

"Walker? Have you hurt yourself?"

"Darling girl, I'm talking about an escort to parties. This one happens to be a friend. His wife is in a nursing home. Everyone understands the situation."

"You'll never give up."

"Not until I fall off the perch. Tonight we're going to an opening night at the Met. A new production with ladders and blue searchlights. Some people complain, they say they want the old period sets, but the place is vibrating these days. There's outreach. Come down and see for yourself."

"I will." A pause. "By the way, I've just had coffee with James and Seth Barzalon."

"Oh? What have you done to deserve that?"

"It was to do with the foundation. I see what you meant about James. He oiled his way around the floor, only this was The Café at the Taj Boston. He likes to go there, but he's too cheap to pay the bill."

"I'm not surprised. He's a great one for façades. Expensive tastes, but God knows where he gets the money."

"You told me the story, but it's really Seth I'm calling about. He sat there, acting like a world-class thug. You said there was a covered-up scandal in Italy. How bad was it? I need to be prepared for the worst. On account of Vanessa."

"Darling girl, I'm not his lawyer, I just hear the gossip."

"I thought your friend Maisie's husband was one of his trustees."

"He is, and it's a wretched job. Seth is always in some kind of trouble, always needing money, but when Nick tries to reason with him, he runs away."

"He has that foundation."

"Which he tries to milk like a cash cow. Enough of the Barzalons. There's bad blood there. Men?"

"Not in the way you mean."

"Emma, I despair. I really despair. How often do I have to tell you that you're a rich, good-looking widow? You should be out there playing the field."

"It will happen."

"Just don't wait too long. Darling girl, my masseuse is standing here, waiting, hands covered with oil. Love you."

"Love you, too."

eighteen

By half past five, the stage was set. The fire was burning. Fresh flowers stood on the coffee table. The ever helpful room service had produced wine, crackers, and cheese.

Unable to sit still, I went to loosen the flower arrangement and throw away the heavy ferns. My wardrobe was limited—tonight I was wearing a black cashmere sweater and tan twill trousers. I had made an effort with my face, but even heavy makeup couldn't cover the circles under my eyes.

At half past six I was pacing the room, regretting the impulsive invitation. That look by the elevator. His words. ". . . get away . . . be together." He could be looking for comfort in a very basic way. I was looking for information.

Resiliency. My new mantra. I must apply resiliency. When the knock came, I went to the door and opened it. He was standing there, wearing the same dark suit. His thin face looked strained to the breaking point; I had seen it before, the look of a tormented person held together with string.

"Sorry I'm late," he said. "Something came up at the last minute."

"It doesn't matter. Really. Welcome to my gilded cage."

"Not bad," he said as we went into the sitting room.

"No, but gilded cages can pall. Pour yourself some wine."

"Can I get you something?"

"I already have mine." Stiff, guarded words, when once we had been relaxed and easy. He poured himself a glass of red wine. I motioned him to the love seat and sat down on a chair.

"Cheers. You look as if you needed this."

"It shows?"

"Yes, but Seth was acting like one of the Sopranos. What's his problem?"

"Same old story. Money. To be first on the market with a big moneymaking drug."

"He needs a kick in the ass. My God, what more does he want of you?"

Greg shook his head. "Forget Seth. It's been a bad day. A bunch of city inspectors suddenly descended on us. Routine, they said, but it upset the staff. What's the story about your apartment?" An abrupt switch.

"About my apartment? Nothing good. It's an old building and the plumbers found asbestos in the kitchen tiles. That means waiting for specialists in asbestos removal. You wouldn't believe the rules and regulations."

"Lawsuits." A pause. "To be honest, you look a little stressed out yourself."

I hesitated. It wouldn't be easy to juggle two balls in the air: the mourner and the information gatherer.

"That's because I am. *Very* stressed out about Cathy Riordan's suicide. We're all asking ourselves why we didn't see it coming."

"I had a friend in college who hung himself when he didn't make the Dean's List. Last year a colleague who was going through a divorce turned on the engine in his garage. You always wonder what you could have done."

"True." I crossed my legs. "The thing is, none of us can understand the reason. That's why I went out on a limb and asked Seth about Terry Gallagher."

"You got your answer. He was fired."

"Yes, but I wanted to hear more. I think he may have had something to do with Cathy's death."

Greg's hand tightened on the glass. I could see that the knuckles were white.

"What makes you think that?"

"There was a drink in Paris. A trip to Venice in the plane. I know he saw her in New York, Monday night, and something must have happened. When I talked to her the next day she was very upset about him."

"Do you know why?" There was no mistaking the urgency in his voice. The muscles in my neck tightened.

"We were going to have lunch. Then she killed herself. Did you notice Seth's reaction when I asked him about Terry? It was a deluge. Not the usual two-second sound bite. He knew something about Terry that he wasn't telling me." A carefully casual voice. I watched Greg's face.

"I didn't notice. What matters is that you got what you wanted. Seth isn't going to be hounding your niece."

"True. Good riddance."

We sat in silence. Had Greg come to get information from me? After a moment, he cleared his throat. "Seth did me one good turn. I met *you*."

"Oh?" I stared up at the portrait of the woman above the mantel.

"A very good turn. I held back when you were so worried about your niece. It wasn't easy. In fact, it was hell. Now I want to be part of your life. More than dinner and a concert. There's a place in northern Vermont that belongs to a colleague, another researcher. A ski lodge with a great view of Mount Mansfield." A pause. "I was hoping we might go up there tomorrow. Get some good clean air. Relax."

"Tomorrow?" I kept my eyes on the woman's black lace dress. It had come, the invitation I was expecting, but something about it seemed forced, wrong, as if wrung out of him against his will.

"What do you say?" He was staring at me, a look that was almost pleading. I folded my hands in my lap to keep them from twisting.

"You know, I'm afraid that won't work for me. Not at the moment. I'm still getting over my husband's death. It takes time."

"I understand. These things can't be rushed. It's just that we've come to know each other very well. It would be good to take the next step." He put his glass down on the coffee table and leaned toward me.

I shifted in my chair. "I'm sorry. I know what you're saying, Greg, but the answer is no."

"Are you sure?" He raised his arm—a sweeping gesture. His hand hit the glass. Red wine poured over the glass top and down onto the carpet.

After a horrified second, I stood up. "Oh no—I'll get a towel."

"Blood." The word came out in a gasp.

I jumped. "It's wine."

"Blood. Your blood." He leaned forward and put his head in his hands.

"*Greg.* It's *wine.*"

He raised his head and gave me an anguished look. "Sorry. For a moment . . . sorry." His whole body was shaking.

"Are you all right? Shall I call a doctor?"

"No doctor." He put his head in his hands again.

The wine on the carpet was spreading. I stood there, helpless and unnerved. Was he going out of his mind? Somehow I must get him out of here.

"Listen," I said loudly. "Listen to me. You're exhausted and no wonder. Go home and get some sleep."

"Yes." He got up and began to walk toward the foyer, moving like a sleepwalker. As we reached the door he turned. Again, the anguished look. "Emma. I'm sorry. I never meant it to happen."

"It was an accident. Go home. Look after yourself."

"I never meant it to happen."

"Of course. Get a taxi. Go home."

Quickly I closed the door and ran back to the sitting room. It was too late to keep the stain from spreading.

For what seemed like hours, I blotted and scrubbed. Poured on soda water. The stain turned from red to pink, but it might never come out.

Finally I sat back on my heels. Mopped the coffee table and picked up the glass. The white towels looked as if there had been a bloody murder in suite 954. A murder without a corpse.

It was only six thirty. I got to my feet. Put the glasses and half-empty bottle back on the side table. Went to the love seat and put a pillow over the stain that looked like blood. My blood. Rodale and the Superintendent must be told about Greg's strange lapse, but not until I could pull myself together. Turn around and go down a frightening new path. *What* hadn't he meant to happen? Why the invitation to go off with him? What did Greg want from me?

Taking deep breaths, I began to by-pass angst and put myself in Greg's mind.

The day Vanessa got sick he was over at the foundation. Suddenly there's a call from his boss, Seth Barzalon, ordering him to go to Boston General. Get info about a Vanessa Metcalf. Make contact with her aunt.

At first he was just to get close. Keep his ears open. Then comes the unwelcome command to put in listeners in her apartment. Then, when it became clear that she was part of an investigation, he's told to go through her apartment. Find names and telephone numbers.

Terry, the Barzalon pilot, kills for the second time. The situation is now out of control. The aunt is a threat who must be silenced. Greg is caught in a trap. He snaps.

A police car went screaming down Arlington Street. I stood still, trying to make sense out of this new crisis.

Another police car went screeching by. I put my hands to my ears and tried to dig deeper. Unless I was very wrong, the man who had helped me with Vanessa had been sensitive, loved music, was dedicated to his work. Yes, he was carrying out orders, using me as a conduit, but something had happened during that last meeting with the Barzalons. Something bad enough to break him down, make him act like a man torn into pieces.

A heavy piece of equipment rumbled by, a fire engine letting out short blasts on the horn. An accident—or a fire. I looked at my hands. There were stains on the ends of the fingers, shades of Lady Macbeth, only in this case I was the victim. The one who had been deceived. Taken in. I must go and wash them. Then make my calls to Rodale and the Superintendent.

nineteen

I slept for a few hours. Toward morning I dreamed that I had fallen into a well. The water was rising and I was scrabbling for a foothold, but the stones were slippery. I called for help. Greg appeared, he was holding a wineglass. He gave me a desperate look, then turned away.

Now, as I lay under the down duvet, I was beginning to realize how much I was hurting. I had imagined that we had a future together. I wanted to pick up the phone and call him: "Greg. What's wrong? Tell me, please tell me, that whatever horror is happening has nothing to do with you."

At eight o'clock, the waiter Ron wheeled in the breakfast table with my coffee and cereal. Ron lived in Brighton and had three boys, all in college. The housekeeper, Anna, had seven grandchildren. At nine, she came in wearing her black uniform with white apron and white collar. She cut off my abject apologies about the wine stain.

"These things happen. I'll do some spot cleaning; then Maintenance can have a look after you leave."

I hadn't expected to see Superintendent McNulty, but by ten he was standing in front of the portrait in my sitting room. Listening as I gave him a verbal version of what had happened last night.

"His wineglass was on the table. Red wine. He waved his hand and knocked it over. He thought it was my blood. He fell apart. He was shaking from head to toe. I barely managed to get him out."

"Any ideas as to cause?"

"Yes. Seth Barzalon was putting pressure on him to speed up his antiviral, but it was more than that. I think Seth was using him to spy on me. Find out what I knew. I think he was told to take me off to Vermont and get more information. Maybe in bed."

"A reasonable assumption. Atkins had access to your apartment. A chance to install the listeners. What exactly was your relationship?"

"He helped me get through my niece's illness. I admired the way he's working on an antiviral that could save lives. Now this." No way was I going to admit that I had ever thought of a long-term relationship.

"Right." A pause. "This may tie into the latest developments. A few days ago London instructed us to look for individuals who have access to private labs. Look for any possible connection to a crime syndicate. Dr. Atkins headed the list. We've been in touch with the lab where Dr. Atkins worked before coming to the foundation. We were told that he was considered brilliant, visionary, but unstable. That was the word they used, but it looked as if they were sitting on something far more damaging. No chance of promotion there. My guess is that Barzalon offered him a chance to work on this antiviral and he jumped at it."

I nodded, seeing Greg's agonized face. "He was dedicated to his work. My sense is that if he took the job in good faith, then found out that Seth Barzalon was involved in some kind of crime, something that escalated into killing people, it would be enough to make him snap. Go off the rails. He would know that refusing to take orders would cost him his job. His life's work."

"In any case, after last night we'll be taking a hard look at Dr. Atkins." A pause. He glanced at his watch. A large Rolex on a large wrist.

"Last night I had a report from the detective assigned to look for witnesses in Mrs. Riordan's neighborhood. A teenager, hurrying to a party, says he saw a couple coming out of the building around nine o'clock. According to his story, her legs weren't working right; the man was half-carrying her to a car. The boy figured she was drunk. He couldn't give a description, he was in a hurry, but he says he knows a drunk when he sees one."

I put my hand on the back of a chair. "She said she wouldn't see him again."

"It's possible that he forced his way in. Injected the drug."

"It had to be him. Gallagher."

The Superintendent held up his hand. "There's still no evidence. There may have been others involved."

"What about the search?"

"I was coming to that. All we have is a signal from Ireland. An agent at the car rental desk in Shannon Airport thinks he recognized the picture that went out to all airports."

"But he's not sure?"

"No, he's not, but it turns out Gallagher has a police history over there. Nothing was proved, but his name was attached to a bank robbery in Donegal in the eighties, back when the IRA was raising funds for guns."

"Does that mean they'll be looking for him?"

"Not unless there's new evidence." He looked at his watch again. "Mrs. Streat. About your situation. You can't stay here indefinitely."

"I certainly can't."

"On the other hand, you need protection. As I say, there may be unidentified others involved. I'd like to move you to a place we use for just such contingencies. As soon as possible."

My hand tightened on the back of the chair. Going to a safe house would mean isolation. Separation.

"Mrs. Streat?"

I stared at the large Rolex watch. Rodale had talked about hounds keeping their noses to the ground, losing the scent, then going on. This was no time to be grounded. Cut out of the loop.

"Actually, I have a better idea," I said.

"Which is?"

"For me to go to Ireland. With Cathy's ashes."

Superintendent McNulty rocked back on his heels. He gave me a quick look.

"What do you think you could accomplish?"

"I'm a dangerous loose end. Terry wants to get rid of me. He walks into a trap. The goat staked out to catch the wolf."

"Not feasible," the Superintendent said flatly. It was easy to guess what he was thinking: Case of delayed shock. Better nip this in the bud.

"Why? Her cousin is flying over with the ashes. I'll be with her on the flight. After that, agents could be watching. I wouldn't be alone."

The Superintendent touched today's tie. Brown, with cream stripes. "There's no way Gallagher would know you are in Ireland."

"There is. I call Greg Atkins. I say I'm sorry about last night. Tell him that I'm going to Ireland with Cathy's cousin and where I'm staying. If he's involved, he'll pass the word along. If not, no harm done. I go over, representing the family, and I come back."

"Can't be done, Mrs. Streat. Far too much risk with little guarantee of a good result."

"Maybe, but if it's the last thing I do, I'm going to see Cathy's killer behind bars. Are you saying you won't help?"

"I'm saying this is not a workable way to apprehend him."

"You mean it's not the usual way."

"In any case, it's out of my jurisdiction. You would need a high level of protection from the Irish police, the Garda."

"You're forgetting one thing. I'm a free agent. I can always go on my own."

Silence. I kept my hand on the chair. Superintendent McNulty walked toward the door. After a moment he turned. His face was impassive, but his neck was red.

"I hope you realize you're putting me in a difficult position, Mrs. Streat. This will have to be taken up on a higher level," he said, and the door closed behind him.

I stood still, holding on to the chair. There it was again, the quick temper and impulsive behavior my mother had struggled to change. Over the years, I had made impulsive decisions, some good, others bad, but never before had I deliberately put myself in danger. The next step was to beat the Superintendent to Rodale.

Luck was with me. A moment later Rodale was on the line.

"Emma. Good timing. You'll be glad to hear that your tip

about the gondolier in Venice has paid off. Late last night the Questura intercepted a handover at a trattoria. The gondolier Fausto was picked up with a package of viruses in his accordion case. Destination a lab in southern France. The Colonel sends his respects."

"That *is* good timing. You're not going to like this, but I want a payback. A big one."

"That sounds ominous."

"A man forced Cathy Riordan out of her apartment and into that hotel. It has to be Terry. I gather he may have bolted to Ireland."

"It's a possibility. We're putting out feelers."

"If he has family and friends, he'll be hard to find. Cathy Riordan's cousin is taking her ashes to Ireland. I want to go with her."

Rodale cleared his throat. "Why, may I ask?"

"Because if he knows I'm there, he may come out of the woodwork."

"Speculation, my dear. Pure speculation."

"Maybe, maybe not. I couldn't give details in my message yesterday, but something very peculiar is going on. Seth is losing his cool. Dr. Atkins went off the wall when he was here with me last night. Spilled red wine and thought it was my blood."

"Good God."

"Exactly. It looks as if three people are involved at this end. I think Seth Barzalon ordered Dr. Atkins to spy on me. Now Dr. Atkins is having a conscience attack. I want to tell him that I'm going to Ireland. Be the goat staked out for the wolf. Lay the killings on Terry so thick that steps will be taken."

"The classic bait and catch, but if the operation is beginning to unravel, these people may get jumpy. You'd need good security around you."

"My handler the Superintendent wants to send me to a safe house. I'm tanking over his head, calling you for help."

A long pause. I waited, trying to steady my breathing. The bastard owed me. He *owed* me.

"Emma?"

"Yes?"

"You can stop the arm-twisting. I'll deal with the handler. Tell him that you have a track record for smoking individuals out of the woodwork. If you're willing to go out on a limb, then it's worth our while to support you."

"You'd tell him that? You have that much faith?"

"Spare me. He'll provide security for the flight. I'll arrange for backup over there. Just recognize that no security is one hundred percent effective."

"Not a comforting thought."

"It's not meant to be. It looks as if the stakes in this operation are high enough to kill anyone who gets in the way. Fear of exposure is a very powerful motive. If you're having second thoughts, ring me back. Now is the time to change your mind."

There were no second thoughts. Suddenly the clock was ticking. Plumbers brought clothes from the apartment. A warm coat and something black for the funeral. I wrote letters to Jake and Steve, telling them that I was proud of them. Telling them that Ned and Cassia would step in and make a home for them if anything happened to me.

I was finishing a letter to Ned when the Superintendent called.

"Mrs. Streat? You'll be going to Ireland. You've met Agent Rudnick. She'll fly over with you and stay on as part of your security. Her cover is that she's a cousin. There mustn't be the slightest suspicion that you're part of a police operation."

"I understand. I liked Sally."

"Agent Rudnick is very capable. Once you're in Ireland, the Garda will provide backup if needed."

"Thank you. Very much. I'm afraid I've given you a lot of trouble, but I appreciate the way the Boston Police Department has handled a . . . a different kind of situation."

"There's still work to be done. A good deal of work." A pause. "Good luck, Mrs. Streat. I mean it. Best of luck. Take care of yourself."

"I will." Under the impassive surface, this was a kind, competent man. In fact, as soon as I got back I would write a letter to the papers, praising the Boston Police Department.

There was one more river to cross. I stood in the middle of the sitting room and stared at the stain under the coffee table. More deception. More lies. Not the way I wanted to live, but there was no alternative.

Greg answered on the second ring. "It's you," he said. "I didn't think I'd ever hear from you again. What I did was unforgivable."

"You've been under a strain. We're still friends. I was calling to see if you're all right."

"As well as can be expected, after landing you in such a mess."

"The housekeeper did miracles. Anyhow, I'm leaving. I'm off to Ireland."

"Ireland." A pause. "Did you say Ireland?"

"My old nurse came from Killarney. I've always wanted to go there, and now there's a reason. Cathy Riordan's cousin is taking the ashes back to her parents. A little village in county Waterford. One of the Metcalf family should go and Vanessa certainly can't."

"When do you leave?"

"Day after tomorrow. The cousin will be coming back after the funeral, she has a job, but I'm going to stay until I can get back into my apartment. There's a little place in County Waterford. The Fitzgerald Arms. I'll make that my headquarters."

"Sounds like a good change."

"For the better, I hope. I've had enough of the Taj." I began to pace, clenching the cell in my fist. "But now I have another reason. It's so upsetting I can hardly talk about it."

"What?"

"I've just been talking to the police. You remember I was the one who went to the hotel and identified Cathy. They called and gave me the autopsy report. They said it wasn't a suicide. They said she was injected with a lethal drug. Her death is now being listed as a homicide."

"Good Lord. I'm sorry."

"I told the police that Terry Gallagher had frightened her. They've been investigating and they think he may be in Ireland. I tell you, I've never been so angry in my life. All I know is, I'm going to find that man. Make him pay for what he did to that girl."

"You don't know that he's responsible. Let the police handle it."

"I don't have that much faith in the police." My voice was shaking—but that fitted the lies. "What's more, as soon as I get there I'm going straight to the Garda. Before she died, Cathy told me something that ought to put him behind bars. For life," I added. Would he ask the telling question? It came.

"What did she tell you?"

"Something only the police should hear. Anyhow, I have to run. Don't work too hard," I said, and hung up. There was no room for doubt. He was Seth's tool. He was going to spread the word.

twenty

It was late afternoon, Irish time. The Aer Lingus plane was making its last run into Shannon Airport, descending over a patchwork quilt of little fields, each a different shade of green.

I turned to Maura Riordan. "My old nurse used to say there were fifty-two shades of green in Ireland."

"She had the right of it. If things were different, I'd be beside meself with the joy of coming back."

"It's hard," I said, and glanced at the carry-on bag stowed under the seat in front. Human ashes were surprisingly heavy. For some reason I had expected Cathy's cousin to be older, running to plumpness. This woman was thin as a lathe, with short dark hair and hands always in motion. It hadn't been easy for her to sit still for five hours. She had talked about Cathy and the family.

"They don't know yet that the poor lamb was murthered. I'll have to tell them. I'm thinking they'll find some comfort that she didn't commit a sin."

The plane was sinking slowly toward the small green fields. I pulled my seat belt tighter. Leaving the plane meant stepping out of a safe cocoon, but Agent Sally Rudnick was with me, guarding my back. To the other passengers, we must look like two ordinary tourists. Sally's long blond hair reached the shoulders of a swinging black leather coat. I had settled for the old black pants suit and my signature Hermès scarf.

"My cousin is between jobs," I had told Maura. "Between jobs and boyfriends. The last one wanted a mother."

"Shame, and she so friendly. Perky. Will you bring her to the wake then? She'll be very welcome. You have the directions."

The tarmac was coming up to meet us. With a roar, the wheels touched down. Everyone cheered and the cabin erupted with excitement. A nearby group was going to a wedding. Others were going home. "Will Dermot be there to meet us? Will he bring the twins?"

As we left the plane and started through the terminal toward the baggage carousel, I resisted the urge to look around. If Terry were here, he wouldn't show himself. Or maybe he would look like an elderly man or a woman.

A delegation of Riordans, young and old, was waiting at the gate. There were hugs for Maura, introductions and handshakes for Sally and me. They were all doing their best to hide the pain.

"You were good to our Cathy," her father said. "She wrote how much you helped her, you and Miss Metcalf."

"I loved her. We all did."

"We'll be seeing you at the wake, then, you and your cousin."

"Mrs. Streat?" A ruddy-faced man wearing a tweed cap had pushed through the Riordans. "Oliver Rafferty, your driver. I was given a description and told to get you out as quickly as possible."

Sally stepped forward. "Are you from McNulty in Boston?"

"I am. Follow me. I know a shortcut around the Duty Free. If you can manage with the hand luggage, I'll deal with the cart."

Moving fast, he led us along several back halls that ended in a parking lot used for deliveries.

"Welcome to Ireland, ladies," he said as we climbed into a green Ford sedan parked beside a Guinness van.

In a surprisingly short time, the sprawl of airport had become open country. The leaves were changing, but the colors here were muted compared to the New England triumphant brilliance. A gray sky pressed close, enfolding us. The air coming through the open window was soft and damp.

"Feel that air," I said to Sally, sitting beside me in the back. "Like skin lotion."

Oliver laughed. "It'll be yer first time here, then?"

"Yes. The first time," Sally said. "What instructions did you get?"

"To be on call around the clock. I'll be giving you a number. Whenever you go out, I'm to drive you."

I leaned forward. "The Fitzgerald Arms. Is it far from here?"

"A little over an hour. They'll make you very comfortable. It was a coach stop in the old days and people still use it to meet. The hunting crowd comes in after a day over the walls. Locals, too. The manager, he's a fine lad."

We were reaching a crossroads. The signs were in English and Gaelic. Oliver slowed and turned off the main road. "This way is longer, but anyone following would be seen."

The new road was narrow, enclosed with tall hedgerows. We passed an old stone cottage behind a crumbling wall. Then a stretch of small fields.

"Look at *that,* will you?" Sally said, pointing. "Over there. Straight out of Harry Potter."

I looked. A round stone tower stood at the summit of a gentle hill. The top had fallen away, leaving it open to the rooks and the rain.

"It must be very old," I said. "Imagine living in a little winding space, maybe fighting off marauders. My old nurse came from Killarney. She used to tell us stories about fairy rings. Leprechauns, the little people, who wore shoes no bigger than her thumb. She saw one, she says. It was real leather, with tiny little stitches."

"You didn't believe her."

"Seeing that tower, I'm not sure."

For a few moments we sat still, not talking, looking out at the peaceful land. Suddenly the road curved sharply. Oliver braked. A large road sign stood on the bank. White, with a black circle in the center like a bull's-eye. Two words had been painted on it: "Black Spot."

"Black Spot," I said. "What on earth is that?"

"D'ye not have them in America? It means there was a terrible motor accident at the spot. People will have been killed. 'Black Spot' is a warning, you might say."

As we came into the first small town, I studied the row of gray stone buildings with faded signs above the doors: Mulvany Wines and Spirits. Patrick McGrath Quality Meats. Noel Cusack, Turf Accountant. There was a green and yellow telephone booth at the corner. A woman wearing a head scarf and carrying a string bag filled with groceries walked by. Two children with carrot hair pranced ahead, licking ice-cream sticks. Suddenly Oliver slowed.

"Ah no," he muttered, and stopped. A large lorry was stuck in the middle of the street, almost touching the parked cars. As the driver clashed gears loudly, a number of older men wearing tweed jackets and tweed caps appeared.

"Go forward, man," one called to the driver. "Ye've a foot to spare."

"Ye're wrong, Matt," said another. "He'll never make it, going forward. Back, man, back and have another run at it."

"No, no, call Tim. Let Tim come and move his car."

Everyone was talking. All were in high good humor.

We waited. Finally the man called Tim arrived. There was a loud cheer as he got into the small car and maneuvered his way through the space in front of the lorry.

As we left the town, Oliver swung onto a dirt road a few feet wide, then hit the steering wheel with his fist. "Ah, will you look at that. Out of the frying pan into the fire." Just ahead, the road was blocked by a large herd of black and white cows, rumps swinging in rhythm as they walked. A young boy with a stick sauntered behind them.

We began to inch through, so close the rough hides brushed the car. The smell was powerful. As we came to a run-down farmyard, a black and white dog lying beside the road rose up and began to snap at the tires. Sally and I looked at each other.

"Interstate I-ninety-five—not," she said.

"I love it. I'm falling in love with this place. Seriously in love." I leaned forward again. "This village where we're staying. Is it large?"

Oliver turned. His false teeth looked like square white Chiclets. "The Arms and two churches and a few shops."

"Do you live in the village? Do you have a large family?"

"Close by. My wife's in hospital with the gallbladder. She left me in charge of the grandchild that's with us. There's a neighbor coming in, but little Pat's only three. He misses his mam."

"I'm afraid we're taking you away from him."

"Not at all. I'm glad of the work. Here's the wall, the start of the village," he added as we crossed a little river with an arched bridge, passed two houses with thatch roofs, and pulled up in front of a long, low, mustard yellow building. Oliver turned.

"Go on in, ladies. I'll see to the bags. Will you be going out again tonight?"

"No, I'm sure we won't."

"So what time will you be wanting me tomorrow?"

I opened my bag and handed him the directions to the wake. "How much time should we allow for that?"

"Less than an hour, if there's no cows in the way."

"Let's say ten o'clock, then. And thanks for all the information."

"It's been a pleasure. A real pleasure."

The front hall had low ceilings and a worn black leather porter's chair by the door. A young woman came forward from behind a desk. Her round cheeks and sturdy legs reminded me of Cathy.

"Mrs. Streat and Miss Metcalf? I'm Deirdre. You're very welcome."

"We're glad to be here," I said, meaning it. The feeling of warmth and cheer was pervasive. Nearby, through an open door, I could see several men standing at a bar. One had a dog with him, a large brindle greyhound. The dog's light eyes were fixed on his master's face.

"Tim will be taking up your bags," Deirdre went on. "Will you be wanting tea?"

"No tea," I said, and to Sally, "I'm beginning to feel dried out. How about a long, cold drink?"

"Sounds good to me."

I turned to Deirdre. "I think we'll go in there and then to our rooms."

"That'll be fine. When you're ready, you have only to tell me. Our housekeeper, Josie, will take you up."

The lounge was noisy and crowded. A coal fire blazed in a grate. We found an empty table and sat down. There was a long bar with signs for Jameson whiskey, Harp, and Guinness ale. People seemed to be carrying their own drinks. Slowly, the tension in my neck began to ease. For a few hours, at least, I could forget the strain of the past few days. Pretend that I was just an ordinary guest and let the charm of the place sink in.

"What'll you have?" I asked Sally. "I'll get it."

"Something nonalcoholic. A large Coke."

"Right. I keep forgetting you're on duty."

"Something tall and orange and a large Coke," I said to the curly-haired young bartender. "I'm staying here, but I don't know my room number."

"Ye look honest; a name will be fine. Half a mo' while I pour for the ladies in the corner. It's very upset, they are." He nodded toward a group of young women. They were all laughing. One was doubled up, hands over her face.

"They don't look very upset to me."

"Ah, but haven't they made the big mistake? It's off to a two-day retreat they were, all laid on by Father Dogherty. Hubbies and mothers gang-pressed to look after the children. Now they hear the retreat isn't until next week."

I laughed. "So what are they going to do now?"

"Ah, that's the question. Will they treat themselves to a night out before crawling home?"

"Night out, I should say."

"I think you have the right of it. This is their second round."

Next to me, a man missing two front teeth was talking about a place called the Curragh. "Cheerful Rogue, he has heart; there's nothing can touch him. Put your punts on him."

The noise grew louder. I finished my drink and turned to Sally. "That hit the spot, as they say. Maybe we should go up and unpack, then come down for dinner."

"Works for me. I want to call the numbers I was given and check on Oliver. I should have asked to see his credentials before letting him rush us away like that."

"Well, he got us here," I said, and went to Deirdre at the desk. "We'd like to go up to our rooms now. What time do you serve dinner?"

"Seven to nine. This is Josie, our housekeeper," she said as a small, elderly woman came forward. She was wearing a white sweater over a black dress.

"You're very welcome," she said, smiling. "This way, please, ladies." We followed as she opened a door into a dark hall that smelled of furniture polish and led us to a flight of stairs covered with a worn brown carpet and held down by brass rods, then down a shorter flight of stairs that led to a landing, then up again to another hall. I pulled my coat closer. There didn't seem to be central heat. Halfway down the next hall, Josie finally stopped. "Ye're number five, Mrs. Streat. Miss Metcalf is two doors down at number three."

Number 5 was large, with buff-painted walls. Faded hunting prints on the walls. An armoire and a dressing table. Josie went to switch on an electric heater that was sitting in the fireplace.

"There'll be electric blankets on the beds," she said. "You can ring if you'd like a nice hot bottle for your feet." She crossed the room and opened another door. "This used to be the dressing room. Now it's the bath. Just finished," she said proudly. "The water's fine and hot."

The tub was a good seven feet long, with faucets in the middle and a tray for soap. "It's *very* nice," I said.

Josie beamed. "There's a bell and the phone if anything's wanted. Shall I pull the curtains?"

"No thanks. I just hope we can find our way back."

"Ah, it's a rambling old place. I'll be showing the other young lady her room."

"I'll see you later," I said to Sally. "An hour, let's say. I wouldn't mind a quick nap. Maybe a hot bath."

"Sounds good."

As the door closed, I went to a window and looked out. The room was at the rear of the building, away from the road. There was a neat vegetable garden with beds of winter vegetables. Two staked rows of fall dahlias. A white van with a logo for garden fertilizer was parked against the far wall.

The sky was darkening, almost touching the ground, with a look of impending rain. Even with the electric fire, the room was still cold. A long steam in that vast tub would take away the stiffness that comes from being immobilized for hours.

I was crossing the room to turn on the water when there was a knock on the door. I went to open it. Oliver was standing there, cap in his hand.

"I'm that sorry to trouble you, Mrs. Streat, but it's about to-morrow. The woman who looks after the grandchild was called away. I may have to send someone else in me place."

"I see." A cool tone of voice. There was no need for him to come up to my room. He should have called from the desk or his cell. "Don't bother to get someone else," I said. "I'm sure the Arms can find us a driver."

"Will ye call them now?" He took a step forward, as if trying to see into the room.

"Good night." I started to close the door.

"Ah, now." With one quick motion, he had a cloth around my mouth. I opened it to scream for Sally. No sound came out.

Seconds later I was being propelled down the dark hall, half-lifted off of my feet. As we reached the end of the hall, I tried to kick my way free.

"None of that." He gave my arm a twist as we hurtled down uncarpeted back stairs and out through an open door. The white van was pulled up, motor running.

"In with you." I fell forward into the backseat. The door slammed shut. Half-blinded by fear, I beat at the door. It was locked.

"Sit still," Oliver growled. The van began to move. We emerged out of an alley and started down the street.

"Faster," Oliver called to the driver.

"Are ye mad? I'll not risk being stopped." A woman's voice. Just now Oliver had looked into my room to make sure no one was there. He had known the layout of those back halls. My brain seemed numb, but one thing was clear: Greg had sent the message. A team had been assembled. I was in trouble.

The car gathered speed. I tried to speak, but my mouth was full of wet wool. My saliva. Oliver's arms were holding my shoulders. He smelled of stale tobacco and sweat. Somehow I kept myself from retching into the tight cloth. Oh God, Sally's instinct to check Oliver's credentials had been right. How long would it take her to realize I wasn't in my room? An hour, maybe more, if she was wallowing in a hot bath.

It was getting dark, but the headlights showed that we were on an isolated road with no houses in sight. Going fast. Where?

Suddenly the van slowed. The driver pulled to the side of the road and stopped. Oliver leaned forward.

"Ye know the plan?"

"Meet you the other side of the mountains. I know the place."

"Right." And to me, "Easy now and ye won't be hurt." With a twist, he pulled off the cloth and hurried me out of the van.

A car was half hidden behind a stone wall close to the verge. Oliver's green Ford sedan. He pushed me into the back and climbed into the front seat. In seconds we were going forward through a gap and onto the deserted road.

"Good evening, Mrs. Streat. We meet again."

My head jerked around. James Barzalon was sitting beside me. In the dim light from the dashboard, I could see that he was smiling.

twenty-one

I didn't move. My mouth was too dry to speak, but disconnected thoughts were racing through my head. Terry should be sitting there. Or Seth. According to Caroline, James Barzalon was nothing but a hanger-on whose main function was to escort ladies to charity balls.

He cleared his throat. "Rather a chilly night. Frankly, I hadn't expected Ireland to be so cold, but my Irish friends tell me they find our summer heat unbearable. Would you like the heat turned up?" A smooth, solicitous voice.

"No," I said, trying to keep my voice steady. "Mr. Barzalon, why are you here? There must be some mistake."

"Mrs. Streat—may I call you Emma?" James Barzalon raised his hand and smoothed the shock of beautifully cut silver hair. "You are quite right, but the mistake was for you to come over to find Terry Gallagher. I couldn't allow you to succeed."

I swallowed. The tight cloth had bruised my mouth and

throat. *He* couldn't allow me to succeed? "I don't know what you're talking about," I said.

"My dear young lady, don't insult me by playing the innocent. You forced me to change my plans. You called in the police. You've been working with them from the time you were in Venice. In fact, you've caused me a great deal of trouble."

His plans? I dug my nails into the palms of my hands. Greg had dismissed him as a useless parasite: "Once in a while he puts his oar in and muddies the water . . . has attacks of thinking he's a man of business." Seth had called him a nuisance. Had they deliberately thrown up a thick smoke screen?

I turned my head and looked at him. "Frankly, I think Seth has been telling you a pack of lies. I still don't understand why you are here."

"There's no need for you to understand, my dear."

"But you, of all people. Were you forced to come? I mean, is Seth using you to cover his mistakes?"

"I? Used?" The words came out like bullets. "No one uses *me.*"

The anger in his voice was unnerving. I moved into the corner. "Sorry," I said under my breath.

"Ridiculous. The very idea is ridiculous. The fact is, I am surrounded by fools. Yes, mistakes were made, but they could have been remedied. Unfortunately, you interfered. Now you must pay."

I sat straight, needing to defend myself. "I didn't interfere," I said. "And I don't see how I could have upset your plans, whatever they are."

"Then you must be made to see." A pause. "Yes, you must be made to see. Telling you can do no harm now." He took a deep breath, as if trying to regain control. "Dr. Atkins will have told you that he was hired to corner the market with a new and more effective antiviral. A much-needed moneymaker."

"Yes, he did."

"New drugs require a long testing process. Dr. Atkins was taking too long to go through the usual channels. I was forced to take steps. It cost me money, a great deal of money, but I was able to acquire a number of live viruses for testing purposes." He stopped.

"I don't—" I began, then bit my lip.

"As I say, in order to save time, I had to take steps. For clinically proven results, human guinea pigs are brought in. Dr. Atkins tried using people off the street. That was unsatisfactory. It became clear to me that we must find a celebrity. A person whose illness and miraculous recovery would attract the attention of the mainstream press. Then, through them, the medical world."

"Vanessa." Whatever was coming next, I didn't want to hear it.

"Precisely. During her stay in Venice, the live virus was placed in your niece's water. The antidote was to be given in Sardinia several days later. She would recover. The press would be informed of this vital breakthrough. Do you follow?"

"Yes." I closed my eyes. James Barzalon. Mastermind. An impossible stretch except that he *had* taken charge of the lunch that day at the Taj.

"Dr. Atkins had a black mark on his career, a matter of plagiarism that had to be concealed. Last year, my son and his pilot were involved in a very nasty crime in Italy. If that had come out, they would both be in jail today."

"Blackmail." My voice seemed to be coming from a great distance.

"In a good cause. I made sure that the viruses I bought were waterborne. Airborne would have been too much of a threat to the general public. Gallagher went to Miss Metcalf's suite to put the virus in her special water. The accompanist caught him in the act. Unfortunately, Gallagher's history, when in trouble, is to kill. His first mistake. There was an autopsy and the police were brought in. From then on, he had to cover his tracks. He panicked. He lost his head and killed Miss Riordan. I think you know why."

Silence. James Barzalon smoothed his hair again. "A pity when a life is needlessly lost, but Gallagher is a fool. My son is a fool. Dr. Atkins is not a fool, but he has been a great disappointment to me. Because you took Miss Metcalf home with you, there was no chance for him to test his drug in Sardinia. He should have pushed his way into Boston General and administered the antiviral. Achieved our goal without these annoying mishaps."

Annoying mishaps. The car was hot, filled with great gusts of sickening heat. My mind lurched back and forth. So much suffering—Cathy dead, Vanessa a human guinea pig because this twisted man had convinced himself that his mad plan to make money would work. He had told me his bizarre story because I was no longer a threat.

We were starting up a mountain; the headlights shone out on bare slopes slashed in places for piles of turf. I stared out, feeling as if we were engaging in some theatrical dialogue, nothing to do with the actual world.

"No security is one hundred percent effective," Rodale had said. By now Sally must have alerted the Garda, but no one would know where to start looking. Ireland was a small country, but finding me might mean an endless house-to-house search.

Time passed. The road steepened; the car climbed slowly, with much shifting of gears. James cleared his throat. "There are very few mountains in this part of Ireland. Down on the other side, in the valley, there's an old place called Ballynarog. It belongs to friends. They rent it out when not using it themselves. I'm told the salmon fishing in the Blackwater is excellent, but I'm afraid fishing isn't on my agenda."

He paused. Three forlorn sheep covered with tangled fleece moved slowly off of the narrow road, almost a path, that ran along the top of the mountain.

"Stupid creatures. Back to you, Mrs. Streat, and that unfortunate impulse to find Gallagher. If, by chance, you had succeeded, he would have implicated me to save himself. On the other hand, your coming may prove to be worthwhile."

"Worthwhile?" I was finding it hard to breathe. The word came out in a wheezy croak.

"At Ballynarog, you will be given water containing the same virus that your niece was given. You will become very ill. Then, at the right moment, the antiviral will be adminstered."

"No." I could feel my body shrink, as if trying to disappear into the dingy upholstery. At Boston General, Vanessa had received the best of care. Doctors and nurses had worked around the clock to save her. Who would be with me when I was out of my mind with fever?

"I've arranged for a nurse to be there," he went on. "The woman who was driving the van, a cousin of Terry Gallagher's. She didn't want him found. In the end you'll have the satisfaction of knowing that it was all in the cause of helping humanity. Keep that in mind. In the end, the experiment on you will benefit humanity."

I opened my mouth. My lips moved but no sound came out. He was enjoying himself, watching me, hoping that I would break down and beg for mercy. Grovel at his feet.

The road had been level, traversing the top of the mountain. Now we were beginning to go down. How much longer? An hour? Maybe less, but I was still alive. If Rodale and his colleagues were sitting here, they would be figuring out a plan of attack. They would never give up until the last breath.

For a long time, there had been no sound from Oliver. I stared at his thick neck—and a plan began to form. How much had he understood? How much had he been paid?

The bare slopes were turning into woods. I clenched my fists and looked at Barzalon. He was so close I could smell his expensive cologne.

"You're doing your best to frighten me, Mr. Barzalon, but it just won't work," I said loudly. "It won't work because you and your helper here have just put nooses around your necks."

"Indeed."

"Tell me this. How did you know where I was in Ireland? You knew because the police in Boston instructed me to call Greg Atkins and spell out my itinerary. The woman who came with me is not my cousin. She works for a Superintendent Mc-Nulty. He arranged for backup from the Garda."

"Idle threats, my dear. You'll never be found."

"By now there may be roadblocks. A dragnet. Your only chance of escaping prison is to turn around and take me back to the Arms. Let me out and drive away."

"Nonsense."

The car didn't turn. There was nothing more I could do. Now the road grew wider. The tops of the trees were showing. I thought about my boys, left homeless with no parent. At least Lewis and I had given them a good start. My brother, Ned, and his wife, Cassia, would look after them with good sense and affection.

We were in the valley. The road was level with the trees. For hours, the only sign of life had been those bedraggled sheep, but now a dark cottage showed in the headlights. Then another. We were coming into a small village lined with houses. There was a green and yellow telephone booth on the corner. A pub. A grocery.

Moving one foot, I began to work at the heel of the other shoe, trying to wriggle it loose. If I was quick enough, I could hit Oliver over the head. Grab the wheel. I might die in the crash, but it was worth a try.

Suddenly the brakes went on with a screech. The car stopped in the middle of the street.

James raised his hand. "Don't stop here."

Oliver turned and leaned over the seat. His ruddy face was sweating. "Ah no. Wasn't I promised fifty punts to drive two ladies to the Fitzgerald Arms. Another fifty to drive the two of you over the mountain." He shook his fist. "Jesus, man, no one told me the half of it. I'll not be the patsy in your dirty business, not just to save Terry Gallagher's skin."

"Keep going. You've nothing to do with this."

"Are ye mad? Ye had me drag the lady out of her room. What's more, it's true what she said about the other one being an agent. At the airport that one asked if I'd had instructions from McNulty. By now she'll be missing Mrs. Streat. Sending out an alarm."

"We're almost there. Keep driving."

"And put me head in a noose?" He looked at me. He was breathing hard. "The Garda station is just there across the street under the blue light. Swear ye'll say I was tricked into this and ye can get out. Make a run for it."

I stared at him. It was dangerous to make promises to a rogue, but I had no choice.

"All right."

"Quick, then. Into the station with you."

I ran. As I reached the safety of the door, I stopped and looked back over my shoulder. Oliver and James had emerged from the car. Oliver was holding James by the arm. "Hit me and run off with my car, is it? There's a few tricks I learned in the army. Like how to break a man's neck." He pushed James toward the curb. Seconds later, the green sedan was speeding down the deserted street.

The front room of the station was small and very warm. Two men were sitting behind a counter. Young men, wearing blue uniforms. They looked up as I came stumbling in.

"Good evening, ma'am," one said.

I ran toward the counter. "Help me. You must help me. There's a man out there—he wants to kill me. Don't let him kill me."

They stood up. The one with red hair cleared his throat. "American, are you?"

"My name is Emma Streat. I'm staying at the Fitzgerald Arms in Tarlow. I was forced into a car. The driver went off, but the man with him is out there. He's the one who—"

"Good evening, Officers." James nodded to them. He walked toward me and put his arm around my shoulders. "I'm afraid we're in need of your help. I rented a house the other side of Lidmere and I want to get there tonight. My wife is—not well. Her talk upset the man who was driving our hired car. He made us get out and then he drove away." There was righteous indignation in James's voice. Every hair was in place.

The Garda exchanged looks. I shook off James's arm. "He's lying. I'm not his wife. He wants to kill me."

"Do you have identification, ma'am?"

"Yes—no, it's in my handbag. In my room at the Arms. It's all there. Please call them. Let them know where I am."

"Just a moment, ma'am. When did this happen?"

"I'm not sure, maybe two hours ago. I've lost track." My voice was shaking. "Look. If you don't believe me, call the Fitzgerald Arms. Ask for Agent Rudnick. We're both working with the Boston police. They're liaising with your people. By now, there should be an alert going out to look for me."

Another exchange of looks. James drew himself up to his full height, an authoritative figure in a dark pinstripe suit. "See here. My wife is ill. She needs care. Is there a car in the village I can hire?"

"There's McMahon," the redhead said. "He might come."

"Call him." With a flourish, James pulled out his wallet. "My driver's license. My passport. I'm a visitor here and may I say that I don't appreciate the way I've been treated in this country. Not when my wife is so ill."

"Would she be needing a doctor? He lives down the street. He'll always come in an emergency."

"No, just the car. But hurry."

There was a strong smell of sausage cooking in another room. I stood there, trying to put myself in the place of these young policemen. Who to believe, a fine-looking American gentleman or a woman babbling about being forced into a car? A woman with hair flying, a crumpled jacket, and red marks around her mouth?

I clutched the top of the wood counter. "He's the one who's crazy and I can prove it," I said. "The police in Boston are asking the Garda here to help them find a man named Terry Gallagher. Ex-IRA with a record. He killed a Waterford girl in Boston. Cathy Riordan. It must have been in your papers. The wake is tomorrow. I came over with her ashes and to work with the police."

"Riordan," one said. "Barry, a word." The two went over to the wall behind the counter and began to talk in low voices, keeping an eye on us. Wondering, no doubt, how to deal with these wildly conflicting stories.

A few feet away, James was tapping his foot, an annoyed visitor to Ireland. "It's getting late. By all means call the Arms if you want to be thought idiots, but first get us the car."

"Right, sir," one said. "We'll rouse McMahon. Sorry for the delay. Perhaps the lady would like to sit down. Have a cup of tea."

Keeping my hands on the counter, I stared down at the scarred brown linoleum. In a few moments McMahon would be here with the car. Screaming and fighting would make me look even crazier. Before it was too late, these two young Garda must see *Barzalon* lose control.

Deliberately, I smoothed my tangled hair, straightened my jacket, and turned. Caroline had showed me where this man was vulnerable. I must go for the jugular. Verbally. This tactic had worked for me before. It *must* work again.

"Mr. Barzalon," I said in a pleasant voice. "Please stop pretending that you're my husband. No one is going to let you drag me out of here against my will. The fact is, you're nothing but a pathetic, bumbling failure. You married for money and your father-in-law tied it up tight. Now you're desperate to keep up appearances, but this plan of yours was insane. By tomorrow both you and Terry Gallagher will be behind bars."

"That's quite enough." James's voice was steady, but a vein throbbed in his forehead.

"Enough? I'm just starting. You're a coward who blackmailed his own son. Forced Terry Gallagher to murder a young Irish girl. When I get back to the Arms, my first call will be to my godmother, Caroline Vogt. You know Caroline and her tongue. The news that James Barzalon is a common criminal will spread like wildfire."

"Enough." His face was red, but he was still in control.

"Oh yes. Can't you see it? Caroline will be in her element. It'll be dinner conversation for months, how you fell flat on your face." I took a deep breath. "Believe me, your troubles are just beginning. Terry Gallagher may get a life sentence, but you'll be a social outcast.

He stood still. I smiled at him. "A social leper. An untouchable. No one you know will have anything more to do with you—"

"Stop." He raised his hands. "You spoiled my plan. You're supposed to die." The words came out in a roar. He reached for my throat.

"That'll do, sir." In seconds the two men had Barzalon by the arms. "None of that or we'll be charging you with assault."

The redhead turned to Barry. "Take him into the next room. I'll get through to the Superintendent in Lidmere. He'd better come quick and sort this out." He picked up the phone, looking shaken, then turned to me. "Hadn't he the smooth tongue and all the time—are you all right, ma'am? Sit down while I make this call."

Without speaking, I turned and went out into the quiet street. Leaned against the hard stone of the station wall and put my head in my hands. It was over, and one word was circling through my brain.

Cathy. Cathy. Cathy.

twenty-two

October 30

Boston

I never got to the wake. By noon the next day, Sally Rudnick and I were on our way to Boston. By evening I was back in my apartment, now a place of painful associations. Vanessa lying on the guest room floor. Pleasant evenings with Greg as his listeners wafted my words into space.

I was brushing my teeth when Superintendent McNulty called. "I have to admit, Mrs. Streat, I never expected this kind of breakthrough. You've kept us all on our toes, the last twenty-four hours. I'm glad you're back."

"So am I."

He cleared his throat. In this flat, concise way, he went on to tell me that Terry Gallagher had been picked up at the house in the valley. Both he and James were in custody in Limerick. A search was under way for Seth. The foundation was closed.

"What about Dr. Atkins?" I had asked.

"Put himself in a private mental institution two days ago. We'll have to wait to interrogate him."

"That's—very sad." I had put down the cell and told myself that any thoughts about Greg must wait until I reached my boys. It wouldn't be easy to explain that once again their mother had been at the center of some very nasty happenings—and that at any moment the media would be in full cry with this eye-popping story of stolen viruses. Murders. Larger-than-life participants. I could hear my sister Dolly: "I don't believe it. How could you be helping the police? You haven't had any experience, any training."

Rodale had left two messages on my cell phone. The first was the standard "well done." The second was to say that he was tied up.

This morning I woke early after a restless night. I was watering Seth's monster orchids, wondering who would take them away, when Rodale called again.

"Sorry for the delay. I'm just back from Ireland. You were lucky that driver had second thoughts. There were viruses packed in dry ice in the boot of the car. A hospital bed waiting for you, with Gallagher's cousin the nurse and Gallagher himself in attendance. He tried to run off into the woods."

"But he was caught."

"He was. Yesterday the Colonel went over and interrogated Barzalon and Gallagher. We now have enough information to close this international operation. By the way, you never mentioned James Barzalon. Was he ever on your radar?"

"Only when we all met for lunch. I had a feeling that he was calling the shots. I should have trusted my instinct."

"No one's given us the details, how you managed to break him down."

"By telling him he'd be a social leper. Bringing up the fact that he married for money and never got it. I think the resentment—and the need—built up over the years and finally erupted into this crazy scheme. Probably in his own mind, he figured he was owed. He probably still does."

"Massive greed and incompetence. A lethal combination."

"What about Seth?"

"Run to ground in Sardinia with a budding Indian actress. She wasn't too pleased when the police arrived. He'll be held as an accomplice. His foundation has been closed. You may have heard that Dr. Atkins took sanctuary in a fancy mental hospital."

"He was about to go over the edge. He should have left the foundation as soon as he suspected any wrongdoing."

"I had a feeling you rather liked the man."

"I did. I should be angry, the way he used me, but the truth is, I'm just upset. There's a quotation that says that only God can see through people. It's incredible, how outward appearances hide so much *evil*. I'll never get over losing Cathy."

"No, but now you can stop blaming yourself. After all, you put the finger on Fausto. Broke Barzalon down in front of witnesses. Helped to put a criminal network out of business. What happened at the Garda station after Barzalon went berserk?"

"I couldn't stop shaking. The Garda made me tea so strong you could stand up in it. Then two men from a station in Lidmere took me back to the Arms. The housekeeper put me to bed with a slug of whiskey and two hot water bottles. In spite of everything, I still love Ireland. I can't wait to go back."

"Not with me." He paused. "Emma. We need to talk about our last meeting. It didn't end well. I'd like to explain."

"There's no need."

"Don't interrupt. I ruined one marriage by disappearing and reappearing with no explanation. After what happened to me in

Ireland, my work always came first. It still does, but I minded leaving you that day. Very much. We should have talked it out then and there."

"I understand."

"Do you? For me, you're a very special person. The one woman who knows both sides of my life. We have an unusual kind of relationship."

"Do we?"

"Look. I know I'm selfish and demanding and one-track-minded, but I want you back in my life. Permanently."

The orchid pot was overflowing. I turned off the water and stood there, holding on to the sink. Weeks ago, standing by a window in that white Palladian house, I had ached to hear words of commitment. Now, out of the blue, he had put his feelings on the line and it hadn't been easy. He deserved honesty—or at least the best I could do.

"Emma?"

"I just don't know," I said slowly. "I just don't know the answer. You've brought excitement into my life. Great pleasure. You're a remarkable man, but I don't have to tell you that. On the other hand, I need to start rebuilding a base for my boys. That's my priority. And it has to be over here."

"Fair enough, even though it's not what I wanted to hear. You need to find someone who can give you permanence, and that would be good. In the meantime—" He stopped.

"Yes?"

"That island in the British Virgins. I remember what happened when I brought it up in Wiltshire. You called me a bastard and hoped some woman would stab me. I deserved it, but I want you to know that the door is still open."

"*Andrew.*"

"Keep your shirt on. We'll need to be in touch as this case unfolds." And then he was gone.

I went into the sitting room and sat down on the white leather sofa. Men. For so many years, Lewis had been the foundation in my life. I needed to talk to Caroline.

She was at home. "Darling girl. I've missed you. I've been trying to reach you."

"I've been away."

"Away?"

"A quick trip to Ireland with Cathy Riordan's cousin. You know, Vanessa's assistant who—um—died. We took the ashes back to her family." With luck, my name would not be splashed all over the tabloids. "How are you? What's going on?" I asked.

"The usual mad scramble. Openings. Benefits. By the way, you were asking me about the Barzalons, father and son."

"What about them?"

"Your going to Ireland reminded me. I had lunch yesterday with my friend Maisie. I told you, her husband is a trustee for Seth. A thankless job, I may add. There's an outsize scandal boiling up in that quarter."

"What kind of scandal?"

"Well, my dear, not many people know yet, but James is being held by the Irish police. Maisie's husband is trying to find out exactly what happened, but the lid is coming off over here. It seems that James owes a great deal of money. So does Seth. All hell is going to break loose."

"Why?"

"Why? Because both of them are in debt up to their ears, running up bills everywhere and living high on the proverbial hog. I've seen it before and it always amazes me, how long people can fool the world just by putting up a convincing front. In hindsight, Grandfather Comstock should never have given Seth that foundation. I always said there was bad blood there, and I was right."

"You usually are." But even Caroline hadn't been able to see through James Barzalon's façade.

"Darling girl, enough of those jumped-up losers. How is Vanessa?"

"Going home soon."

"Your boys?"

"Doing well."

"Any men in your life?"

"No one who counts. I'm about ready to let you pick a number for me. I met a doctor a few weeks ago. Brilliant, interesting, but no future there."

"Too bad. I like the idea of a live-in doctor, and you're not getting any younger. What about the rich peer?"

"He wants to get serious. It bolstered my self-esteem, but I turned him down. At least for now."

"Well, use him as a spa, good for toning the muscles. You're not meant to be celibate. Have you found a house?"

"Um—actually, no. I'm just starting."

"Emma. *Really.* I truly despair. What on earth have you been doing with yourself?"

"One thing and another. Not your intense social whirl."

"Darling girl, let's be honest. My intense social whirl is all I've got at my age."

I frowned and shifted the cell to the other hand. "Caroline, that's not like you."

"True enough. I can hardly bring myself to look in the mirror. All those wrinkles and spots—nobody knew about sunscreens in the old days. Darling girl, my accountant is waiting. Love you."

"Love you, too," I said with a sharp stab of dismay. This was the first time Caroline had ever admitted to growing old. She was seventy-four. Not *really* old, but what if she should fall down, break a hip? *Die?* I would be shattered without her. As soon as possible, I must get down to see her.

After a moment, I went to the window. The woman across the street had put two carved pumpkins on her doorstep. Halloween. Soon it would be Thanksgiving. Then Christmas. There was no time to lose. I checked my Rolodex and found Denise Daniels' number under "Real Estate."

"Denise? It's Emma Streat. I'm sorry I didn't get back to you, but things have been a little hectic around here." A pause. "You were telling me about a renovated barn with a tennis court. On a river. Is it still available?"

"Let me check."

In a moment Denise was back. "A young couple put in a bid, but the wife didn't want to be that far from town."

"Could I see it tomorrow? I need to get out of this apartment right away."

"I'll have to clear it with the owners, but they're going to California and they want a quick sale. Unless you hear back, I'll pick you up at ten."

"I'll be ready."

The first step had been taken. I stood there, looking down at the old brick sidewalks, letting my mind drift. In the last three weeks, the season had changed. There were no more leaves on the trees. The woman going down the street was wearing a sheepskin coat. When Cathy called from Venice, I had been standing at this window, feeling as if my feet were nailed to a bridge. Now I was moving forward. I had work to do—but it was time to have another little chat with those ancient gods on Mount Olympus.

"I'm back," I would say to them. "And this time I have a

wish list. A renovated barn on a river where my boys can come for R and R. A place where my dog O'Hara can hunt for rabbits. Time to look after my godmother."

There might be a rumble of protest, but I would stand up to them. "Look. Fair's fair. You hurled down a life-changing thunderbolt last summer. Then another. I need a break from angst and police and making connections. And—just to keep me out of trouble—you can throw in a good man. And a corkscrew that really works."

epilogue

Halfway across the world, a van waited in an alley, engine running. Two floors above, the man was finished cleaning out his office. The last computer was hanging from the wall. He gave it a tug and it crashed down, narrowly missing his feet. He picked it up, ran down the stairs, threw it into the van, and jumped into the driver's seat.

Pulling his cap over his eyes, he shifted gears and began to back up. In fifteen minutes he would be safe in the waterfront section of a city he knew well. In two weeks he would be in business again.

There was a blind corner at the end of the alley. Even in his hurry, he must exit slowly to avoid hitting a pedestrian and attracting attention.

As he came out, he looked both ways. Looked again. Police cars with flashing lights were blocking the street. Uniformed men with guns were walking toward the van, now loaded with incriminating data.

There was no way to escape. He cut off the engine and waited, cursing under his breath. The tip that client 112 was being fingered had come too late—and he had only himself to blame. He should have followed his primal instinct and cut 112 off in Venice. From the start there had been a doubt in his mind about the Boston foundation—and in the end, one rule held true: A hazardous operation was only as strong as its weakest link.